Was she just a drowning civilian...or an agent sent by a supervillain?

Navy SEAL Max Preston made out a figure as he swam toward the wrecked seaplane. A woman. Hell.

Her head lolled as she was carried along a dark curl of water. It wouldn't be long before her strength gave out. Who in the hell was she?

Spinning her onto her side so she could breathe, he cut smoothly through the water. There was no way to tell her age or background or hair color in the darkness, but her body was impossible to ignore. She was tall for a woman—maybe five foot ten. Her arms were firm and toned. Her waist felt slim, and her breasts...

Max wasn't going to think about that or anything else. If Cruz sent her, she would be tough and experienced, a true veteran alert to any weakness. But Max would have the truth out of her in moments because he was a veteran, too.

When he touched her, skin to skin, she wouldn't lie. *Couldn't* lie. His special Foxfire skill would guarantee that. And for her sake, Max hoped that Cruz wouldn't figure anywhere in those secrets.

Navy SEALs didn't earn medals for being nice.

CHRISTINA SKYE IS CODE FOR ROMANCE AND ADVENTURE!

on CODE NAME: BABY

"Thrilling...fans should eagerly await the next in the series."
—*Publishers Weekly*

"Who can possibly resist the mix of super-smart puppies and romantic suspense? Who could possibly do it better than Skye? The Code Name series is incredibly inventive and not to be missed."
—*Romantic Times BOOKclub*

"A totally different, unique, and wonderfully excellent novel....This is a reading experience you definitely owe yourself."
—*Romance Reviews Today*

on CODE NAME: PRINCESS

"Action-packed.... Snappy dialogue and between-the-sheets sizzle will please Skye's numerous fans."
—*Publishers Weekly*

"Christina Skye expertly weaves sizzling romance and suspense in her lightning-paced tales of intrigue."
—Tess Gerritsen, *New York Times* bestselling author

"With Christina Skye, it's all about the thrill... and her hot, sexy Navy SEAL is to die for!"
—Carly Phillips, *New York Times* bestselling author

on CODE NAME: NANNY

"A fun story blending romance with intrigue. The characters are hot, and so is the book."
—*Hawthorne Press Tribune*

CHRISTINA SKYE

CODE NAME: BLONDIE

HQN™

ISBN 0-373-77123-1

CODE NAME: BLONDIE

This edition published by arrangement with Harlequin Books S.A.

www.HQNBooks.com

Printed in U.S.A.

Writing this book was a special experience for me. Miki was hard to handle, but I had great help!

Thanks to Judy and Christiane for Chinese sesame noodles and morale in the trenches!

Thanks to my wonderful agent, Meg Ruley, and the amazing team at the Rotrosen Agency. You are a writer's dream team.

Finally, my deep thanks to Abby Zidle and Tracy Farrell at HQN Books. Thanks for being so gentle with an author's dreams!

CODE NAME: BLONDIE

CHAPTER ONE

17°30' south latitude
18°52' west longitude

WHY DID SEX SOUND so noisy when it wasn't happening to you?

Miki Fortune steadied her digital camera and tried to ignore the grunts and groans from the nearby tent where her two models were doing the nasty again in full audio. There was no mistaking the sharply heaving canvas where her gorgeous six-foot-one Scandinavian model was getting screwed up, down and sideways by an equally gorgeous male model from Montana.

Satisfied with two shots of the pristine cove, Miki shouldered her camera gear and headed back up the beach. White sand crunched beneath her feet and a warm wind ruffled her hair, but all Miki saw was camera angles and F-stops. Paradise meant nothing when you were trying not to screw up the biggest opportunity of your life, a full-color calendar called *Best Beaches of the World.*

Behind Miki the tent walls shook harder. Panting voices carried on the wind. "Oh, Looogan. That way.

Harder—harder!" The canvas snapped and the sound effect grew more obvious.

Miki scowled. If people wanted to have sex, they should do it in another state.

Logan Brooks, Miki's tanned male model, ground out an urgent curse. Something crashed to the ground beyond the canvas wall.

Disgusted, Miki stowed her camera and lenses, then glanced at her watch. After all the time zones she'd crossed between her home in New Mexico and this beach southwest of Bora Bora, her body clock felt permanently out of synch. But tired or not, she had finished the day's shots without a hitch. Now that her new digital cameras were stowed and their precious memory cards transferred to a portable hard drive, Miki couldn't wait to get back in the air.

Paradise was fine when you were eighteen and crazy in love, enjoying a clothing-optional vacation. When you were working, paradise felt like salt in an old wound, reminding you of all that was wrong with your life.

Which, in Miki's case, could have filled most of Montana.

One of the pilots leaned against a palm tree and peeled an apple, clearly enjoying the models' escapade. An older pilot napped in the shade, hat over his head. Her boss sat in a leather campaign chair scanning the photos she'd transferred to his laptop.

Vance Merchant didn't look pleased. She'd given him her best work, shots that shimmered with dawn light and burned with sunset crimson. There was no possible reason for his frown other than the simple fact that he could. The man knew he held all the power and he enjoyed wielding it mercilessly. He was a tyrant, just the way Miki had heard. Being around him was about as much fun as sharing a cardboard box with a scorpion.

But the job was important, her first chance at national commercial exposure. If the calendar was a success, Miki knew she'd receive dozens of travel assignments, a fiercely competitive category of photographic work. So she dug her toe slowly through the warm sand, fighting uneasiness as she waited for Vance's verdict.

Her balding boss looked up as the tent shook one last time. Moments later Miss Finland 2002 emerged, stunning in a black string bikini that hugged her body like butter. When her partner appeared, he was rumpled and languid, his shirt buttoned wrong and his zipper still open.

Someone snickered. The men looked up as Miss Finland stretched languidly. Vance smiled and started to make a comment.

Miki cut him off. "Can we go now?"

The model, who currently worked under the name of Jasmyn, stretched slowly while she toyed with her tiny bikini top, aware that she had all the men's attention. "Me, I am hungry with appetite. I can eat very big horse right now." She frowned beautifully. "Anyone have very big horse to give?"

Miki's boss muttered something to the older pilot. Miki ignored them.

Sometimes men had all the subtlety of boa constrictors. And now three new bruises darkened Miss Finland's elegant neck. They'd have to be digitally removed, the same way Miki had removed the other bites and scratches incurred from St. Thomas to Tahiti. Luckily, Miki was very skilled at both cosmetics and Photoshop.

Vance Merchant looked up and waved his hand at the younger pilot, who climbed aboard one of the two amphibious Cessnas rocking in the water. As the models waited, the pilot revved the engine and gestured from the small cockpit.

About time, Miki thought, heading toward the plane. This place was getting creepy. Besides, the wind was picking up.

Vance caught her arm. "Not you. I need a dozen more shots of the reef before we leave, babe."

"You've got to be kidding. I filled a flash card this morning."

Her boss's eyes narrowed. "I'm the one who decides when we're done, honey. Remember that." He tossed her his big Nikon, careless of the $10,000 piece of equipment. "Get moving."

Vance Merchant could afford to buy a camera a day for the rest of his nasty life. His silver spoon came from his father's success in coffee commodities—and his mother's good fortune in being an oil heiress. The man's trust fund was obscene.

As Miki checked the camera, the balding businessman slid an arm around her shoulders. "I can see that taking orders is a problem for you. We'll have to do something about that."

She pushed his hand away smoothly and thought about decking him. One solid chop to the collarbone and he would be moaning. On the other hand, physical assault didn't get credits on a job resume.

Excellent lighting skills. Inventive with neutral density filters. Crushed the supervisor's collarbone. May be unstable and probably dangerous.

Not the best path to career advancement. Miki sighed. She needed to stop drifting and start being serious. Photography was in her blood, a passion since she was ten. Day and night images haunted her thoughts, burned into her head. The problem was getting someone's attention so that she'd have the backing to shoot for a living. She had finally grown up and started to take her work seriously, which meant no decking the boss.

The Cessna's motor turned over. The models were aboard with all their gear, and the pilot was checking his equipment.

"What's he doing?"

The Cessna began to pick up speed. Miki felt a sudden sharp uneasiness at how isolated they were on this speck of an island. "They're leaving ahead of us? I thought we were flying out together for safety."

"If you do your job, we'll be flying out in a few minutes." Vance glanced at the older pilot, and a silent signal seemed to pass between the two men.

"What do you mean, do my job?" Miki frowned at Vance. "I think we've got enough background shots for ten calendars."

"*You* think? Who's paying *you* to think, babe?" Sunlight burned on Vance's yellow silk shirt as he traced Miki's neck. "The sooner you stop whining and start shooting, the sooner we take off."

"You can't let them go ahead of us, Vance."

"I just did, babe. Move it because your stalling is costing me money."

No point trying to change his mind. After three weeks of travel in close quarters, Miki had figured out that the man was impossible. She stalked over the sand and leveled Vance's Nikon, trying to ignore the roar of the other Cessna as it prepared for take off. Palm trees waved, the ocean glittered—and clouds piled up to the south.

Miki couldn't shake a sense of unease. When she finished two dozen new shots from different angles, she gritted her teeth and turned back to her boss. "I'm done here. Why don't you take a look so we can go?"

"Cool your jets, babe."

Babe? If Miki never heard that word again, she would die a happy woman. Was it stupidity or arrogance that made men think women actually liked that name? Of course, *Babe* was better than *Blondie*. For the last five years, Miki had dyed her natural blond hair to a streaky brown in order to shield herself against the wrong kind of male attention. From bitter experience she knew that being blonde automatically took off five years and ten pounds. The only problem was that being blonde also knocked fifty points off your I.Q. in the eyes of most men. Some women seemed happy with the tradeoff, but Miki wasn't one of them. So why the hell was she back to bubblehead blond now?

When she'd heard about the team shooting an exotic calendar called *Best Beaches of the World,* Miki had instructed her photo agent in Santa Fe to accept the offer with no negotiation. At first her agent had been discouraging. "Waste of time, Fortune. Vance Merchant only hires blondes because he thinks they're good luck." The agent had rolled his eyes. "That means all blondes, all the time. Besides, Merchant is a little hard to work with."

Miki was too enthusiastic to let the offer slip away. That same day she had dyed her hair to its original streaky gold, angry but determined to snag the job.

Unfortunately, her agent had neglected to mention several details. For example, Vance Merchant's interest in blondes usually took on touchy-feely overtones by the second day of a shoot, and Miki soon tired of dodging the producer's fast hands. Between the constant travel and the isolated location shooting, she could never seem to escape him.

Not that she would whine. She could handle a weasel like Vance Merchant. The trick was finding a way to rebuff him without costing her the job.

All her irritation snapped into sharp focus as she waited for the balding California millionaire to amble across the beach in his $800 handmade Panama hat.

When she held out the camera, he moved in close, pressing against her shoulder while he looked into the LED screen.

Miki controlled her irritation by imagining a few more zeroes in her bank balance. "So what do you think?"

"Nice cloud detail. But I keep telling you, we're here for the sex and the skin. That's what sells, not your artsy nature shots."

Miki bit back a hot answer, reaching for the camera, but Vance moved out of reach. "You screwed up Jasmyn's close-ups today. Where's the mineral oil I told you to use on Jasmyn? There's no shine, no sizzle. Are you a total idiot?"

I'll give you shine, Miki thought. "Vance, you didn't tell me—"

"Can it, babe. I need a dozen more windward shots across that slope. Then I can crop and insert some shots of Jasmyn later in post-production. Get to it."

"Now?" Miki started at him in disbelief. The other Cessna had taken off five minutes ago and the dark clouds were getting closer. Was the man crazy?

"Are you coming or not?"

She ached to tell Vance where he could put this job and his expensive Nikon, but somehow she swallowed her pride and nodded. Why did all the good jobs come with jerks in charge? Was there something wrong with her?

"Fortune, are you listening to me?"

"Yeah, sure."

Vance muttered as he vanished behind the low sand

dunes. As soon as Miki crossed the slope, she saw a shirt spread out on the ground. Vance was standing beside it, tugging at his belt.

She went absolutely still. "What are you doing?"

"Don't be so damned uptight. It's just sex, something to loosen you up and get your creative juices flowing. I saw you staring at Miss Finland and the hunk. All that noise got you excited, didn't it? You want it."

"Excuse me?"

Vance's belt hit the sand. "You're wasting time. Get naked."

"You're nuts as well as a creep. The only thing I'm doing is boarding that plane. You handle the sex by yourself. I figure you usually do that anyway," she added grimly.

"In that case, you're fired." Vance made the little Donald Trump hand gesture, his voice icy. "Take your choice."

Did he always get away with this, Miki wondered? Didn't people file lawsuits for this kind of behavior? As the tropical wind ruffled her hair, she saw her career going up in smoke and was too angry to be diplomatic. Enough was *enough.* What she did next was for her and all the other women Vance had suckered over the years.

She kicked sand toward him, pleased when he yelped with surprise. While he was distracted, she followed with a roundhouse kick from one of her many hours of classes. She wasn't coordinated, but her blow to his ribs got the job done, making Vance gulp, caught in mid-curse. He lurched sideways and landed face down in the sand.

A noise drew Miki's gaze. She saw the first Cessna circle high, dipping its trim wing once before heading east. The plane's receding outline left her with the cold feeling that she was cut off from civilization, stranded forever.

And this wasn't a reality show. *This* was her life.

Grabbing her camera bag, she sprinted for the remaining plane, ignoring Vance's threats. *Get in line,* she thought. She had car payments due, credit card bills to pay and now she'd blown her best job in months.

Sand hissed behind her. The millionaire producer huffed over the sloping crest of the beach, red-faced. There was a fresh bruise on his flabby right shoulder.

"You're through, Fortune. There's no city *small* enough for you to hide. Forget about taking pictures for a living. Forget about portraits or calendars or greeting cards. You're over, honey. I'm going to see to it personally as soon as I get back to L.A."

Miki resisted an urge to hit him again, instead dredging up a cloyingly sweet smile. "If I'm over, then it won't hurt me to file a nice sexual harassment suit against you, will it? Won't that look lovely when it hits the papers? You sell a lot of calendars in college bookstores, don't you? I'd say your sales are going to tank when the female students hear about your problem keeping your pants zipped."

Vance's face turned an even deeper shade of red. "You little bitch. You are dead as far as new photographic work is concerned."

Miki returned his cold stare. "Try it, Vance. If you do, my agent will enjoy contacting every female photographer in America so they hear about your little scam," she blustered.

Meanwhile, her teeth were chattering. Fired and now blacklisted. Could her life get any worse?

At least she had new photos for her portfolio, taken on her free time during this trip. Several freelance sales should help make up a month's lost salary and the cost of her new camera equipment.

Vance puffed past her, smiling. "You didn't read the last page of our contract, did you?"

"What do you mean?"

"Stupid move, babe. I mean you can forget having anything for your portfolio. It's all mine—every print and digital image. Your film agent wanted to reject the clause, but it was nonnegotiable if you wanted the assignment. That means you get no use of anything without my approval—and trust me, you won't *ever* be getting that." His lips curved. "Unless you want to reconsider my offer."

"You mean the quickie in the sand?" Miki squeezed her hands together to keep them from lunging at him. She'd purchased a new camera and lenses, slaved for three weeks, and now the weasel had cut her out of rights to her own work.

Stupid move.

Vance was right about that. She should have listened to her photo agent and negotiated harder, but she had been too afraid of losing the job. She had decided to stop coasting or being casual about her life plans. That meant no more whining.

And look where that had gotten her.

She knocked Vance's sweaty fingers from her shoulder. "I'd rather suck glass chips through a straw." She stalked to the Cessna and climbed abroad. The pilot barely noticed her, too busy staring at the dark line of clouds covering the horizon.

Miki turned, following his gaze. "Is something wrong?"

"Not really. We've got a little weather moving in, that's all. Where's Vance?"

"Back up the beach. Probably grabbing his gear."

"He'd better hurry up." The pilot rubbed his neck. "Once we're up in the air, you should check that your cameras are stowed. That storm is moving in faster than I thought."

16°58' south latitude
152°12' west longitude

MIKI COULDN'T DRAG HER eyes away from the wall of gray clouds. Slouched beside her, Vance muttered crossly, avoiding eye contact. Dutch, the pilot, hadn't spoken since they'd lifted off, but he'd consulted his watch twice and his fingers were tight on the controls.

A pilot with white knuckles was never a good sign.

"What the hell's going on out there?" Vance snapped.

"You said that tropical depression was moving to the south. You said—"

"I was wrong." The pilot didn't glance up. "And if you're asking why I didn't know sooner, it's because you insisted on renting the oldest plane you could find. I told you the nav and comm equipment was out of date."

Miki squirmed uneasily. Old equipment and a cheap-skate boss. How could her fantasy job get any worse?

She peered at a dark wedge of clouds to the south. "Shouldn't we be halfway to Bora Bora already? We can outrun the storm."

"A Category Five storm can pack crosswinds above 160 miles per hour. If we'd left when I wanted to, instead of waiting for you two to do the dirty in the dunes, this storm wouldn't be a problem."

"That wasn't my idea," Miki said angrily.

"You wanted it," Vance snapped. "Don't give me that bullshit."

The engine sputtered, cutting off Miki's angry response. Dutch pumped a control beside his knee, his mouth a flat line.

"What's wrong?" Vance swung around. "What was that noise?'

The grizzled pilot didn't answer, fiddling with a row of controls.

"Damn it, I asked you a question, Dutch."

"Trust me, you don't want to hear the answer." The pilot leveled a cold look at his employer. Miki realized that Dutch wasn't looking bored and lazy any longer. "Get your seatbelt hooked, the way I told you."

"Why should I—"

"Because I *told* you, damn it, and I'm in command here."

Vance looked startled, then angry, but he did as he was told. He wiped sweat off his forehead as he stared out at the gunmetal sea below them, alive with boiling waves. "What are we going to do now?" His voice was petulant.

"Praying wouldn't hurt." Dutch fingered the radio and waited, but all that came back was static.

The engine coughed again.

They were in real trouble, Miki realized. Trouble as in mayday and life jackets and forced sea landings. Her fingers dug into the sides of the seat as she fought back terrified questions.

Dutch looked back at her. "You strapped in, Blondie?"

She nodded mutely, cheered by his thumbs-up gesture. They were in a seaplane, she told herself. Dutch was an experienced pilot. He could bring the plane down, land at sea and radio for help. Someone was bound to find them. There had to be major shipping lanes nearby.

But she wasn't thinking about pontoons or shipping lanes when the engine sputtered and died completely. The plane nosed forward and shuddered. Cold with fear, she squeezed her hands against her lap as they plummeted toward the angry water.

Dutch gripped the radio microphone. "This is

Cessna ID number three—niner—four—zero—niner broadcasting on Mayday frequency. I repeat, this is a Mayday call…"

MAX PRESTON HAD NOTHING good to say about airplanes. The ground was better than the air, but water was where he felt most at home, thanks to both instinct and long training.

Right now he was thirty thousand feet above the Pacific, the sun brushing scattered clouds as he secured his jumpsuit. In approximately six minutes he'd hit the plane's jump door and drop into a two-minute free fall.

He still couldn't get over the Labrador retriever nearby, strapped into a vest and parachute of his own. "Is Truman prepped?" he asked.

His commanding officer nodded briefly. "The dog is A-okay, Preston. He'll be on oxygen via mask, just like you. Are you clear on those codes we went over? 92 for visual on Cruz or any hostile forces in the area. 705 for sighting of the missing weapon."

Max shifted his parachute slightly, straightening the line of his oxygen mask. "Good to go on the codes, sir. Two short burst signals, 606, for probability on the weapon device and 797 in the event emergency extraction is called for. But I won't need extraction." The Navy SEAL's face was calm as he slipped on the thin but highly tensile gloves that had become a staple during his long covert training. From now on his skin contact would be limited. His senses were too special to risk sensory overload.

Wolfe Houston, team leader of the government's secret Foxfire program, crouched down and patted the big Lab beside Max. "Hustle my man right in and right out, Truman. You okay with that?"

The dog barked once, tail wagging. He jumped up, licking Wolfe's face without the slightest tension.

"Good dog. You can give us the top ten list when you get back."

Though the Lab had plenty of jump experience, Max still felt odd jumping with an animal—even a veteran like Truman. But that was the new Navy for you. Always innovating. And in Truman's case, there were more surprises. The program's medical team told Max to expect unusual strength and intelligence, along with other abilities that hadn't been confirmed yet.

Max checked the watertight container holding his GPS system and secure satellite phone. After that came a final survey of his oxygen hose and mask. When Houston gave the thumbs-up, Max slid on his helmet, which would provide oxygen and protection in the frigid temperatures at heights above 30,000 feet, where vulnerable skin and eyes risked freezing.

A tall man bearing a marked resemblance to Denzel Washington sprinted down the plane's main deck. "Gentlemen, I just got a weather update." He held up a high-tech laptop and pointed to swirling images on the screen. "We've got a new depression west of Bora Bora that may drive in Category Five winds inside seventy-two hours. In the meantime, I'm tracking convective and boundary layers with real-time analysis from the Naval Research Lab Tropical Storm Center."

"Give it to us in English, Teague." Wolfe Houston crossed his arms. "Is this going to impede Preston's jump capabilities?"

"That's a command decision, sir. All I can tell you is that there's a storm out there and it's one big sucker. Currently we're looking at a forty-eight-hour safety window. If you want to wait—"

"We can't *afford* to wait," Wolfe snapped.

Izzy Teague tapped impatiently on the keyboard. "In that case, I'd say get the hell in and get the hell out."

That was the kind of English Max understood. He gave a nod to Houston. "I'm ready to jump, sir."

Houston stared out at the faint shimmer of the sea below the commercial cargo plane. "All of you know the score. Cruz could be down there already, setting up the deal for his buyers. We can't afford to lose that new weapon guidance system, and we definitely can't afford to let Cruz escape again." When he looked at Max, his face was set. "It's a go. Like Izzy says, get in and get the hell out. Try not to get yourself fried in the process."

"Aye-aye, sir."

Max got the message. Enrique Cruz had once been the leader of the government's select Foxfire team of genetically and biologically enhanced soldiers. Then something had gone wrong. Cruz's skills had shot off the charts and he had acquired the ability to project false images to his targets with complete accuracy, allowing him to disappear at will. But with the new skills had come mental lapses and growing paranoia. He had managed to escape from government control weeks earlier, setting off an extensive but unsuccessful manhunt. As the Foxfire program continued to work out the kinks, it quickly expanded to include service dogs on the team, although details of their use were being kept secret.

Izzy saw Max put a soothing hand on Truman's head. "Don't worry about this big guy. He's already made over ninety successful jumps. Last month he got an honorary medal from the guys at the Army's Yuma Jump School. He'll be fine."

Max gave a crooked grin. "Hell, I thought he was Navy."

"He's whatever you need him to be."

A uniformed crewmember in headphones hurried toward them. "Drop Zone in five minutes, sir. We're keeping radio silence as ordered."

Max tightened his gloves and stared out at the sunny sky. No one spoke.

"Do not engage with Cruz unless prior clearance is received. Remember that, Preston." Wolfe Houston's eyes were hard. "This man is unstable, unpredictable and he's getting more powerful every day. We can't be sure what new skills he's taken on since his desertion. Hell, his adaptability was always part of his success. He used to be one of us, but now he's an out-of-control killer. Remember that." The officer took an angry breath. "I should have taken him out last time when we were in that mine shaft with the dogs."

Houston shot a glance at Izzy. Both had been badly hurt during a nasty encounter with Cruz three months earlier. "Cruz could be capable of much stronger retaliation than we know."

Max felt the silent undercurrents that came with bad memories. "Understood, sir."

"Assume that Cruz is faster, stronger and meaner than you expect and then double that," Izzy said. His fingers idly traced his elbow as he spoke, and Max remembered that both of his arms had been broken in the violent confrontation with Cruz.

"We'll take him out this time." Max moved awkwardly to the rear exit doors, where the crew helped secure his fifty-pound parachute pack in place. As the jumpmaster counted down the final seconds, Max briefly touched the silver scar at his collarbone, one of many he'd received months before during a bungled mission in Malaysia. Though he'd nearly died, those wounds had led to his selection for the ultra-select Foxfire team, so he held no regrets. This team made up of specially trained and genetically enhanced Navy SEALS was the finest group of warriors on the continent—probably on the whole planet—but they were never photographed, never congratulated and never mentioned in any press article or standard government briefing.

Max looked down at the Lab waiting alertly near the

exit door. He checked that the dog's parachute line was clear, properly positioned beside an altimeter that would trigger an automatic chute opening at 300 feet. The oxygen line was already attached to the dog's headgear.

"One minute to drop zone, sir."

Max felt the drum of the plane's engines and the howl of the wind beyond the jump doors. The world seemed to slow down, every atom of his body focused on the here and now as he prepared to jump. He felt his pulse spike. His breath tightened to compensate for the adrenaline surge.

Show time.

When the jump light went on, he moved to meet the air's fury, his body hammered as he followed the Lab out into the void.

CHAPTER TWO

MIKI OPENED HER EYES and gasped as water spilled into her mouth. She was *choking*.

When her terror cleared, she realized the water was coming from a broken plastic sports bottle shoved above her seat. She was dry everywhere except for her face.

Outside the plane was a different story. Angry waves slapped against the Cessna's body, spilling froth over the window.

Vance was slumped forward against the pilot's seat. Blood trailed down both cheeks.

"Vance, are you okay? Can you hear me?"

When he didn't answer, Miki tapped his shoulder to get his attention. Her hand came away slick with blood.

His body slumped sideways, stiff and lifeless, and she caught a breath in horror, gagging.

"Dutch, what should I do?"

The big man coughed and Miki saw him wipe away blood with his left hand. His right arm was out of sight on the seat as he fiddled with the Cessna's controls.

"I've been broadcasting a Mayday on our last contact frequency. They'll have our ID and present position. The radio transponder is set for continuous transmission in case of—" His voice shook as waves buffeted the plane. "How's Vance?"

"He's gone." Miki's voice shook. "Something hit his head, I think." She fought to think clearly. "What are we going to do?"

"Stay calm, that's what. We stay smart and we'll stay alive until we get picked up. I never should have agreed to use this old plane." He closed his eyes for a minute and seemed to struggle to breathe. "Get out of your seat harness. Do it now." His voice was grim. "Head to the cargo door."

"What about *you?*"

"I'm staying. I'll keep the radio alert squawking as long as I can."

"I can't leave you."

"Listen, I got us down in one piece, but Vance is gone and my arm's pretty well crushed by this broken seat. If you stick around, you've got no odds, which is just plain stupid. So I'm ordering you to unharness and ditch. You've got your flotation vest. Pull the cord once you're outside. Someone will come eventually. You can tell them to come back for me." His voice tightened. "Now get going."

"But I—"

Water hammered high and the windshield gave way. The plane pitched hard, driving Miki back. Suddenly she was fighting to breathe as seawater covered her face, and raw instinct took hold. She clawed free of her safety restraint, kicked past Vance's lifeless body and managed to find the rear cargo doors. An eternity passed as she searched blindly for the door latch. Water slashed her face, blinding her as she forced open the hatch. She turned back to search for Dutch and felt the plane shake. Engulfed, she lost all sense of direction, unable to see Vance or Dutch. Desperate for air, she kicked in the direction of a dim patch of light, fighting through cold, churning water.

Her face broke the surface. Her first gasping breath was torn away by the howling wind. Then Miki began to sink and realized that she'd forgotten to open her flotation vest.

After her third try, the vest inflated and she bobbed to the surface. Dragging in air, her thoughts flashed to Vance, lifeless and cold somewhere in the water while Dutch bled in the cockpit, maybe dead already.

Another wave crashed into her face. Everything slid away but survival.

Stay smart and you'll stay alive.

Miki clung to the words as she was yanked up over the lip of a towering wave and dropped mercilessly into a trough.

Someone would come, she told herself. They *would.* All she had to do was stay alive.

THERE WAS A STIFFER current than Max had expected from the prejump briefing. Even Truman was tired from their long swim. Unfortunately, the drop had left them slightly off course and they hadn't been able to make up the distance in their glide before chute opening. As a result, their swim to the island had taken twice the estimated time. But they'd made the beach with no more than a few bumps and bruises. The big yellow Lab had come through like a pro in the air and in the water.

Max's target was a neighboring island separated by half a mile of open sea. This was the spot where recent intel had indicated Cruz was building a covert base. So far Max had found no movement or signs of life, but that meant nothing. Any plan by Cruz would involve elaborate security precautions.

Max put down his binoculars and scratched his canine backup behind the ears. Otherwise, neither moved. The wind was already picking up and gray-green clouds dotted the horizon. The Lab raised his head, ears alert. It was still too early to say if Izzy's storm predictions would be on target.

Max was about to scan the far side of the nearby island when he heard the muffled cough of a motor. Instantly he swung his binoculars up, but saw nothing in the fading twilight. When he swept the ocean, he saw a dark shape hurtle down, hitting the water too fast. A smaller outline separated, bobbing on the gunmetal waves. Focusing his powerful binoculars, Max made out a figure near what looked like the body of a wrecked seaplane.

An accident here, within earshot of Cruz's island?

Unlucky tourists? Max didn't buy it. That kind of coincidence only happened in movies.

But if innocent civilians had been forced to ditch at sea, they could be fighting for their lives. He couldn't let them die without a chance.

Max felt his senses narrow, focused and alert as he grabbed his scuba gear. He wouldn't go in too close, in case this was a trap, but he had to check out the scene carefully. Cruz himself might be out there.

On the other hand, he might run into twenty drunken tourists. The SEAL bit back a curse at the thought of the possible complications. Civilians would whine and make noise, asking questions and demanding to be taken back to Tahiti or Bora Bora.

FUBAR.

After a silent touch command to his dog, Max waded into the restless water, flipped on his mask and headed west into the night toward the coordinates where he had last seen the downed plane.

CHAPTER THREE

SURROUNDED BY SLASHING WAVES, Miki tried to stay calm just the way Dutch had ordered. She kicked her feet for a few minutes and then floated, stretching out her reserves as she was yanked up and down in the choppy water. At each crest she searched in vain for lights or landmarks, and every time panic threatened, she looked up at the sky, where specks of silver glinted between rushing clouds. Taking steady, deep breaths, she forced her mind away from Vance and the wounded pilot she'd left behind.

In and out. Don't panic.

Stay calm and stay alive.

As the sky darkened, her hands turned cold. Her body tightened, shuddering violently. Was this shock or some kind of delayed reaction to the cold? She had no inkling of how long she had been floating and kicking, watching the sky and trying to stay calm.

She cast about wildly for a distraction to hold back her panic. Music fragments slid through her mind like broken time capsules.

ABBA. *Dancing Queen.* Summer of '92. Her first big romance. Her first devastating split one week later.

Eric Clapton. *Change the World.* Christmas 1997. Mesquite smoke drifting in the clear Santa Fe air like incense. Adobe walls along Canyon Road glinting with luminarias and laughter spilling through the cold.

Would she see Canyon Road again? Would she ever get back home to Santa Fe's beauty?

Cold water sprayed her face. She plunged back into fear and exhaustion. How far had she drifted from Dutch and the plane—and how would rescuers find her out here in the ocean, even if they managed to track the distress call?

Something bumped Miki's foot and she screamed in mind-jolting terror. Please God, no sharks, she repeated over and over.

Reining in her nerves, she forced her mind to a place of safety. Battling panic, she began to sing hoarsely—ABBA, Radiohead, Eric Clapton. Sheryl Crow and Frou Frou. Over and over until her throat was raw and there was no more energy, no more strength left.

Again something touched her leg. Water slapped and a weight settled over her shoulder, dragging her under. Miki screamed, fighting the dark thing in the water until the world blurred.

THE DAMNED WOMAN WAS singing, if you could call that ridiculous noise singing. And she was surprisingly strong.

Max ducked back underwater, away from the kicking legs and slapping arms. When she started singing, he'd made up his mind to risk contact. It could still be a clever trick by Cruz, but her terror was real and Max couldn't leave a civilian to drown. He'd thought he was dealing with a man until he'd felt the kicking legs and heard the unsteady, exhausted voice singing an out-of-key pop song he didn't recognize.

A woman.

Hell.

He stayed out of range until she stopped screaming and her body relaxed. He could have subdued her, but out here a mile from land with no raft, struggling would have been a risk he didn't need. So he waited, knowing she was tired and disoriented. It wouldn't be long before her strength gave out.

He saw her head loll, bobbing as she was carried along a dark curl of water. The only sound was the slap of the sea and the shrill cry of the wind as he caught her arm. When she didn't move or fight him again, Max checked the backlit compass on his watch, noting time and location for his next report.

They were over a mile from the island now, but on the way back he'd have the current in his favor. Carrying her would be no problem as long as she didn't wake up and start fighting him again. Then he'd have to knock her out for sure.

Meanwhile his questions remained. Who in the hell was she? Most important, was she connected with Cruz?

Spinning her over onto her side so she could breathe, he cut smoothly through the water, heading back through the darkness. He couldn't see any details of her face. There was no way to tell her age or background or hair color, but her body was impossible to ignore with her hips brushing against him every few moments as he swam. She was tall for a woman—maybe five foot ten. Her arms were firm and toned. Her waist felt slim and her breasts—

Max did an unconscious inventory as he swam. She was soft and full where their bodies met, but he couldn't let himself think about that or anything else. If Cruz sent her, she would be ruthless and experienced, alert to any weakness. But Max would have the truth out of her in moments, whether she wanted it or not—because he was a veteran, too.

When he touched her, skin to skin, she wouldn't lie. *Couldn't* lie. His special Foxfire skill would guarantee that.

Beneath his scuba mask his lips curved. He cut through the water with smooth, practiced strokes. Her body would tell him everything he needed to know. For her sake, Max hoped that Cruz wouldn't figure anywhere in those secrets.

The Navy didn't hand out medals for being nice.

SHE WAS GOING TO THROW up any second. She was cold, suffocating, disoriented.

A sharp movement jerked Miki awake, out of her dreams of nausea and into something far worse. Wind cut into her face out of an endless darkness as an arm locked around her shoulders. By instinct she screamed and terror made her fight with desperate strength, but the grip at her shoulders was implacable.

Where was she?

She tried to see, but there was water in her face, in her eyes. "Let me go," she tried to gasp. "Dutch is back there. I have to go—" The words were only guttural sounds, blocked by a powerful body she couldn't see. Then her stomach clenched hard and she broke into painful spasms.

Hard hands flipped her over sharply and for a terrible moment Miki thought the man was pushing her under, set to drown her. Instead he lifted her, one hand across her mouth.

His dark arm was barely visible against the night. The man was wearing a wet suit. Miki could hear the squeak of rubber as he carried her forward. Suddenly her bare feet hit sand. Glorious, wonderful sand.

She tottered, falling to her knees, but he dragged her back to her feet, every motion made in silence. They were moving up a beach, she realized, the stormy surf behind them now.

She shivered in the wind, waterlogged and exhausted. "Who are you?" she tried to ask, but his hand tightened, and something slid around her mouth.

He'd gagged her. The damned man had *gagged* her.

Grunting angrily, she fought free and toppled onto wet sand, her cropped angora sweater tearing off. The man didn't say a word, efficiently cuffing her hands in front of her, then tossing a blanket around her shivering shoulders.

She muttered her anger at him and tried to stand, but

he turned, striding back toward the water. He hadn't removed his dark swim mask.

He stopped abruptly. "No noise," he whispered. "I'm going back for the other one."

She heard a hiss, like something sliding into place. She stared around her at the darkness. Even the stars were hidden beneath racing clouds, and there was no moon to be seen. Miki had no idea where she was or how she could wiggle free of his restraints. He'd saved her life, but she didn't trust anyone who slapped cuffs on her without a word.

She stumbled forward and a furry body shoved at her leg. A low canine growl rose from the darkness, freezing her in place.

"Good boy." The man's voice was almost too low for Miki to hear. "Guard."

Miki swayed, dazed and exhausted, but determined to escape. She didn't move, listening to footsteps crunch over the sand. Something brushed her feet again.

The dog. Big one. Lots of hair.

She was almost too tired to think straight. Who were they and why where they here—wherever *here* was?

She sank to one knee, too tired to move.

"You won't get past the dog," the man said roughly. "Don't waste your time trying."

Cool air brushed her face. Miki sensed more than saw movements nearby.

And then her rescuer—or her captor—vanished into the water.

Huddled in the blanket, shoeless, cold and miserable, Miki felt her thoughts blur. The world had turned into an endless nightmare. Nothing made any sense. She stared into the darkness, trying to stay awake, but her thoughts kept looping and tangling like cotton candy.

Trees hissed. A bird cried. Then Miki heard a loud splash somewhere to her left. She was certain she'd heard the man call softly to his dog. Then there were faint movements near the beach and more splashes.

She reacted by pure instinct, running in the opposite direction. She had to hide until she understood what was going on and whom she could trust. She tried to move quietly, barely able to see inches in front of her as she crossed the sand, her feet cut by stones and shells.

Must have lost my shoes during the crash. Blast it, she'd loved those bright red sneakers that matched her favorite Hawaiian shirt. Leaning against a tree to catch her breath for a moment, Miki discovered that she'd lost her favorite angora shrug, too. She had designed and knitted the fluffy little sweater with ruffles, during downtime while Vance bickered with the models and Dutch tinkered with the two Cessnas' engines.

Vance.

Dead.

Dutch.

Lost at sea. Probably dead.

Somehow the sweater didn't seem so important after

that. She bit back a sob and kept moving, forcing her way through bushes and tall grass that shredded her feet further. She staggered through a patch of mud, hit water and then stopped to listen for sounds of pursuit.

All she heard was the hiss of the wind.

Her hands hurt where the Jerk had cuffed them in front of her. Wincing, she shoved and twisted against the heavy restraints.

No luck.

And there was no time to waste. Miki remembered seeing the glint of a stream when the creep in the wetsuit carried her up the beach, so she followed the dark curve of water rather than pushing farther inland. Five minutes of steady climbing later she was breathless, standing at a small pool surrounded by tall grass. From the sound of it, the stream fell sharply, spilling into a space somewhere to her left. In the dark she had no idea how far down the waterfall went, and she couldn't distinguish the roar of the water from the rustle of the trees. A bird shot from the right, and Miki guessed that her captor was close.

Exhausted, she sank down on a rock. She couldn't go back and she couldn't go forward. One wrong step would send her out into space, wherever the waterfall went.

She shivered, fiercely cold and badly frightened. Then she closed her eyes, relying on her photographer's memory to reconstruct everything she knew about this place.

Water glinting to her left. Rocks straight in front of her, a dark mass that was probably a cliff. Bushes and grass to her right.

As she stood in the restless night, putting together the pieces from memory, she caught a musty smell. It reminded her of the dust mixed with mold of an old basement. She had gone caving once with Kit O'Halloran, her best friend back in Santa Fe. The experience had been fascinating, and Miki was sure the smell was a current of air carried from underground. Could she find the source by smell alone?

She had to find it. She also had to avoid breaking her neck in the attempt.

She slitted her eyes and looked from side to side, using her peripheral vision, which was more effective in darkness. Working slowly from bush to bush, she came to a wall of rock where the musty smell grew more intense. She followed it until cool air gusted directly onto her face. Kneeling in the mud beside the pool, she searched carefully.

The opening, when she found it, was tiny. Whispering a prayer that she wouldn't meet any snakes, Miki squeezed through and didn't look back.

WHERE THE HELL HAD she gone?

Max stood on the beach, staring at the empty place on the sand where he'd left the woman from the plane. He'd called Truman away briefly when the strap on his tactical vest had broken, and before he had been able to give the dog the defective piece to hide, the woman had bolted.

Truman bumped his leg tensely. Well trained to make no noise, the dog was clearly excited. Max hefted the pilot off his shoulders, set him on the beach, then leaned down to pet the golden Lab.

Bump, turn, sit.

Bump, turn, sit.

The dog was giving Max a message to follow, indicating the direction by the way he sat. The interior of the island.

Max scratched Truman's head and gave the two-tap signal to go. Instantly the dog shot across the sand, silent despite his size. Speed and keen intelligence were his specialties, and Max was glad to have him along as backup. Things were quickly growing messy in ways that no one had planned.

Not that Max had expected this mission to be easy.

The dog slowed, sniffing the ground. When he trotted back, he carried a soggy mass that might once have been white, but now was the color of day-old vomit.

Max studied the wad of fabric in Truman's teeth. He remembered the white thing that had been tied around her shoulders when he'd lugged her out of the water onto the beach. When Truman bumped his leg again, eager to continue the chase, Max gave him the two-tap freeing command. *Go.*

Given the woman's resourcefulness, he had no more doubts.

She had to be working with Cruz. Rescuing the other passenger he'd seen would have to wait.

MIKI HUDDLED IN THE DARKNESS, shivering. What in the heck was she *doing?*

Her knees were bleeding and her cheek was bruised where she'd hit a rock during her blind flight. She was a photographer, not a secret agent, and she was way out of her comfort zone.

She heard a noise behind her, at the mouth of the cave. Pebbles skittered, echoing hollowly. With unsteady hands, she followed the narrow tunnel deeper underground, splashing through an icy pool.

More pebbles rattled. Terror drove her forward, stumbling over fallen earth and boulders, her feet bleeding. Abruptly the cave widened. She pressed on, leaning against the stone wall, following the sound of water. In her panic, she stumbled. Her ankle twisted and her head struck a ragged piece of limestone. Even then she tried to crawl forward, but the ground had begun to whirl.

Something splashed through the water behind her, and she lost her balance, going down hard. She was angry that she wasn't faster, angry that she'd lost her favorite shrug.

Angry that she'd screwed up yet again.

A sharp pain throbbed in her forehead. She kept crawling right up until everything went black.

CHAPTER FOUR

MIKI AWOKE WITH SAND in her mouth.

She was flat on the ground, her clothing still damp. Her hands were behind her back now, aching in plastic wrist restraints. How much time had passed since her fall?

She tried to free her hands, and instantly felt hot canine breath on her face, a silent warning. Miki tried to clear her fuzzy thoughts, remembering her escape and the pursuit. Her wrists hurt, but by wriggling slightly she could relieve the pressure. Tilting her head back, she looked up, searching vainly for familiar constellations. With the clouds gone, the darkness was alive now, filled with glittering white specks that dotted a sky untouched by any other light. None of them meant a thing to Miki. She barely recognized the constellations back home in New Mexico.

She was on a beach somewhere. That much she knew, but nothing else. Wincing, she glanced carefully around and froze at the sight of the pale shape stretched out nearby.

A *really* huge dog. Some kind of retriever.

Now you've stepped into it, Miki thought. Fired, wrecked, ditched, then lost and half drowned. A hysterical laugh bubbled up inside her, but she cut off the sound, remembering Dutch's final order.

Stay smart and stay alive.

The dog gave her no choice. She shuddered at the thought of sharp teeth lunging at her throat. Guard dogs were taught things like that. They could kill in seconds, according to Miki's best friend, who trained service dogs for police and military units. Now Miki wished she'd paid better attention all those times Kit described how she trained her dogs.

If she ever got back.

Blocking a wave of hopelessness, she watched a dark shape feather across the moon. She recognized the leaves of a palm tree, and that meant she was still in the tropics. Given the silence, it had to be someplace remote. Since she'd come awake there had been no lights, either at sea or from passing planes.

Very remote, she thought grimly.

Her head began to ache, and she remembered bumping it back in the cave. Now her whole body throbbed along with her head, but pain or not, she had to do *something* before the creep in the wetsuit came back, even if one escape effort had failed.

But that left the dog. If she moved very slowly, she could try to make her way back to the water, since dogs couldn't carry a scent over running water. She remembered hearing Kit say that.

Carefully, Miki eased onto her side. The wind rushed over her face, but she was certain the dog couldn't hear her anyway. Her confidence growing, she moved another few inches.

Still no warning growl.

Her pulse hammered as she moved again, her face against the wind. She heard a sucking noise and sand skittered over her feet. The sound came again, and the blackness materialized into a column. Miki realized the man was back, her worst nightmare in the flesh. Over the slam of her heart she heard a soft groan that seemed familiar. The noise came from what appeared to be a large object.

Dutch?

Recognition made her try to stand. Had he actually found Dutch out in the dark water? She could barely believe it.

Her urgent questions were cut off by cold gloved hands at her mouth. "No noise," he whispered. Kit felt him bend down, checking that her restraints were in place.

Then sand squished and he drove her across the beach. She felt sand give way to dirt, the waves sounding muted behind her.

A light flickered and disappeared and his low voice came at her ear. "Four steps down."

The first drop took her by surprise and she stumbled, her ankle twisting. Gloved hands caught her and she slammed against a hard chest.

A door hinge whispered. Light flared, blinding her.

She could see the creep for the first time, his body covered by a black wetsuit and black gloves. He was carrying a pair of heavy night-vision goggles, and in the light his eyes snapped with command, somewhere between blue and gray. Miki couldn't seem to focus, but when he undid her restraints and set her down, Dutch was at her feet, sickly white. A long gash ran down his right cheek.

"You got him," she whispered, kneeling beside the pilot. She didn't look up, gripping Dutch's cold fingers. "Thank you. I didn't think anyone could do that."

"Don't thank me yet." He tossed a silver thermal blanket over Dutch and tucked the foil around the man's motionless body. As he moved his light, Miki saw that they were underground in some kind of small room. Near her feet were a large metal case and half a dozen tins that looked like MREs. The dog sat beside the case, ears erect, body alert. Spotting her sodden camera bag on the floor near Dutch, Miki reached out, but the dog seized the handle in its teeth and tugged it out of reach.

"Hey! What do you mean by—"

"No noise." The man looked at his dog. "Sit."

Instantly the powerful body dropped, Miki's camera bag still between his front paws. The dog nosed the bag and suddenly flattened on the ground, his hackles rising.

The man spun around. "Target?" he said softly. "Alert."

Target? All Miki had in the bag were clothes, a few sundries and her camera equipment. Everything was likely to be ruined from the seawater.

The dog sniffed the ground, sniffed Miki's satchel, then laid one paw across the leather bag and didn't move.

"Confirm."

The dog sniffed her bag again, and the motion made something shift inside an inner pocket. There was a small *pop* and fragrance blossomed, filling the cramped space. Miki realized it was her best French perfume, the same fragrance she'd worn since she was seventeen, taken everywhere as a good luck talisman. Unfortunately, she'd been in a rush that morning and had shoved the bottle into an empty lens pouch rather than wrap it carefully the way she usually did.

Judging by the sharp odor, the bottle had just broken.

The dog sneezed loudly. For some reason this made the man angry. He flipped off his penlight, then opened the trap door, letting the dog race up the small wooden steps.

Miki started to blurt another question but one cold look stopped her. Her captor looked furious. Silent and controlled, he pulled a plastic bag from a black tactical vest near the metal case. His mouth set in a thin line as he opened the camera case, saw the overturned and now lidless perfume bottle. Quickly he closed the lens pouch and then zipped the bottle inside.

"What are you doing with my stuff?" she hissed. Since when was it a hostile act to wear nice perfume? Miki's irritation swelled when he dropped her lens case and camera inside a larger plastic bag, then locked everything inside the metal case.

"Hey, you can't—"

"No noise. No perfume or scent of any sort. You understand that?"

Miki stared at him, cold, tired and furious. The man was unhinged. Sure, he'd saved her and then gone back for Dutch at considerable risk to himself, but he'd also cuffed her. Now he was the perfume police? Maybe he was one of those neatness freaks she saw newspaper stories about, people who wash their hands fifty times a day and don't let anyone touch their personal belongings.

The sudden sound of Dutch's labored breathing made Miki forget about her expensive perfume. The pilot didn't open his eyes as his lungs moved in strained bursts. Even to her untrained eyes it was clear that he was in bad shape.

"He needs a doctor," Miki whispered.

Her rescuer raised two gloved fingers, tapped her mouth and shook his head.

Clearly, noise was another one of his problem areas.

She decided it would be best to play along. Right now he was her only contact with civilization, even if he appeared to be two tortillas short of a combo meal.

But he looked competent as he knelt to check out Dutch, cleaning the gash at the man's stubbled cheek and unbuttoning his shirt to check for other trauma. Miki thought the pilot's chest looked odd, slightly concave, and the deep bruises streaking his ribs made her breath catch.

Deftly the man checked Dutch's pulse, eye reflexes

and temperature, then put away his black case and medical supplies. Oddly, he never removed his black gloves.

Too weird, Miki thought. At least Dutch appeared to be stable now. She retreated to the far wall, waiting tensely. Though her nursing skills rated a negative ten on a scale of one to five, at least she could provide some kind of moral support to the pilot.

Over her head paws scraped against the trap door, and Miki heard a dog's muffled sneeze. Was the dog bothered by perfume, too?

Hit by a sharp wave of dizziness, she closed her eyes and prayed she wouldn't throw up, wincing as her stomach continued to gurgle and churn. She'd swallowed seawater nonstop after the crash and now her feet and ribs ached. Exhausted, she leaned back against the underground wall, her eyes closed despite her efforts to keep them open.

It felt as if a week had passed since they'd left the beachside hotel in Bora Bora, with Vance muttering and complaining about every delay and expense. Now he was dead, his body lost somewhere at sea. Miki shivered, aware of how close she and Dutch had come to dying with him.

A scraping sound brought her around with a start. The small room was quiet, both candles out. "Hello?" she whispered into the darkness.

There was no answer.

She rose and felt her way along the wall past Dutch's cot. Fumbling, she found the four steps beneath the sloping entrance. With shaky fingers she searched for the metal door, pushing upward until the hatch squeaked, rising slowly to reveal a gray bar of predawn sky above angry clouds.

But before she could savor her little taste of freedom, a dog's face appeared at the door's edge. He sniffed intently, and his mouth curled, baring his teeth.

Miki shut the door quickly. The creep was gone, but he'd left the dog as a guard. Probably he kept the poor Lab underfed to make it hostile. She hated people who were vicious to animals. If he hurt the dog in any way, she was going to make him very sorry.

Assuming she was still alive by then.

CHAPTER FIVE

ENGINE TROUBLE.

A plane crashes at sea. Two survivors in the wrong place at the wrong time. Coincidence?

"FUBAR." Max spoke softly, scratching Truman where he liked it best, behind both ears. The Lab had been edgy from the first moment Max had carried the woman out of the water. But then had come her escape and now the perfume accident. The woman could have slept with Cruz in the last five hours, but Truman wouldn't be able to pick up a trace due to the perfume's mix of volatile oils, sterols and alcohol overwhelming his keen sense of smell.

Max had found the woman slumped over beneath the ridge after she fell and hit her head during her escape.

Once she was secured, he'd thoroughly searched the plane wreckage and floating debris, but found nothing useful beyond camera equipment in a watertight bag and some clothes. He'd checked the identification he'd found on Dutch, and the passport and U.S. driver's license looked genuine, though good forgeries could be deceiving. The woman's ID had eluded him in the limited time he'd had to search at sea. He couldn't risk using a light after full dark. It would have shone like a neon sign against the water. Why couldn't women just carry their IDs in their back pockets the way men did?

Shaking his head, he moved behind a line of trees and fingered his satellite phone. He couldn't chance a real transmission this close to Cruz's island, but three short bursts would let Foxfire HQ know that he was safe and his reconnaissance was proceeding as planned. Longer communications would wait until he accessed secure equipment at sea. He'd have to deal with his two new arrivals according to his own judgment for now. Since both were possible hostiles, Truman would keep them contained underground where they couldn't do any harm.

Neither one carried weapons or communication devices—Max had checked carefully before bringing them back to shore. The pilot was in poor condition, his lung compromised, but Max's mission was clear. He had to stay quiet, stay out of sight and track the stolen weapon guidance system. Cruz wasn't going to escape a second time—not on Max's watch.

At least Truman had recovered from the initial shock of the perfume cloud on his hypersensitive nose. Max opened a zipper on his vest and pulled out a bag. Immediately, the Lab pushed closer, sniffing the plastic eagerly until Max gave him the beef treat inside. The dog was superbly trained, his medical enhancements as sophisticated as those that Max had been given, but a dog was still a dog. Beef treats were special.

When his own stomach growled, Max dug into a different pocket and pulled out a fat gray bar that looked like chalk. Tasted like chalk, too, Max thought wryly. The components were carefully selected by the Foxfire medical team to provide minimum bulk and maximum nourishment for high-energy work. Max didn't particularly mind that the bar would be his major food source until he finished up his work here.

He wasn't used to fine living or creature comforts. He'd never had a normal life as a child since he'd spent most of his boyhood in institutions. Not until he was adopted at the age of ten did he find out how it felt to have a normal family—if you could call his spit-shine admiral father "normal." He smiled at the thought of the bossy, demanding man who'd taken him in, taught him discipline and given him pride in his successes. Work was his life now, just like the Admiral's.

He still called his adoptive father "Admiral" and he knew the grizzled old veteran was probably worrying about him right now, though he'd never admit it.

A faint line of pink marked the horizon to the east. Max figured he had thirty minutes until full light, which would give him time to swim out to the derelict Japanese gunboat that rode atop a nearby reef. The support people at Foxfire had managed to slip in a radio transmitter and emergency water, along with food stores and ammunition. If necessary, Max could hole up there indefinitely, keeping Cruz's island under covert surveillance.

No one had counted on two civilians plummeting out of the sky in the middle of the op zone. But as a SEAL, Max was trained to expect the unexpected, so the show would go on. He wouldn't worry about the woman with the expressive eyes or the body that was tempting in all the right places, even buried beneath soggy jean shorts and a baggy Hawaiian print shirt.

Come to think of it, why was she dressed like a college student on spring break? How could a college student afford the expensive camera and lenses that he'd seen in her leather bag? He'd have to search for her ID again later while she slept.

First he had to swim to the reef and complete a secure transmission back to HQ. After that, he'd stockpile more medical supplies, transferring them from the beached gunboat to the underground bunker. If the pilot took a turn for the worse, Max wanted to be ready. He was no surgeon, but he'd had training in field medicine and Izzy Teague would brief him on what to expect from lung complications.

After a final scratch and a touch command to his new best friend, Max slipped on his breathing gear and headed back to the water.

"YOU'VE GOT *WHAT?*" Lloyd Ryker, the head of the Foxfire research program, sounded worried.

"Two civilians from a ditched Cessna, sir. Vehicle ID

number Alpha seven—one—niner—four—two—zero. The pilot's passport reads Jase Van Horn, and the woman called him Dutch. He's in bad shape, sir."

Ryker muttered a few choice words. "I'll put our tech man on when we're done. He'll handle the medical end. What about the woman?"

"Not much to tell. Blonde hair, maybe five foot ten. Speaks English like an American and seemed pretty strong for a woman."

"No ID?"

"None that I could find, sir."

"And there's been no sign of your target?"

"Not yet." Max sensed Ryker's growing tension that Cruz hadn't been sighted.

"Did your friend show any scent alerts for these two?"

He meant Truman. "Nothing that was clear. He was edgy, and he checked out the woman briefly, along with her bag. Before he got very far, a bottle of perfume broke inside her case. That pretty much blew any hope of a clean scent."

"Accident?" Ryker snapped.

"Unclear."

"No weapons on either of them?"

"No, and no communication devices," Max said tightly.

Ryker drummed his fingers loud enough for Max to hear over the static. "They could be civilians, but you are to treat them as hostiles until we have confirmation of their aircraft number and passports. We'll have an answer by your next check-in. What happened to their Cessna?"

"I drilled the pontoons and sank it, sir. Figured we didn't need any floating debris to trigger alarms."

"Good. Keep focused out there. Here's your tech contact. You've got ninety seconds. I won't risk detection."

"Copy, sir."

Static crackled. "You've got a possible lung compression there? Give me the vitals," Izzy Teague said briskly.

When Max finished his report, Izzy was silent. Paper rustled, then Foxfire's techno wizard cleared his throat. "There's good news and there's bad news. Your man there is in bad shape, but he appears stable. That could change fast, of course. For now, just keep him warm and hydrated, and watch for signs of infection. Keep me updated, if possible."

"Will do." Max watched the sweep hand on his luminous watch. "Time's up."

"Give 'em hell. Oh—give your friend a nice scratch from me." Izzy was careful not to mention Truman by name in case the message was picked up. He was chuckling when he cut the connection.

Quickly, Max stripped down the phone and hid it in a false compartment inside the ship. Then he sealed extra medicine inside his watertight kit for the swim back. His watch vibrated, signaling that it was time to leave, and Max knew he was cutting things close if he hoped to miss first light.

With his swim fins over one arm, he climbed the rusted companionway of the old gunboat, wondering what tales the walls could tell of Japanese sailors sent out to this remote island to watch for enemy activity. The ship's log indicated that a storm had run the ship onto this reef and put it out of operation. The captain had committed suicide, shamed by his carelessness.

Shadows moved along the companionway as Max made his way to the middeck. He understood the weight of duty and self-sacrifice. There were worse ways to go out than falling on your sword.

But Max wasn't about to let his own mission run aground.

As he slipped on his mask and breathing gear, he focused on the woman. Maybe she was the pilot's daughter. The age difference was about right, and she seemed genuinely concerned—assuming this wasn't one more part of an elaborate act.

He smiled as he went backward into the water. If she was lying, he'd know soon enough.

There weren't many ways to keep secrets from him.

WHEN MAX REACHED THE beach, Truman was waiting. The dog looked up, wagging his tail but holding his down position above the well-hidden bunker.

There were no signs of footprints or boat draglines along the sand, and Truman would have signaled any visitors. With the perimeter secure and full light due any second, Max opened the trap door and headed underground.

The pilot was breathing fitfully, and the woman was curled up on Max's cot, her Hawaiian shirt tugged around her shoulders and her arm propped against the wall of the little room. Every time the pilot made a noise, she gave a jump, then sank back into deep sleep.

Max checked the pilot's vitals as Izzy had specified, frowning at his low temperature. Silently, he covered the man with another blanket. Pulse and heart rate were in acceptable limits, which was good news.

Time for work. The kind of work that the Foxfire team did best. He studied the sleeping woman, considering his best avenue of approach.

Not the hands. After too long in the water the skin usually became risky to read due to contamination. Not the legs or chest, since he didn't want to risk waking her yet, and moving her clothes would almost certainly wake her. That left the face and neck. Swimmers always tried to keep both above water, which would help him pull a better impression.

Silently he pulled the soft leather glove from his right hand. Breathing deeply, he rested his fingers at the nape of her neck. He made a preliminary scan, checking for the most reliable scent and steroid markers.

With each biochemical marker, his senses tightened, drawing him deeper. His eyes narrowed and his breathing slowed as he focused. The tactile scan wasn't magic and it wasn't superhuman, but it might have appeared that way to an uninitiated observer. What he did was the result of medical enhancements and a third-generation sensory biochip, courtesy of the crew of eggheads that Lloyd Ryker kept on tap at the Foxfire lab. Max had trained hard to master a huge range of human steroids, hormones and man-made chemicals. When carefully recorded, they presented a picture of the subject's recent activities, where they took place and the emotions that were present at the time.

To a civilian it would look like witchcraft, images pulled from thin air. But every scan had its price, demanding absolute focus as well as psychological risk. Like Truman, Max's amped-up senses were vulnerable to every stray chemical, whether human-based or manufactured. For his own protection, gloves were required gear, keeping his senses clear for mission work. At the beginning he had missed casual skin contact; now it was his normal mode.

He felt the hairs stiffen at the back of his neck as cool air brushed his palm. It felt odd to have his hands free. It also felt damnably sensual.

Frowning, Max shoved that thought from his mind. Skin was skin and a woman was a woman. There was no big deal about either.

Through his sensitized fingers he picked up the faint sweetness of her spilled perfume and the tang of sweat, some of it his own. Even without touching her, he knew he'd find a welter of female hormones layering her skin. If somewhere in those tangled scent layers he found Cruz's markers, something Max had been keenly trained for weeks to pick out…

In that case, he was under orders to extract all possible information via any means necessary. No questions would be asked later, as long as he succeeded in his mission. Ryker had made that clear.

And Max was committed to success. This was his first mission since the incident in Malaysia that had taken his jump partner's life and left Max in a surgical ward for eighteen hours. This time, failure was not an option. He had too many debts to repay—and too many demons to silence after the harrowing, predawn raid that had taken seven lives.

In the darkness the pilot shifted as if he was in pain. When his blanket fell, Max straightened it, careful to use his covered hand. In the narrow space every movement seemed loud, each rustle of fabric sharp. Even breathing seemed intimate.

It was strange how often you came to feel a physical connection with your subject, Max thought. When the hormones came into focus, you picked up fragments of over-the-counter sleeping pills or antihistamines, hair dye and sunscreen. In a wave that seemed to come out of nowhere, you knew your subject better than you knew your own friends or family. People thought your smile was just a sign of polite interest or concealed boredom. They didn't suspect that you were picking up their medical history, reading their whole life in a simple handshake.

In the Middle Ages this sort of thing would have gotten you burned at the stake. In the Navy, it earned you a medal—even if it happened to be a medal that no one saw, because the whole program was code-restricted to a handful of outsiders.

Frowning, Max focused on the woman's face. Even in sleep she was in motion, her eyes fluttering, her hands moving back and forth across the wrinkled shirt with the outrageous red flowers and pink parrots. When her hands curved, he had the feeling she was dreaming about holding something. A camera? She'd had enough equipment in that big leather bag he'd found drifting in the water.

She muttered a name—Vance or Lance? Her mouth thinned and she shoved at the wall, banging her elbow. Max saw his moment and took it, curving his palm over the skin just behind her ear and under her hair.

Information washed over him, swift details of disparate chemical nuances. Hair spray. Wax, probably from an expensive candle, judging by the high amount of distilled perfume oil. She'd touched coconut oil recently, the food-grade kind, thick and unhydrogenated, without perfume additives. Below that was a layer of some kind of silicone.

Max frowned. Expensive mascara. Also some kind of high-quality hair dye. He didn't move, settling down into a spiral of hexones and fragrance oils as he picked up the threads of her life. There was some kind of personal-use lubricant, scented and very thick.

His lips twitched as he searched his memorized catalogue of ingredients. Was it regular moisturizer or the kind of lubricant you bought for a rough and wild Saturday night with your latest lover? His hand tightened and he forced his gaze away almost instantly. You never second guessed the layers. You kept the sensory flow straight and clear, chemicals and hormones only, no counting on outside cues from clothes, complexion, age or anything else.

Clean and simple. That was rule number one.

Max figured that the rule applied to a whole lot more than his Foxfire observations. In life, clean and simple was the only thing that made sense. It was too bad more people didn't seem to know that.

But there was more to feel and he needed to work fast before she awoke. He moved his hand inside the curve of her ear, gentle as a whisper of air, searching for any chemical signature that would connect her with Cruz. The rogue Foxfire operative hadn't known that one of his last chips was a scent marker designed to convey information unnoticed by the human nose but registered clearly by a trained government animal like Truman.

Or by a special forces agent trained and enhanced the way Max was.

He traced her ear gently, finding the small curves where wax clung, the places most likely to hold other scent clues. He found a hint of cigar smoke, the coconut oil again, more of that damned expensive perfume she seemed to love. Sunscreen. A little bit of very dry champagne, as if someone had sprayed her recently.

A wild midnight party?

But there was nothing else. Not a hint of Cruz's marker. Nothing that suggested the special lubricants used in the stolen inertial guidance system. Nothing even remotely close to what Ryker was looking for.

Max wasn't sure whether to be irritated or relieved as he knelt beside her on the ground, watching her hair fan across her cheek and the faint trace of veins beneath her eyes.

Feeling her skin, feeling her pulse. 98.4—she was probably in deep theta, given her heart rate. She'd had dental surgery within the last month. One or two fillings, since he could pick up the faint but acrid hint of mercury on her skin. That was one of the first ingredients he'd been taught to identify.

She sighed and turned onto her side. Her hair spilled over his wrist, warm and soft, the sudden contact like a fist slammed into his chest. He picked up the hormone array of a vital woman in childbearing years. He read estrogen and cortisol, from stress and physical exertion, but he figured she was also a coffee drinker because he picked up kona notes, too.

What would it be like to drink in those layers, to feed her chocolate and a fine roast coffee, letting the taste hum right down through her senses into his? Through her, lifted from her mouth and skin—

He cut through the image, disturbed at his primal male reaction to her. When had his thinking turned *personal?* His Foxfire training had eliminated the concept of personal from his physical contacts.

Or so he'd thought.

Something pricked at the back of his neck. He was

trying to figure out the source of that sharp sensation when she turned and flung up her arm, hitting him in the shoulder. The breath whooshed out of his lungs as he was caught in blurred impressions. Sea water and sunscreen. More of that damned Chanel No. 5, but still nothing that connected her to Cruz.

He stood up quickly, catching his breath, distinctly disoriented.

She reached out, this time her arm slamming against the cool earth wall. The impact made her breath catch and Max heard her gasp. Her eyes fluttered.

He leaned down to check the man she'd called Dutch so she wouldn't realize that he'd been touching her neck.

She came fully awake and frowned at him. Anger blazed over her face. "What are you *doing* to him?"

"Be quiet," he said tightly.

"Why do you keep saying—"

"Do it." Cold. Leaving her no doubt that he was deadly serious.

She glared at him, then lifted her shoulders in an irritated shrug. Even this she did expressively.

And bravely. She had no clue to his identity, no certainty of the risks before her, yet she faced him squarely and demanded answers. She'd make a damned good solider, Max thought. She prioritized in an emergency, handling what she could control rather than spinning her wheels over what was unchangeable.

He realized that in the faint light of his Mini-mag with its narrow blue field she was striking. Not beautiful, but unusual. Probably a lot of men had told her that. Probably hearing it had gone to her head. With wild blonde hair and cheekbones like that, he figured she knew all about manipulating men with a single glance, a teasing smile and the lure of that rich body.

Not that it mattered to him.

She crouched beside him. Bending closer, she whispered in his ear. "How is he doing?"

"Stable."

"Then why do we have to whisper?"

"I don't want to take chances."

"Chances on *what?*"

"Keep quiet."

She moved back to the nearby cot, looking irritated. "He needs a doctor. A *real* doctor," she snapped.

"He's going to be fine."

She continued to stare at Dutch. "What happens if he gets worse?" Her voice had turned uncertain.

Max didn't answer. He knew she wouldn't want the truth, and tactically it was best not to lie any more than you had to.

She looked down suddenly, rubbing her arm. "What did you do to me?"

"Nothing." His voice was a whisper. "You were lurching around in your sleep and you hit the wall."

Her eyes said *yeah, right.*

Max figured it was time to ask his own questions. "I don't know your name."

She stared at him. "That's right, you don't. Yours first."

"Max."

"Max what?"

"Massey." He lied without hesitation.

A frown worked down her forehead. Probably she was surprised by the quick answer and after that she was trying to figure out if he was telling her the truth.

"My name's Jones. Ella…Jones."

"Sure it is. I'll just call you Blondie."

That seemed to irritate her. "No blonde jokes or it won't be pretty."

Max shrugged. He wasn't up on current entertainment due to months of medical recuperation, followed by round-the-clock training at the Foxfire facility. "So where are you from, Blondie?"

"Detroit." She sat up slowly and rubbed her elbow. "Dad was a cop. Mom was a school nurse. Dinner conversation got pretty raw sometimes, what with sucking chest wounds and infectious impetigo." She pulled the shirt around her shoulders, her eyes locked on his face. "What are you doing here?"

The question was casual, Max thought. Like she had no particular interest. If she was working for Cruz, she was damned good.

Of course Cruz would insist upon that skill in an operative.

"I do chemical work." Max used his arranged cover, every detail well rehearsed. "Microscope and chemical assay for hire, world wide."

"What kind of chemical work?"

"Oil fields, that kind of thing."

"I guess that's important." Her eyes moved over the room and its small crates of stored equipment, and Max could see her putting the pieces together. "Why did you tie me up at first?"

"Lady, you came down in a plane right at the epicenter of my exploration zone. I'm taking no chances. I've been alerted that two other oil companies may be sending in unlicensed investigators, and that could cost my employer millions. Money aside, freelancers don't always have scruples about how they get the job done. It's the Wild West every day, everywhere when you're talking about oil. We have a closed contract for exploration here for another two months, and no one is getting in here before that."

"People do that kind of thing? I mean, they steal corporate information in a deserted place like this?"

Max thought she sounded surprised. Either she was very naïve about how business worked, or she was one very smart woman putting on a great act.

He shrugged. "Where money's at stake, people will do anything."

"You're probably right." She studied his Mini-mag. "So you're here doing x-rays, things like that?"

"More or less. Since it's proprietary, I can't really discuss it." Max pulled his canteen out of his vest and held it out for her to drink. "You should rehydrate."

She took the canteen eagerly, then gave the opening a quick scrub with the hem of her shirt. "Nothing personal, but I don't know you from Adam."

"Always smart to be cautious." He watched her drink. There was something fascinating about the way her muscles rippled. Her hair was wild, a dozen different shades of blonde. Beads of water trailed from her mouth, over her chin.

What would they taste like, mixed with her unique scent blend?

Enough. You know she's probably connected to Cruz. There are damned few coincidences in this line of work.

When she stopped drinking, Max took the canteen, then raised Dutch's head and poured a small amount into his mouth.

"How is he doing?"

"He seems stable. Heart rate in the normal zone."

Her eyes narrowed. "You know about stuff like that? Hardly standard procedure for engineers."

"I go into some pretty desolate areas, so I have to know basic bush medicine."

She appeared to think this over and then nodded. "What's wrong with him?"

"I'd say it's his lungs. His chest looks like it took some trauma, and he may have compression in the right side."

"How soon can we catch a plane back?" Her voice tightened. "You must have some way to communicate with your headquarters, right? They can send a plane for you."

"Not yet, they can't."

"Why not?" She shot to her feet, banging her head on the earth ceiling. The woman was tall, Max thought, and she looked more than a little klutzy. Probably that was part of the act, too. "I want to leave now."

"Open your eyes. Did you happen to see any planes in the area?"

"So call someone. Use a radio. You must have something."

"There's a storm heading into this area. I doubt that any planes are flying right now."

"So when?" She winced, rubbing her head. "Dutch looks bad. I don't think we should wait."

"I'll try calling again soon. The weather situation could clear by then." Like hell he would, Max thought grimly. He held up a cardboard-covered tray with a prepackaged meal. "Are you hungry?"

"I guess I should be, but I'm not. I had breakfast back in Tahiti and some coffee and a protein bar at the beach where we were shooting—"

"Shooting what?"

"Swimsuit stills and tropical backgrounds for a calendar."

"You're a photographer?"

"For ten years. I can't think of any work I'd like to do more—and I've done most of it, believe me." Something haunted filled her eyes. "I guess that's all off, now that Vance is…gone."

"Vance was the other passenger? Big guy, balding?"

"That's him. He wasn't breathing when I woke up. There was a lot of blood on the seat. You found his… body?"

Max nodded. The sight hadn't been pretty, the body swollen and pale.

She cleared her throat and looked at him uncertainly. "Could I have more water, or is that something we need to ration?"

"We should have enough, but don't overdo it."

She took the canteen and splashed a little on her hand, then rubbed her face. "I'm sticky from seawater. What I wouldn't give to clean up."

"Afraid I don't have bath facilities."

She squirmed uneasily. "But you must have—I mean, what about the necessities?"

Max pointed over his shoulder. "When you need to go, you find a quiet spot and do what you have to do. But be sure to bury everything. This is a fragile ecosystem," he added, pretty sure that this would register.

"Of course." She turned and stared pointedly up the steps. "At least I can go back to the waterfall and wash my face. Unless you're going to lock in me again."

"One, I didn't lock you in. The door was always unsecured. Two, I left the dog so you wouldn't wander out in the dark and hurt yourself. When I called him off, you went straight out and did just that."

For the second time, her eyes said *yeah, right.* "Well, it's not dark now, so how about opening that door? I want to get some fresh air and clean up."

There was an answer to her question. Max just couldn't think of it right that second. He could strong-arm her into staying. He could probably frighten her badly.

On the other hand, what if she really *was* an innocent bystander having one nightmare day? Hell, she didn't look or act like a trained professional. Her blond hair was matted from seawater, she had mascara clotted under her eyes and her legs were scratched up. Max had dumped her sweater outside, some kind of short, clingy thing that barely covered her arms, much less her chest. Now he noticed that stray white hairs covered her Hawaiian shirt.

He plucked off one of the strands and held it up. "You're shedding."

"It's from my shrug."

"Beg your pardon?"

"Shrug. A short sweater…the new, new thing." Her voice was ironic. "Actually, it was my own design. I knitted it between shoots back in Tahiti. Or was it the Marianas? After a while, all beaches start to look alike. Did you find it?"

"Back on the beach."

She seemed relieved, smiling suddenly. The curve of her mouth fascinated him so much he almost didn't hear her next question.

"Why the leather gloves?"

"Chemical sensitivities."

Miki frowned, then broke into a hacking cough. "Great. Seawater in the lungs. I think I swallowed some really nasty algae, too."

He thumped her hard on the back. "Dulse and sea plants are an excellent source of nutrients. The iodine and mineral salts are invaluable."

She stared at him. "Don't tell me you're a nutritionist along with knowing field medicine. That's pretty impressive."

Max noticed that she didn't bat her eyes when she said it. No simpering, either. He needed to decide if she was very innocent—or very clever, carefully trained by Cruz. He had a feeling that either way this woman was going to be big trouble.

Since he couldn't give her a good reason to stay underground and out of sight, he decided stalling was the best tactic. Fingering the white piece of thread, he sat down on the steps leading outside. "What do you call this stuff?"

"Angora. As in rabbits and goats."

"And you used it for that…sweater thing you were wearing. How?"

She stared at him, looking impatient. "I knitted it. Two sticks, one string. You may have heard of it," she said dryly.

"I don't think I've ever seen anyone actually do it." Max rubbed the back of his neck. "How long does something like that take?"

"Three or four days, more or less. It depends on how complicated the stitch is and what needle size you're using." She put her hands on her hips. "You don't have the slightest interest in knitting. You're just trying to keep me in here. Why?" she demanded flatly.

Max didn't move. "Actually, I am interested. How does it work?"

She stalked across the small space, angry and determined like a storm that couldn't be contained. "Enough of the inquisition, buster. Let me out of here now or I'll do something you don't like. And trust me, whatever it is, it will be really *loud*."

CHAPTER SIX

"HOW ABOUT YOU RELAX?"

"I *can't* relax. I've been in a plane wreck, nearly drowned, and now I'm incarcerated with a crazy person. Also, I've got to tell you that glove thing of yours is too weird. I don't buy that sensitivity story, either. You know what I think?"

Max watched her, fascinated by the color pulsing through her cheeks and the anger in her eyes. Was she always so intense? "No, I can't even imagine."

"I think you're a criminal who came here to hide out. Probably you're the kind who uses his brains more than brawn. Maybe you're a high-tech thief, someone who masterminds money laundering. Not the chump change kind either, but a business that's huge and far-flung and multinational. Out here you think no one can catch you."

"You've got quite an imagination." Max watched, fascinated by her energy as she ran into a crate, stubbed her toe and hopped around awkwardly. "You may want to cool down before you hurt yourself."

"That's very funny. You couldn't care less about me.

First you lock me up here in this…this awful cavelike place while you—"

She stopped as Max stood up and calmly pushed open the small metal door, revealing a perfect turquoise sky.

"Go on."

She stayed where she was, her face uncertain. "Right now?"

"Right now."

Wind ruffled her hair. "Up there? You won't stop me, or send that big dog of yours after me?"

Max reined in his impatience. It was a calculated risk to let her out, but risky moves could yield the best results. He figured she would need to find temporary bathroom facilities soon anyway. "You've got four minutes. There's a place inland with some hibiscus plants to give you privacy. When you're done, you can scrub your face with sand and a little water from the stream there. Don't dawdle."

She looked at the canteen he was holding out. "You want me to wash with sand?" She caught a shaky breath. "I guess I shouldn't be complaining. I could be dead right now, half-eaten by fish. What's a little sand in comparison to that?" She took his canteen of water. "So I have four minutes?"

Max nodded. Following her moods was like trying to catch minnows in turbid water. One minute she complained, the next she was logical and full of apologies. He moved aside, slanting her a warning look. "Remember the time. It's important."

"So you keep saying." She raised the canteen against her chest, climbing past him up the stairs, but her bare foot hit an uneven plank and she fell sideways.

Max caught her quickly, his gloved hand circling her waist. Her hair brushed his face and her body slammed against him, surprising them both by the contact. Beneath the damp clothes her skin radiated a subtle but distinct heat, which he felt through the leather of his gloves. He put her down as soon as he could, dropping his arm and trying not to remember how warm she had felt.

A sudden wind filled the small space, ruffling her hair. She cleared her throat and pulled away. "That was clumsy of me."

"No problem." Max put more space between them. "No more perfume because it bothers my dog. And no noise." When Max followed her outside, little flecks of white yarn drifted back from her shoulders. She swung her arms wide, trying to balance in the narrow doorway, and in the process nearly knocked him in the face.

He ducked by reflex, wondering if she was always this clumsy. If it was an act, it was very well rehearsed. Something tickled his nose, squeezing his throat and he sneezed hard, which sent more angora fluff up into his face and nose. Max brushed it away, frowning. The noise discipline rules applied to him as much as her. Cruz could be on the other island waiting and watching right now.

One mistake could get them all killed.

Cruz didn't believe in giving second chances.

MIKI STILL COULDN'T FIGURE out if he was a recluse or some kind of white-collar criminal. He might even have been a mercenary, she thought. He had the cold eyes to be all of those things. His story about oil field exploration made sense, but she still didn't buy it. She had been a photographer too long not to have a sharp eye for details and faces, and Max Massey was no pencil-pushing engineer. She was equally certain that his big, intelligent dog wasn't along as a passive companion. The lab had the same intense focus she'd seen in her friend Kit's animals. Frankly, *both* of them gave her the creeps, and the sooner she got away from them, the better.

She looked around, committing the terrain to memory. Since she might be stuck here, she needed to stockpile as much information as possible. Meanwhile the clock was ticking and she had no doubt that Mr. Hard-as-nails would enforce his four-minute warning.

The hibiscus bushes were right where he had said, providing a nice wall of privacy. When she'd finished the more pressing necessities, she grabbed his canteen and a handful of sand and went to work on her face and hands. The sand stung her arms, but she managed to remove most of the stickiness left over from the seawater. Closing her eyes and scrubbing her neck and chest, she fantasized about a bar of French milled soap and a loofah sponge. As she tilted her head, a cool wind brushed her face and she almost forgot that she was stranded and she had blisters on her feet. There was no point trying to do anything about her hair. There was no way for a decent shampoo with only a little water and a handful of sand.

Her time was up, so she tugged her shirt back in place, picking up the canteen from the ground. But a flash of color caught her eye and she leaned down to study a small pink flower. Miki felt a wave of excitement as she recognized a rare orchid, its bright petals soft and fragile. The scene would have made an award-winning photo, if only she had her camera. Maybe if she groveled, the Jerk would return her camera bag and equipment for a few minutes.

A hand gripped her arm and closed, pulling her to her feet. How did the man manage to be so quiet? "What's wrong?" she hissed.

He didn't speak, pointing at his watch.

"That's a very rare orchid," she whispered excitedly. "I could win a prize with this. You have to let me—"

He cut her off with a gloved hand to her mouth. Miki felt the soft leather against her mouth as he turned her slowly, looking down the beach. He seemed to be scanning the water, and she realized there was a larger island glinting in the sunlight, its central mountain ridge wreathed in clouds. Though Max's breathing was low and steady, she felt his tension clearly.

When she tried to talk, his gloved fingers cut off the sound. His body was absolutely still.

Why was he looking at the beautiful coves? Did he expect trouble from there? She didn't struggle when he tugged her back toward the hidden door and the big dog waiting beside it. She took a last deep breath of clean air and then went back down the steps she was already beginning to hate. As soon as the door was in place, she rounded on him.

"That was a very rare flower back there. I could have gotten a thousand dollars for one shot. You want to tell me again why I can't have my camera bag and why I can't make any noise?"

"I already explained. You should have listened then." He pushed her back toward the one spare cot. "Sit down."

"You think I'll do whatever you ask? Forget that. I'm tired of taking your orders."

"I said to sit down."

"Go eat sand." Miki crossed her arms, furious.

When she didn't move, he caught her shoulders, and she tried to push him away, but the man wouldn't budge. For someone lean, he was incredibly strong.

Furious, she watched his fingers open, then brush her hair. If he thought this would be some kind of kinky prelude to sex, he had a major surprise coming.

His thumb combed through her hair, and Miki was amazed at how gentle the movement was. Her confusion grew as he leaned closer, sliding his arm around her shoulder.

She felt his muscles tighten and his breath play over her cheek.

"Don't move."

Like hell, she wouldn't move. He'd saved her life, but that didn't entitle him to grope her. Enough was enough.

When she tried to move, his hand twisted in a blur of motion.

"Stand still," he whispered. "Completely still."

Her breath caught as something appeared in his hand. Miki saw that it was long and small and frantically alive, wriggling against his glove.

"Centipede." He frowned, holding up the restless mass of legs. "Poisonous variety."

She gulped air, feeling faint. She hated bugs. Really, really hated bugs. "On me? In my hair?" She swallowed. "How poisonous?"

"Let's just say that you wouldn't have felt your fingers in a few seconds."

She fought a shudder as he carried the centipede up the stairs. "Aren't you going to kill it…or something?"

"Why? This is its home. We're the intruders here. I'll put it where it won't bother us."

Miki stared at him. It was poisonous and he wasn't going to kill it? That was either religious or downright weird. Just when she thought she had a handle on the guy, he threw her a curve ball. On the other hand, he could be faking. She'd noticed that men did that a lot.

He turned around, disappearing up the steps, the centipede in his gloved hand. Suddenly escape was all she could think about. She couldn't stand the thought of the dark, cramped space or the poisonous bugs hidden in the dirt or waiting on the walls. She began to sweat, panicking. She needed open sky and fresh air around her. She needed time to think, away from constant observation.

Even though she was surrounded by water and there had been no sign of passing boats anywhere, she had to try. The sooner she got away, the sooner she could find help for Dutch.

She waited until there was no sound from the open door, then crept up the steps. Sunlight spilled over the long curve of the beach, and she saw the glint of the open sea. The Jerk was standing about twenty feet away, giving something to the dog.

Miki ran for the line of boulders at the top of the beach.

CHAPTER SEVEN

IT WAS GOING TO BE CLOSE.

Panting, Miki dug her feet into the sand, throwing all her strength forward as she ran. She was only eight feet from the first of the rocks, and once she was out of sight, she would sprint for the dense trees at the top of the hill.

Her heart pounded, and sand flew in her face. She squinted, afraid to take her eyes off the tree line as she ran.

Something cut across her path—the big gold Lab.

She turned sharply, sprinting for a different opening in the rocks, its shadows three feet closer. There was no noise except the thunder of her heart and the slap of her feet.

But then a low whine filled her ears as her pulse hammered and sweat trickled down her back. Dimly she realized the sound came from the sky overhead.

Silver wings glinted, breaking through a wall of clouds. Miki looked up and screamed, jumping wildly and waving her arms at the plane.

A moment later she was tackled from behind, driven facedown into the sand. She wheezed as a powerful body dropped flat on top of her and a hand gripped her mouth.

"Stop moving," Max hissed, his mouth to her ear.

Like hell she would.

Her fists flashed, pummeling his shoulders while she kicked wildly. But there was no way to shift his powerful body. As the drum of the engine grew louder, she fought to break free, but he kept her pinned beneath him while she sputtered curses beneath his gloved hand. The thunder of her heart was so loud that she barely heard the airplane drone off into the distance.

Tears burned. There was no way anyone would see her now. There was no hope of escape.

Caught between fury and crushing disappointment, she jammed her elbow upward, aiming for his neck, pleased to hear him give a tiny grunt, but she might as well have tried to dislodge a Sherman tank with a flyswatter.

His thighs opened. He wrapped one foot around her ankles and their bodies ground together intimately. He was stronger than she'd realized, stronger than any man she knew, and she was his captive with no way to escape and nowhere to go even if she succeeded.

Miki's face flamed at the pressure of his thigh wedged against hers. She jammed her other elbow upward, fighting blindly. This time he didn't grunt or show any sign of contact. What kind of man *was* he? A direct blow like that should have hurt him somewhere.

As she struggled, she had a glimpse of his face, cold and determined above her. The smooth surface of his leather glove traced her flushed skin.

His fingers opened at her jaw, tightened.

He was going to choke her. She twisted as she felt

his hands tighten on her neck. He seemed to search her skin carefully, pressing a spot at her ear.

White lights burst behind her eyes and Miki felt the world drain away to black around her.

THE FREAKING WOMAN HAD done it now, Max thought. If Cruz had spotters in that plane they'd be down on this beach in minutes.

He'd had no choice but to knock her out while he tackled damage control. His eyes narrowed as he swept both sides of the beach. There was no sign of a response yet. No energy signatures that matched Cruz's.

Max swept her limp body over one shoulder and sprinted for the bunker. After dumping her on a cot, he grabbed a wide palm leaf and worked his way back along the sand, methodically wiping away all their footprints.

He tapped his leg, summoned Truman and swept away the dog's prints, too. With the beach clean, Max studied the sky to the west. There was no further sign of air traffic, nor any movement at sea, and he hoped it would stay that way. He would have to face Cruz soon, but first he needed more information about the fortifications on the nearby island.

Max brushed the sand around the door, and as a final precaution, scattered twigs and torn palm leaves randomly throughout the area. When he finished, untrained eyes would have sworn they were standing on pristine beach.

But Cruz didn't have untrained eyes. He had been the first and very best at reading energy trails, and his skills had grown stronger since his escape from Foxfire custody.

Max had to assume they had been spotted by the plane, their hiding place blown. Once he was back underground he slung Blondie over his shoulder, grabbed a pack with extra supplies, pressed a spot in the wall and watched the cement slowly part to reveal a hidden tunnel.

TWENTY MINUTES LATER, Max scrambled up the hillside beneath a cover of trees. He'd left Blondie unconscious and secured out of sight in a nearby cave, then retrieved his gear and set up an alternate camp at a spot overlooking the beach. Now he was in the process of carrying Dutch to safety, with Truman walking point. The Lab stopped every few moments, head raised to sniff the air, his eyes on the horizon, but so far there had been no alerts to indicate danger.

Max's shoulder felt the first hint of strain from five trips up and down to the beach, but beyond that he'd barely broken a sweat. *Good genes,* as Wolfe Houston liked to say with a wry smile.

As he climbed the rim of a rocky slope, Max heard a low vibration behind him. Truman had already stopped, his ears raised, studying the clouds to the south. Racing back, the dog bumped Max's leg.

Danger alert.

A small seaplane appeared, no more than a smudge

against the racing clouds. Truman looked up at Max, as if asking for orders.

"Out of sight ASAP, buddy. Double-time it." Max sprinted up the steep slope, careful to stay under cover of scattered trees. As the motors droned closer, he calculated the distance to the cave.

He wasn't going to make it. Carefully, he lowered Dutch to the ground, hidden beneath an overhanging bush.

"What's—wrong?" The pilot roused, his voice cracking. "Have to land. Strict…orders. No time."

"It's okay, pal. Take it easy."

But the pilot had already slipped back into unconsciousness. Max made certain he was out of sight, then turned to gauge the distance to the hidden cave.

Something prickled at his neck. A weight seemed to fall without warning, pinning him to the ground.

Cruz. Foxfire's ex-leader could distort and project any kind of energy until Miami Beach looked like Nome, Alaska. If he didn't know better, Max would have sworn he was being crushed by a chunk of that plane overhead. With focused concentration, Max cut through his sudden immobility and sprinted up the hill, Truman inches behind him. Even at top speed it was going to be damned close.

The prickling at his neck grew into a sharp stabbing, and Max had no more doubts: it had to be Cruz carrying out an energy scan from the approaching plane.

A cloud covered the sea, casting a shadow over the slope. Truman brushed past Max's leg and turned, very still, face to the sky as the wind riffled his hair. The dog's tail flattened to a rigid line.

"Take cover, Truman." Max snapped the order, aware that precious seconds were passing. He brushed his collarbone, pressing an implant in the bone to set off a localized energy disturbance, but he knew the field wouldn't last long—or possibly not at all, if Cruz's skills had grown sharp enough to see through this recent Foxfire innovation.

He glanced back at his training partner. "Tru, *heel.*"

But the Lab didn't move, body stiff, face toward the sky.

Something drifted out of the air. Light and cold, it danced over Max's cheek and then vanished. Another speck swirled through the air, and suddenly Max was surrounded by white flakes drifting out of a sunny sky.

Snow? Impossible.

As the engine whine grew closer, the delicate flakes seemed to blur, whirling above Truman's head. Darkening, they gained substance and rippled into a wall of fog, dense and moist, shrouding Max and the dog in an impenetrable curtain.

The airplane shot past, engines throbbing. Max felt the hairs stand up along his neck as a bar of energy probed the spot where he had been standing moments before. As the fog pressed at his face, he heard the plane bank and circle, dropping lower.

The energy signature retreated, and still Truman hadn't moved, his head raised alertly to the sky. The possibilities left Max stunned. This was the new skill that Ryker had hinted at, glimpsed only once before in the training facility. Whether it could be controlled and harnessed, Max didn't know, or even how long the dog could maintain the effect. Max knew how draining a small image distortion could be, and an intense weather disturbance like this had to have cost Truman dearly.

The plane circled again, and Max breathed in relief as it droned away into the distance. Seconds later the prickling at his shoulders vanished.

Over his head the fog began to fade. Max picked out the outline of nearby trees as a gust of wind swept up the slope, scattering the unstable gray veil. In a surreal moment, mist gave way to sunlight that beat hot on Max's neck. If he had not stood here in the middle of the phenomenon and experienced it, he would never have accepted any of it.

He rubbed a hand over his eyes, but the sunshine remained. He looked over at Truman, shaking his head. Wait until Ryker heard about this.

"Pretty smart, aren't you?" Max knelt and raised one hand. "How about a high five for a fellow SEAL?"

Truman turned around in a circle, tail wagging happily as it banged Max in the face. Then the dog sat, raised one paw and waited.

High five.

Damned if he didn't know *that,* too. Filled with a wave of pride, Max laughed as the big dog licked his face. "Is there anything you can't do, champ?"

Truman's head cocked. He panted hard, tongue lolling. Then he shuddered.

"What's wrong, Tru?"

The dog whimpered softly. Then he collapsed.

Truman felt cold as Max picked him up and sprinted uphill. Because this was new behavior, Max had no idea of how to treat the dog or even the nature of the problem. The Foxfire science team had given him a medical kit with nutrients, so Max figured he'd start there.

"What's wrong with your dog?" Blondie was sitting against the cave wall, her hands on her forehead as if it hurt. "While you're at it, why do I have the mother of all headaches and how did I get here?"

Her questions didn't surprise him. She wouldn't remember the last minutes before he had put her out. No one ever did. "I knocked you out," he said curtly. "The men flying in that plane could have been dangerous."

"You think *everyone* is dangerous." She started to say something more, but instead she frowned and crossed to sit beside Truman. "He doesn't look right. Did he fall during that fog?"

"Not exactly. Hell, what's your *real* name? We both know it's not Ella."

She chewed at her lip and stared back at him, then shrugged. "Miki—like the mouse."

Max filed the name away for future reference. He had a hunch that she was telling the truth this time.

"What's wrong with Truman?"

"Something happened after that fog came in off the sea." Max chose his words carefully. "You saw that, did you?"

Miki nodded. "At first I thought I was imagining it." She ran a hand slowly along Truman's head. "He feels cold. Can't you do something for him?"

Max found a package of green gel nutrients and squeezed a tiny amount into Truman's mouth.

The dog didn't respond, barely breathing now. Max lifted him gently onto his lap and stroked his head.

"What happened?" Miki asked anxiously.

Max shook his head. "One minute he was fine. Then the fog came and he just collapsed. Maybe it's some kind of canine virus."

Miki pushed closer, rubbing Truman's stomach. "Poor baby," she crooned. "Move over," she ordered. "Then go get me a blanket."

"Why?"

"Because he's cold, stupid." Miki nudged him away as she scooped Truman closer, smoothing the fur across his back. She lifted one of the Lab's eyelids carefully and frowned. "No pupil response. That's a bad sign."

Max stiffened. "You know about dogs?"

"I told you before that my friend is a trainer and one of her dogs had a habit of getting sick. He's a real handful, but he likes me, so I help take care of him." Miki felt Truman's chest. "Where's that blanket?"

Max didn't have a blanket in his pack, so he pulled off his T-shirt and draped it over the Lab's motionless body. He realized Blondie was staring at his chest. "Something wrong?"

Her eyes were wide. She took a little gulping breath. "You— Your chest. It's…strong," she said hoarsely. "But the scars…"

It had been so many months that Max had actually forgotten the silver network that laced his ribs and shoulder, relic of a mission gone bad in Indonesia. "I had a car accident," he said tightly.

Her hand rose involuntarily, almost as if to soothe and comfort. The sight made Max's stomach clench. When had a woman last touched him to comfort rather than in the heat of sex?

He cleared his throat, annoyed at the sharp image of her fingers tracing all his scars while her soft mouth offered whispers of praise and desire.

"Shit."

"What's wrong?" Her brow wrinkled. "Do they hurt—your scars, I mean?"

"No, they don't hurt. They haven't hurt for months." He was angrier than he should have been. "Forget about it."

"I can see how you'd be sensitive about them. I'm sorry."

"Look, I'm not—hell, forget it." Max jammed a hand through his hair. "They're ancient history."

He saw her eyes linger on his stomach and he realized there was appreciation, not distaste in her glance. Instantly his body hardened in an erection.

Talk about rotten timing, he thought irritably. Silent and controlled, he pulled a syringe from a sealed packet of the medical kit. Ryker had told him the high potency stimulant was strictly for emergencies. Max figured this fit the definition.

Kneeling beside Miki, he brushed aside the fur at Truman's chest and broke the seal off the packet.

"Is that adrenaline? Do you think it's his heart?" Miki's voice was tight with concern. The name suited her, Max thought. Restless and quirky. Unusual.

Not that any of that mattered to him.

"Try to hold him. He can be very strong, I warn you."

"Just *do* it," she said tensely. "We'll be fine, won't we, honey?" She stroked the dog's silky head.

Truman lay limp and cold. Max could no longer feel a pulse. He found the carotid artery and injected the stimulant. If this didn't work, he could do CPR—even a cardiac thump, part of his advanced field training. But beyond that…

He forced away the thought. He'd never left a man behind in battle and he damned well *wasn't* going to lose Truman. The injection done, he smoothed the Lab's fur, checking for a pulse.

Nothing.

Miki watched his face, her fingers smoothing the Lab's soft hair. Their shared worry tightened, a thread of emotion that built until it stretched between them, deep and tangible. Max could almost feel her anxious breath, the brush of her thigh, even though they weren't touching.

Suddenly Truman wheezed. His tail banged Max's

leg weakly. With a sharp surge of relief, Max saw the dog's eyes open. The Lab twitched hard, looked up at Miki, then lapped her face with his wet tongue.

Most women would have gasped and squirmed away. But this woman laughed in pure exuberance, brushing Truman's nose with hers and ruffling the dog's fur. "About time you came around, big guy. Come on, give Aunt Miki a kiss."

Limp but eager, Truman burrowed closer against her chest, his nose shoved under her shirt directly atop her breast.

Smart dog, Max thought wryly.

"I don't think we should move him." Max straightened his T-shirt over the two of them. "He still feels cold."

"Of course we can't move him." Miki sounded indignant. "He almost died, so he gets whatever he wants." She looked around in excitement. "I still have two sticks of beef jerky in my camera bag. And you should bring my shrug. It's light but warm."

Max gave a little half smile. "Any other orders, ma'am?"

"Yes. Cover us up. Your shirt just slipped again."

Max made a mock salute and did as Miki ordered. "I need to carry Dutch up here. Then I'll go back for your sweater and more supplies."

Her eyes darkened. "I forgot about Dutch. How is he?"

"Stable." As Max straightened his T-shirt over Miki's arm, his fingers brushed her cheek. Something filled the air between them, sharp and electric, making him keenly aware of her skin, her energy and the questioning look in her eyes.

She cleared her throat. "Thanks for the shirt. And thanks for pulling me out of the water after the crash."

Truman made a tiny huffing noise and rested his head across her arm, sleeping deeply. Max looked down and shrugged. "No need for thanks. Keep an eye on Truman for me. I won't be long."

IT WAS GETTING HARDER AND harder to dislike her.

The woman could be irritating, but she had also helped save Truman's life. She was stubborn and outspoken, yet Max sensed that she was working hard to hide deep layers of vulnerability beneath her stubborn facade. But the questions remained: who was she and why was she here?

Max hoisted Dutch up on his shoulder once more. The pilot roused at the sudden movement and frowned. "Who…are you? Man on the phone? My plane—" Agitated, he tried to sit up and see the sky. "Where's my plane? What happened to Miki?"

"Take it easy. Miki's doing fine." Max didn't mention the plane, which was gone forever. "What went wrong out there?"

"Wrong? Maybe—fuel line. Vance was cheap. He—cut corners on repairs." The pilot's eyes narrowed. "Who are you? Don't…know you and I want—my plane." The pilot struggled blindly, wheezing for breath, then lapsed back into unconsciousness.

When Max entered the cave, Truman opened one

eye, wagged his tail and tried to sit up, but Miki held the dog tight against her chest. "You just stay here and rest, honey. Aunt Miki has another beef treat for you when you're ready, assuming the big, mean man says it's okay." She shot a level glance at Max. "Maybe even if he doesn't." She laughed as Truman licked her face with sudden energy. "It's you and me against him. How does that sound?"

Truman burrowed closer, his face disappearing under her shirt.

"I'll take that as a vote of agreement." But her smile soon faded. "Funny, I can't remember much of what happened right before I got here. I remember running—and then nothing. I was trying to get away, wasn't I?"

"You seem to do that a lot," Max said tightly.

"Because you're a stranger and I don't trust you." Miki wriggled as if it was possible to get comfortable with one hundred pounds of dog sprawled on top of her. "And I know you're only telling me half of what's going on here."

Max started to answer, but she shook her head. "Save your breath if it's just another story you made up. Tell me the truth or don't tell me anything."

He could have lied or sidestepped her question. Instead he nodded.

"It will save us both a lot of trouble if you remember that." She smoothed Truman's head. "And I know something happened. First there was a loud noise and then I saw that strange fog drift up the hill." She frowned at

Max. "But it was clear and sunny. I don't remember any clouds."

"The weather can change in seconds here. I wouldn't get too upset trying to figure it out."

There was a faraway look in her eyes. "I wish I'd gotten a picture. It would have been one in a million. The light was so strange and the ocean changed colors." Her face filled with a longing so intense it made Max's throat tighten. "If you miss a chance like that, you never get another one."

She knew about missed chances, he thought. That would explain part of her vulnerability under that mouthy exterior. "Have you lost many pictures?" He told himself it was simply to change the subject, but he knew that was a lie. He cared about her answer even though he shouldn't have.

Far more dangerous, he was starting to care about *her.*

"More than I should have." Her voice was quiet, wistful. "First I was too young, then I was too stupid. Later I was too lazy. There were always good excuses and a thousand reasons why the important work could wait one more day. Then one morning you wake up and realize you've wasted your life on a string of nothings."

Max wondered what had left her with such pain and regret in her eyes. The thought that it was a man filled him with icy fury.

But things were getting too personal. When you joined Foxfire, you gave up all rights to downtime and a personal life. It was part of the deal you made with Uncle Sam.

Clean and simple, Max thought. It had always made perfect sense to him before. He wondered why he was questioning the idea now.

Miki winced slightly. She looked more uncomfortable than ever, trying to move her leg without shifting Truman's body.

"What can I do?" Max asked quietly.

"A Brandy Alexander with one of those cute little umbrellas would be nice." Miki gave a crooked smile and then yawned. "A pedicure and a deep tissue massage would be a bonus." She yawned again. "Barring that, maybe you could—"

Max bent beside her, noticing the slab of rock that dug into her shoulder. Carefully he lifted her up, slid his folded vest beneath her side and neck, then settled her back on the ground. "Better?"

She stared at him, looking tired and more than a little dazed. "Who are you *really?*" she whispered.

Max walked around her and picked up his canteen. "I'm the person you're going to have to trust."

The silence seemed long and far too heavy. Then she shook her head. "Wrong again. I make it a firm rule not to trust anyone but the face that looks back at me in the mirror every day. Sometimes not even her."

"Anybody ever tell you that you've got issues?"

She gave a tired shrug. "A few. I didn't pay attention because I didn't trust them." She smiled crookedly, her eyes closing. "Shut the door on the way out," she murmured, snuggling closer to Truman.

They made quite a sight, Max thought. Truman's head rested on her chest, his body half covered by Max's black T-shirt. Right now both of them were oblivious to the world.

Max tried to look away, but something held him immobile. Simple weariness, he thought. But there was something deep and real about the bond of trust he sensed between woman and dog. There was no questioning, calculating or negotiating between them. It simply *was*. Max wasn't sure he had ever trusted anyone that much, outside of his Foxfire teammates. He wondered how it would feel to let down his guard that way. Just once.

Clean and simple, he told himself harshly. No strings and no emotions. Attachments broke your focus during a mission, but emotions could get you killed faster than bullets.

Max wasn't taking chances on either.

CHAPTER EIGHT

THE SEA WAS A RESTLESS curtain of silver beneath a darkening sky. Enrique Cruz sat without moving, hands locked on his seat. His focus was cold, intense and impenetrable. For a moment there had been a stirring of something familiar below him between the stretch of open sea and the dozen small islands scattered along the horizon.

He had sensed familiarity. And danger. He had seen what looked like fog, and the weather pattern continued to bother him. Now he opened his awareness, scattered a broad net of energy and waited for a response. The process had always seemed a little like sonar, except the trigger was his mind, focused like a weapon. Once he had been Foxfire's best weapon, the first in a team of deadly warriors who fought in silence with skills no machine could detect.

Now Cruz fought only for himself. And his greatest wish was to cripple the men who had studied him, caged him and made him into a lab animal.

One day soon they would pay for that.

Sweat dotted his brow as the small seaplane circled.

Once he sensed something…familiar, but he couldn't trace it to a specific location. Give it time. Soon he would be able to verify his suspicions. "Go back," he rasped. "Thirty degrees north. Hurry."

His brother shifted uncertainly. "It is too late. Our fuel is already low. We must land, *jefe*. Tomorrow we can—"

In a savage movement, Cruz shot around in his seat and gripped his brother's throat. "*Now,* I said! Never argue with my commands, *imbecil*. Tomorrow will be too late. He will be gone, hidden like the snake that trained him."

The three other men in the plane's small cabin watched in horror as Cruz slowly choked his own brother, but none dared to say a word for fear of a similar fate.

White-faced, Cruz muttered vows of death in a mix of Spanish and English. Then his hands opened and he took a harsh breath, staring at his brother, now unconscious. "Never mind. We will return tomorrow after my brother recovers," he said unsteadily. "The snake can live for one more night."

The pilot nodded, too afraid to speak. The small plane banked and circled back to the east, swallowed by a wall of sullen clouds.

The sun vanished over the ragged horizon, pulling behind it an endless curtain of night.

CHAPTER NINE

MIKI SAT UP ABRUPTLY and felt the ground spin.

She whimpered as the world went black and tilted sharply. Cradling her head, she opened her eyes slowly.

Truman was still asleep, draped over her chest, and Miki's head felt as if it had been run over by a cement mixer. She had a vague memory of the fog that had come out of nowhere and Truman's collapse, but the memories were little more than fragments strung together by threads. She couldn't seem to hold any of them long enough to figure out how they fit together.

But something had happened, and it had been *important.*

Images began to return. She remembered how gentle Max had been with the dog and how carefully he'd arranged his vest under Miki's head. He'd seemed vulnerable then, even wistful, and Miki hated that she had flinched at the sight of his chest and its web of silver scars.

What kind of car accident could have left him so badly hurt? Probably she would never know. He never talked about himself unless she probed hard.

Wind sighed outside the mouth of the cave. From

where she lay, a corner of velvet sky burned with scattered stars that looked close enough to touch. Miki smoothed Truman's head and fell back to sleep. Though it made no sense at all, she felt safe for the first time in weeks.

MAX DIDN'T CURSE, BUT he thought about it. Cool air rushed over his face as he moved silently through the night. With the probability that a hostile force was watching the nearby island, either directly or indirectly, he had only a few more hours to finish his surveillance, locate the target and extract—all without tipping off Cruz.

Now he had two civilians gumming up the works, and one of them was in bad shape. As for the woman, he still couldn't decide whose side she was on or why it was starting to feel like a personal question.

Max studied the spot where he'd buried her shrug—or whatever the little sweater was called. He still couldn't understand why she was so protective about a piece of clothing, especially one as beat-up as this was.

Crouching on the sand, he studied the darkness that stretched to the neighboring islands. He wouldn't make radio contact until just before dawn, when he took his next trip out to the beached gunboat near the reef. That would give him enough time for a brief coded update about Truman's condition and the airplane flyover.

After removing a camouflaged pack that he'd hidden in the sand, Max trotted into the trees and set up a sniper scope to view the ragged cove at the far side of the bay. As before, there was no sign of human presence. There had been no returning airplanes, either.

After an hour of continuous surveillance he stood up and stretched, working out the tension in his neck. From his cover behind a wall of bushes he could see the opening to the cave. So far Miki had stayed out of sight, along with Truman.

She had great legs, he'd give her that. None of that perpetual-teenager, skinny look too many women went for. The rest of her body wasn't half bad either, though she was a little tall for his taste. What man liked to stand level with a woman when they kissed?

Max frowned, wondering where the idea of kissing her had come from. Probably it was due to their cramped quarters. He was a healthy male, after all. Like it or not, there was a quirky vitality about the woman that was…

Out of bounds.

Dead stupid and possibly dangerous.

Without making a sound, he crossed the moving shadows into the jungle. There was a higher vantage point two clicks to the south, and he wanted to make another long-range surveillance there. Once he was finished, he'd check the cave, but this time it would be quick and clinical. No personal questions and no intrusive thoughts about her body and that soft, full mouth.

Ryker had taught him well.

Rule #8. *Never tell the truth when a lie will do.*

Most important of all was rule #9: *Never forget that*

you're different. This one was the easiest because Max's life experiences hadn't given him any opportunity to forget that fact. Being abandoned at birth in a cardboard box between the ammo and the valve grease at Wal-Mart left something of an impression when a person thought about his roots.

That was one of the reasons that Max didn't dwell on the past. The memories of living through a string of foster homes that had taught him to be tough and keep his feelings hidden weren't exactly Hallmark card-worthy. The present was a damned sight better, and Foxfire was the only family he needed.

Shouldering his second canteen and the sniper rifle, he set off for the cliffs. Soon he was swallowed up by the restless wall of the jungle.

THE SKY WAS STILL BLACK when Miki awoke. Though she tried not to move, Truman came awake, too, wagging his tail and licking her face eagerly. Miki watched the dog jump up and prowl the cave as if he had never been weak, let alone close to death. Only when the Lab found Max's canteen and carried it to her did she realize how thirsty she was.

"Smart guy, aren't you?" She smoothed Truman's fluffy fur and laughed at the silly idea that a dog could read her thoughts. But her smile quickly faded. There were three who needed water now, so she would have to be economical. She gave a small amount to Dutch, listening to his steady breathing. Then she poured several inches into a small depression in the rocks, smiling when Truman finished it off enthusiastically. She took only one drink for herself. Max had made it clear that going outside could be very risky, and this canteen was their total reserve. Now it was half-empty. When it ran out…

Miki stood up, feeling shaky. The ground spun for a moment and she slammed into the wall of the cave, her arm striking rough rock. Pain shot up to her shoulder and when she cupped her elbow she felt blood on her fingers.

Stupid. She hated her clumsiness, which seemed to have gotten worse in the last few months. It had begun the summer she grew four inches, and her grace had never returned. Great genes, she thought.

But no more excuses. Something wasn't right about her arm. As much as she hated doctors, she would schedule a complete physical once she got back to Santa Fe.

Assuming she lived through this nightmare.

Cupping her bleeding arm, Miki searched for the Mini-Mag light she had felt in Max's vest. She hadn't wanted to use it until necessary so she could conserve precious power. Now, in its clear beam, she saw rough walls gleaming with quartz fragments.

Something scuffled through the darkness at the cave entrance.

"Truman?"

There was no answering movement. The dog was gone.

Feeling a sudden stab of loneliness, Miki studied the small cave. She couldn't stay here and do nothing. At least she could explore a little and look for a source of drinking water. They were going to need that soon.

She shoved up her sleeves and searched the other pockets on Max's vest, hoping he might have a compass stashed there. She wasn't an expert at orienting by the compass, but she knew enough of the basics to find her way back.

Before she could finish her search, Truman shot toward her, licked both her legs and then sniffed her right arm thoroughly, back and forth. He pressed his nose against her bloody fingers and licked her arm. With each pass the Lab seemed to become more excited, turning in sharp circles and bumping her leg.

"Take it easy, honey." Miki held out her hand.

Truman backed away from her and bared his teeth. His head cocked as he took a hostile stance.

"Truman, what's *wrong?*"

The Lab turned in another tight circle, his ears flattened against his head. Then he shot out of the cave and vanished into the darkness.

Miki stood frozen, confused by this sudden, inexplicable hostility. In the silence she felt a pang of utter loneliness. Truman had been the closest thing to a friend she had on this island, even if he was just a dog. His flight was unnvering. Sighing, she ran a hand through her hair, wincing at the tangles. It was going to take a week to clean up after this ordeal. A nice long bath with ylang-ylang oil was tops on her list after being rescued.

She stared around the cave restlessly, raising Max's

light for a closer look. Near the bottom of one wall she could see signs of earlier digging. Water had left a dirty trail in one spot where the floor was uneven, scored in deep lines. Miki had read about the complex fortifications used by both sides during the Pacific campaign of World War II. Once a natural cave, this space had probably been excavated for storage defenses. There could be dozens of hidden bunkers like this scattered across the island.

Holding the light in her teeth, Miki crouched down and ran her fingers over the cracked concrete. When she was nearly at the floor, she saw that something was off. After several minutes, she realized that the cracks were uneven and the stripes in the cement didn't match. Even stranger, fresh cool air touched her face.

As realization hit, Miki began to smile. Could the manmade cave lead to a tunnel that had been sealed up and long forgotten? She had a hunch her search had just struck gold. Running her fingers along the floor, she searched for an opening or hidden latch, but all she managed to do was break two nails and skin her palm badly.

After ten minutes she sank down against the wall in exhaustion.

Her foot bumped a ridge on the floor.

Suddenly stone grated against cement, and the wall slowly began to move. Blinking, Miki watched a long crack appear, barely wide enough for her to squeeze through. After giving Dutch another small drink, she grabbed Max's vest and pushed through the rough opening, gripped by excitement.

The air was thick with mold and rust, along with an ammonia smell that probably came from bird droppings. Bird droppings meant that the tunnel had been open to the outside at one time. With luck it would still be.

The current grew stronger, riffling her hair. In the tiny beam of her light Miki saw that something was moving on the uneven cement floor. Red eyes flashed, and she nearly screamed as a huge rat shot past her feet.

Fighting down her fear, she moved along the sloping tunnel, careful to keep the cool air in her face. As she climbed, the smell grew more intense, and she covered her face with the sleeve of her shirt to keep from gagging.

Suddenly wind gusted into her face. Directly overhead a tiny spot of light glinted from a distant star. Kit O'Halloran's brother had been fanatic about studying the sea battles of World War II, and since Miki had a huge crush on Trace O'Halloran for most of her teenage years, she had studied the subject, too. *That* was before she had wised up and realized that if you had to change who you were to suit a man, he wasn't worth having. But those old library books were priceless now because of their elaborate diagrams of fortifications on Iwo Jima—and her photographer's eye, which never missed a detail. Miki remembered picture after picture of underground corridors with vertical access via ropes.

She looked up. She could still see one blinking star, a speck of hope in the colossal mess she'd landed in. The roof was fifteen feet high, too far to reach, and no ropes were visible in the shadows. Besides, any ropes would have rotted in the decades since the war ended.

Exhausted, she tried to think.

But calm planning had never been her strength. Recklessness, yes. Creativity, absolutely. But planning and continuity had always bored her senseless. Kit called her the Queen of Dropped Projects.

More red eyes flashed around her, and something jumped across her ankle.

Rats. This time she did scream, dancing from foot to foot. They had beady eyes, sharp teeth, nasty karma. Not that she knew if rats had karma or not, but if they did, it would definitely be nasty.

Gripping Max's light, she started forward. A spider web hit her face, clinging to her hair and eyes despite her frantic attempts to wipe it away. As panic closed in, she forced herself to take deep breaths, trying to stay calm and ignore the gleaming red eyes all around her. Then something else brushed her face.

Raising her light, Miki saw a rusting metal ladder strung from wire in the darkness above her, its end lost in the shadows over her head. Once there had been two sides, but one end had fallen. Now only a single knotted cable held the corroded rungs.

Back in sixth-grade gym Miki had *sucked* at climbing. Her gym teacher had sworn that someday she would find a use for that particular skill, but Miki had never believed it. Until now.

As rats skittered around her in the darkness, she held the light in her teeth, grabbed the ladder and started to climb.

Despite her karate classes, she was no Jackie Chan, and her movements were clumsy. Her shoulders ached and she could barely manage to hold on. Three times she lost her grip and slipped back to the ground, tearing welts across her palms. Angry, but on the verge of panic, she was almost ready to give up when a rat jumped up and nipped at her bare calf.

Miki screamed and shot up in the air, throwing hand over hand and straining upward while the wire swung wildly. Shadows danced on the rough cement shaft and she was almost too exhausted to feel the gust of wind that slipped through her hair where the shaft opened at the top.

Her shoulders throbbed, her whole body neared exhaustion as she clung to the twisting cable. Looking up, she saw a metal grate blocking her way out, but how could she hold on and push the metal lid open at the same time?

With clumsy movements, she caught one of the rungs under her left arm, and looped the wire over her shoulder. With her right hand, she banged hard at the circular piece of metal. Dirt and leaves tumbled down, blinding her. Her hand slipped.

She dropped three feet, gripped the line and climbed slowly back up, finally able to reach up and shove away the rusted grate, then pull herself out onto cool, rocky soil.

With a tortured gasp, she collapsed on the ground. One leg still dangled over the black hole, but she was too tired to crawl any farther.

A canopy of stars twinkled above her, the most beautiful sight she had ever seen. She raised her head, listening for sounds of water, but all she saw was dark ocean and darker land. Then through the starlight she saw a narrow trail between big boulders. Exhausted, she stumbled down the path, stopping every few minutes to rest.

Her hands ached. Her hair was covered with dirt and leaves. When she pressed her palms against her shirt, she saw the dark imprint of drying blood.

High above her head a shooting star blazed through the sky in an arc of light. Miki didn't move, barely able to breathe. When she looked down, she saw a narrow ledge whose rough face fell away into a sheer cliff. The shooting star had saved her life.

One more step would have sent her to her death in the ocean two hundred feet below.

Shivering, she inched away from the edge. But then a rat raced past her and she jumped aside in surprise. As one foot hit loose gravel, she lost her balance and grabbed wildly at the air. The shrill cry of a sea bird carried on the wind as she pitched forward into darkness.

IT WAS PITCH BLACK, AND Max liked it that way.

Hand over hand he climbed the stone cliff, muscles straining. There was no movement of the equipment strapped to his waterproof vest. Every piece of ammunition and all sensing devices had been carefully taped in place, secured in zippered compartments. Silent and lethal, he scaled the rocks, swinging effortlessly from handhold to handhold until he was eighty feet above the ocean. Wedging his foot into a narrow ledge, he looked inland, his thermal camera clicking softly. In a little over two hours, the sun would burst in a red cloud across the eastern horizon. He had to be out of sight well before that. But first Max needed high-resolution images of three locations on the nearby island, visible only from this high vantage point.

When he had taken two dozen thermal images, he stowed the camera in a watertight pocket and checked his watch. Quickly Max rechecked his equipment and then made his way back down the cliff by rope, repeating his swim through the choppy, predawn waters.

At the edge of the beach Truman was waiting for him, edgy and alert. He gave no sign of his earlier collapse, running in tight circles, tail wagging. But when Max started toward the bunker, the Lab cut him off, tugging hard at his leg. At this clear alert, Max's hand went to the revolver inside his waterproof vest. He watched Truman make a half circle, then paw the ground.

Danger.

The big dog sniffed the wind, looked at Max and headed north parallel to the beach.

Max was right behind him.

CHAPTER TEN

MIKI'S BODY TWITCHED. Darkness stretched around her and small creatures skittered through the night, but she didn't wake, drifting through a landscape of broken promises, fifteen again. In that world of dreams, her father was gone, her mother facing a crippling fight with cancer, dying in Miki's arms.

Once confident and enthusiastic, in her dream Miki again pushed everyone away. Her last two years of high school had been spent with an unmarried aunt who was clueless about the needs—and fears—of a high-strung teenager. Only with her camera had Miki felt in control of her world. Only with her lens did she forget her awkwardness, her height, her pain.

Caught in bleak memories and anxious dreams, she climbed mountains, running from her past. Her hand reached out, digging into the warm dirt to frame a picture that would never be taken.

She didn't feel the rat crawling over her hand. She didn't see the bank of clouds move in from the west and extinguish the stars one by one.

MAX'S FINGERS CLENCHED ON the grip of his gun as he followed Truman into the jungle. They had already crisscrossed the beach, and Truman seemed more agitated than usual, unable to focus. The Lab had a matchless reputation for terrain reconnaissance, but some part of Max's mind couldn't relax as he crept through the shadows beneath the rustling trees. The hell of it was, the island would have been beautiful under different circumstances. The air was balmy, scented with night-blooming jasmine. It was the perfect spot for an upscale resort catering to vacationing honeymooners.

But now it was a place of shadows and danger.

Truman turned sharply, following an incline dotted with boulders. As they climbed, Max looked down and saw the cave directly below them.

Gravel skittered in the darkness. Max heard a squeak as a dark shape shot past Truman.

Rats.

Max gave a mental curse as he scanned the terrain. Like all the Foxfire team, he had perfect vision up to 500 yards at night, due to extensive photoreceptor enhancements. He calculated their location, pinpointing the top of a rocky promontory that overlooked the beach, waiting for Truman's next alert.

The dog moved forward slowly, then sank onto his haunches. *Follow with caution.*

Carefully Max crossed the slope and within two steps he heard a low moan. Truman sat down next to a dark shape, unmoving between two boulders. It was Miki. She rolled sideways, gasping as her head struck a rock.

"Relax," Max whispered. He slid one hand over her face, feeling for blood or signs of trauma.

She took a sharp breath, trying to sit up, but his hands tightened, holding her where she was in case of trauma. Of course, if she had incurred spinal or other neurological damage, there wasn't a damn thing Max could do to help her.

Even if he did break cover to radio Ryker, they wouldn't be able to get a team here in time to make any difference. That was one of the reasons he'd locked her up in the bunker, protection as much for her as for him.

"Throat hurts." Her voice cracked. "Dry."

Max tipped his canteen, wetting her lips, but giving her no more than a taste. He didn't want her choking.

Even without direct contact, he picked up her stress and confusion like a weight across his own shoulders.

"Why were you—"

"Save the questions." He checked his watch, anxious to get her down the hill and out of sight before first light. "Can you walk?" he whispered. "Don't answer. Just nod your head for yes."

She moved cautiously, as if checking for anything broken, then her head moved up and down.

Yes.

"Put your arm over my shoulder and get up slowly. It's about fifty yards down the hill. Understand?"

She nodded again.

Silently, Max checked her for signs of blood, but found only dried patches on her shirt and jean shorts—a very good sign. When he tightened his arm around her waist and helped her stand, she kept as much distance between them as possible while Truman shot ahead of them, following a narrow path between the rocks.

In growing impatience, Max urged her forward. As the slope grew steeper, she tried to pull away and nearly fell. Without a word, he swung her over his shoulder, ignoring her gasp of surprise. They weren't going back to the bunker yet. He had had a clear impression of Cruz in the passing airplane, which mean he couldn't risk returning yet. Instead Max scanned the shadows below.

An open stretch of sand separated them from a partly beached Japanese gunboat. Truman sniffed the air, waiting expectantly. At Max's touch command, the Lab shot over the sand toward the old boat while Max followed, carrying Miki. He tried to ignore the pressure of her hips and the chance movement of her arm against his thigh. The fool was lucky she hadn't broken her neck, he thought grimly as he climbed onto the rusting deck and carried her down a listing companionway. The lower deck had one tattered mattress in a cramped bunk bed, and he left her there.

"I'll be back." Before she could ask more questions, he retraced his steps, found a large palm frond and brushed away all traces of their steps while working his way back to the boat.

There was no movement at sea. A faint skein of pink

unraveled across the horizon and shimmered over the gray water.

Dawn coming.

Even before he reached the companionway, Max had his questions ready. "How did you get outside?"

She stared at him, exhausted but defiant. "I found a tunnel. Truman acted strange and ran off, so I thought I'd look for some water. Where did *you* go?"

"I was getting supplies."

Never tell the truth when a lie will do.

She winced, cupping her right ankle. "Who are you really working for—what branch of the military?" She stood up awkwardly. "Not that I really care. All I want is for you to take me to that radio." She glared at him and jabbed one finger at his chest. "I'm tired and I'm sore and I want to go somewhere—anywhere—that has running water and hot coffee. Your business is your business."

Her weight shifted to her right foot as she glowered at him, only inches away, and Max was pulled into the scent cloud of her spilled perfume, faint but still disturbing to his heightened senses. Heat rose from her body, her female chemistry conspiring to distract him, even without direct contact. He picked up stress and fear along with an edgy restlessness that held the scent code of sexual desire.

The combination was like a sucker punch to his gut. He'd never felt a connection so strong before, and that made Max distinctly uneasy.

"Well?" Her face was pale and strained. "When do we leave?"

"After you explain what happened to Truman."

"How should I know? It started after he brought me the canteen and I hurt my arm—come to think of it, how did he know to bring the canteen? Did you train him to do that?" She frowned. "My friend's dogs are smart but I don't think they're that smart." She cradled her arm a little, as if it hurt. Then she turned, looking a little unsteady. "I don't feel so good." She shook her head, swaying.

"Have you drunk any water?"

"Not th-thirsty. I was at first, but Dutch was weak, so I gave him my water. I was afraid we might run out." She was shivering, her body stiff. "That was all the water we had and I didn't know when the heck *you* would come back."

"So you haven't had any water at all since I left?"

"I *told* you, no. Well, one sip right before I hit my arm and Truman acted strange." She blinked at him, looking almost drunk. "How did you get to be so strong? I bet you eat raw eggs and chlorella powder, don't you? And you probably do about a th-thousand sit-ups every day." She took a ragged breath. "Why do I feel—"

She swayed and Max caught her with one arm. "You're dehydrated. Sit down on the bed."

For once she didn't argue, sinking awkwardly onto the tattered mattress. "Dehydrated? No way. I'm just tired." Her body shook and she clamped her arms over her knees. "A little stiff, too."

"That's from salt depletion, electrolyte imbalance and dehydration." Max dug in an interior pocket of his field vest and found a salt tablet. "Swallow this," he said flatly. "Then finish off the water in that canteen."

Her eyes narrowed. "You're not a doctor."

"Stop talking so you can take this."

She studied the white tablet suspiciously. "What is it?"

"Salt. No more questions."

She was shaking now, her arms locked at her waist, and Max started to be worried, even though he didn't know what kind of rational person gave up all their water to someone else. Self-preservation was primal behavior.

Miki took the pill he held out, slid it around slowly on her tongue and grimaced. "Disgusting."

"I didn't say it would taste good." He held out his canteen. "Drink some more water."

She took a sip, then closed her eyes, gripped the canteen and pulled it closer, sucking greedily until every drop was gone. After that she ran her tongue around the opening.

Something about the way her mouth hugged the metal rim, searching for every bit of moisture, made muscles clench all along Max's body, right down to his groin. He couldn't fight a wave of hot images detailing other things she could do with that full, soft mouth. "I think you got all of it," he said gruffly.

"I want more." She pushed the canteen against his chest, frowning. "Now."

Opening his vest, Max took out a reserve canteen. This time when she drank, he looked away. Watching her mouth was making him painfully hard.

She finished drinking, sighed in satisfaction and

wiped her mouth with two fingers, then pushed the canteen back at his chest. "Maybe I was wrong. Maybe you're not a complete jerk. But you should have left us more water. Truman needed some, too." She looked around the dusty room. "Where did he go?"

"He's up on deck."

She nodded a little sadly. "I missed him. He looked… strange, so hostile. It all happened so fast." She sighed, stabbing her fingers through her hair. "I don't think I did anything wrong. Most dogs like me."

There was something wistful in her voice that made Max frown. Her hair had dried in unruly waves, probably because she kept running her fingers through it every two minutes, and the chunky edges suited the strength of her face. But the real problem was he couldn't keep his eyes away from her mouth, soft and full, the color of raspberries just on the verge of ripeness.

Hell, he was doing it again. Why did he keep thinking about kissing her?

"I'm going to call Truman down here," he said curtly. "I need to see how he reacts."

"Sure." She shrugged. "But if he bites me, I'm going to sue you." She was still shaky, her arms tense.

"Maybe you should lie down," Max said, touching her arm.

Miki's eyes flashed to his gloves. "Do you wear those things *all* the time?"

"Yes." When Max tried to urge her to lie down, she winced.

"Hey, watch it." She frowned as she rubbed her arm gingerly. "No need to get violent."

"Something wrong with your arm?"

"It's been bothering me the last few weeks ever since a jerk bumped me at the Java Express back home. First the creep spills a full caramel macchiato all over my arm, then he vanishes. No apology or anything." She rolled her shoulder carefully and winced again. "My arm's been bothering me ever since."

"Did you see a doctor?"

Miki shrugged. "He said it was a second-degree burn. Everything healed up except for an ugly scar, but it keeps bothering me."

Max felt a tickle of uneasiness. "Bothering you how?"

"Itching sometimes. Throbbing and burning other times." She passed her hand through her hair again and he watched, fascinated by the colors and textures. There was a whole realm of reckless life in that one simple movement, and Max had a sudden feeling that trying to pin this woman down would be like trying to catch sunlight in his hands.

"Why are you asking all these questions?" She rubbed her forehead. "I want more water."

"After you tell me about the jerk with the coffee."

Her eyes looked unfocused. Max knew she was still feeling the effects of dehydration. Now was the best time to question her, while her guard was down. He wanted every detail of Truman's behavior.

"The jerk in the Java Express, you mean? What's to tell?

He was about 170 pounds. Short build. Dark tan, red hair going gray. He had a small mole above his left eyebrow."

"You saw all that?" Max frowned. "How? It couldn't have been more than twenty seconds."

"Ten. I'm a photographer, remember." There was a note of pride in her voice. "If I can't see, I can't work. We see when we're kids, but time goes by and life starts creeping in. First the colors go, then the imagination. Pretty soon you're seventeen and you can't *notice* things anymore. At least not the things that matter." She sounded wistful when she said the last part, and Max found himself wondering why.

"Something happened to you, didn't it? You want to tell me about it?"

She looked away, shrugging. "It's history. I never do the past. No point." Her voice was firm, cutting off that line of discussion, which left him more curious than ever.

As he leaned down, he caught the hint of her perfume and the faint citrus scent of shampoo. Ignoring a warm nudge of desire, he raised her sleeve. "You're bleeding."

"I told you, I bumped that spot on my arm."

Max pulled out a sterile wipe and cleaned away some of the blood.

Miki flinched and gave a sharp yelp. "Watch *out.*"

"What's wrong?"

"I felt some kind of jolt, almost like you hit a nerve."

Max knew he hadn't come close to any nerves. "Let me take a look."

She didn't move, looking tense and still wary, and he

wondered if she had any idea how vulnerable she appeared to him.

"Look, Miki, I need to check you out. If something's wrong, I'll know it."

"I told you, the burn is completely healed."

"Maybe, maybe not. You could have torn something open during your fall." He dropped his medical kit on the empty cot. *"Sit."*

"Do you always snap out orders to everyone?"

"Mostly, yes."

"Then you must not have many friends." She didn't sound snide, merely curious. "What do your girlfriends have to say about that bad habit of yours?"

"Girlfriends? How many do you think I have?" he said grimly.

"Quite a few. You don't look like the type to settle down. Definitely not the type for celibacy." She studied him gravely. "Nope, no monogamy for you, not even serial monogamy. You're definitely a play-the-field, go-for-the-action kind of a guy."

Max shook his head, irritated at her assessment and wishing it hadn't been so accurate. "You don't know anything about me."

"So tell me." Her face was intent. "Married, divorced, what?"

"Neither."

"Not ever?"

"No." He didn't know why he answered her. He *never* discussed his personal life.

"Steady relationship?"

Max shook his head.

"Bingo. Mr. Play-the-Field, just like I said. Bet you've got a woman in every port."

"Stop trying to sidetrack me. I need to see your arm," he said gruffly. "And my private life is *none* of your damned business."

"Touchy, touchy." Stiffly she held out her arm, but instead of taking off her shirt, she merely pulled up one sleeve and kept the rest of the cloth clutched to her chest.

She didn't trust him, Max noted.

That was fine, because he didn't trust her, either. He was still distracted by her perfume. Even worse, there was an irritating whine in his ears when he sat beside her. Was there a fly somewhere in the cabin?

Ignoring the whine, he pulled up her sleeve and studied her bare arm. The wound was right where she'd said, stretching from her elbow toward her shoulder. The scar had faded to pale silver, and there was no sign that anything had torn open.

"Well?" She sat stiffly, her body angled away from him. "Is it the burn or something else? Maybe there was something in the water. Jellyfish can sting, can't they?"

"Trust me, you'd know a jellyfish sting," Max said grimly. He'd had a few nasty encounters on prior missions in the Pacific, and the memory was still unpleasant. "Stop squirming." He shone his light on the scar, looking for recent cuts or trauma, but he saw only a little blood where she'd scraped her arm. "Make a fist and show me where it hurts."

"It hurts near the old scar, just like I told you." She did the restless hand thing again with her hair, and Max felt his eyes drifting over the bright tangles, then down to her soft mouth. He wasn't used to being around women during a mission. Hell, he wasn't used to being around women, period. After he'd joined Foxfire, his free time was almost nil, and any limited female companionship had been arranged by Ryker's people. It was simple sex, hot and fast, a means for physical release. And his body was reminding him that it had been too long since he'd had even that kind of encounter.

"Stop moving," he muttered. "Is the pain above or below the scar? Right or left?" The whine in his head had grown to a buzz, but Max could find no source. Could this be some kind of delayed chemical reaction to fuel contamination from the crashed plane?

"I can't tell. The pain comes and goes, but it's gotten worse in the last few hours."

"Touch the closest spot where you can remember having pain." Max knelt beside her, watching her arm flex as she traced the right side of the scar.

A wave of dizziness hit him. He steadied himself with one hand on the edge of the cot beside her leg.

"Don't you ever take them off?"

He ignored her question, waiting for the dizziness to fade. He'd had a physical a few days before he'd deployed, but his newest chip was a prototype. Possibly some kind of malfunction. Just great.

"Are you listening to me? You look really weird, Max."

He definitely felt weird. "I always wear the gloves," he said tightly.

"Even during…you know."

He smiled thinly. "When I eat?"

"Actually, I meant when you—"

"I know what you meant."

Of course he knew what she meant. Even the scientists back at the Foxfire base had wanted to see how his tactile sensitivity would affect his sexual encounters. Lloyd Ryker, Foxfire's head, had gone so far as suggesting that Max keep a detailed journal of his reactions. According to Ryker, knowledge of a woman's body chemistry during her peak arousal of sex could have some tactical use for covert operatives.

Max considered himself as loyal as it got, but he had ignored that particular order. His skills were too new—and occasionally too unpredictable—for him to guarantee their value during sexual encounters.

But it was hard not to wonder what full body contact, including his hands, would be like. He had never taken off his gloves with a woman in intimacy, not since a Foxfire surgeon had slipped a tiny electrode into his brain and linked his tactile sense with his sense of smell. There had been more procedures after that, each one amplifying his abilities. It had taken weeks for him to learn how to identify the complex chemical formulas picked up through his skin.

But now the identification process had become second nature. He had accepted the personal restrictions because they protected him and made him a better soldier. Going back simply wasn't an option.

The dull throb centered behind his right ear. Probably stress, he told himself. If not, he'd put it down as a chip malfunction. For that Ryker would give the science team hell when Max got back.

As far as he knew, he was the only Foxfire member using the third-generation tactile chip. It was too new to have any record of failure rates yet.

He recalled the single wrong note he had picked up when he'd first carried Miki to the bunker. Something had drifted among those faint chemical layers of seawater and engine fuel, but it continued to elude him, even though he was trained to recognize everything from mouthwash to nuclear waste. He should have recognized whatever he'd picked up on her skin, but he couldn't.

As Max stood up, fresh pain dug at his eyes. He would get some air, clear his head and then call Truman down.

Something circled his wrist. He frowned when he saw Miki's fingers tighten against his gloves.

"This isn't leather," she whispered. "It's too soft, too thin. What *is* this stuff?"

A manmade fiber that had taken ten years to perfect in the Foxfire labs, Max thought. The exact components were still highly classified.

Her voice echoed a little and he realized his hearing was affected now, too. He looked at her fingers, strong and pale against his glove, and he thought about the brush of her skin everywhere. He wanted to touch her and taste her while she was lost in passion. Hell, there was no point in pretending she hadn't gotten under his skin.

But he wasn't going to do a damned thing about it, Max swore. He pulled away, his expression masked. "Stay here."

"Where are you going?"

"For Truman." He watched her face for signs of tension or evasiveness, but he saw neither. She just nodded calmly.

"You should make sure that he's completely recovered." She sat up quickly, looking pale. "What if he's collapsed again? Wait, I'm going with you," she said firmly. "Then we have to check on Dutch."

"You're too weak to go anywhere."

She took a deep breath and stood up slowly. "Not anymore. I'll be fine." She crossed the cabin, her face determined. "What are you waiting for? I want to check on Truman."

Max opened the rusty door. Instantly the Lab appeared in the companionway, ears high. He circled warily, then shot forward, sniffing Miki's arm. Very carefully he pressed his nose to her elbow, licking her scar.

She didn't move. A frown worked down her forehead. "He's doing it again."

"What do you mean?"

"He's smelling my hand like he did before. Now my arm. Why?"

Before Max could answer, Truman turned in a tight circle, sat down and sank into a prone position. His head rested on his front paws as he stared intently at Miki.

Max didn't move.

Foxfire's canine prodigy would take this position for only one reason. He had just picked up a scent signature for Enrique Cruz, the man who had stolen the government's newest billion-dollar weapon guidance system.

That meant Blondie here was up to her neck in deep shit.

CHAPTER ELEVEN

"WHAT'S WRONG WITH TRUMAN?" Her voice was low and a little hoarse. "Why did he lie down suddenly like that?"

Max kept his face blank. "Probably tired."

"I don't think so. I think he was trained to do that." She stared at the dog. "My friend's dogs do things like that all the time, especially the little one." She moved, her hands restless. "I don't like any of this and my arm hurts. So why are you *really* here?"

Max stripped off his heavy waterproof vest. He had to get answers from her. She was implicated now beyond any possible doubt.

Sand had blown over the lower deck during past storms and broken seashells were mounded against one wall, but Miki didn't seem to notice. Her gaze was locked on Max's face. "What is so important that you can't leave this deserted speck of land and you won't let us leave, either?"

Max cut her off. "I'll ask the questions. Let's start with how you got up that ridge."

She studied him in stony silence.

"How did you find that tunnel so easily?" The most logical answer was that Cruz had *told* her it was there.

She shook her head, not answering.

"Tell me about Cruz." He moved in, pinning her flat against the wall, with no place to go and no place to look but his eyes.

Color filled her face. "I don't know what you're talking about. Cruz who?"

She was damned good, he thought. There was just the right touch of wariness and innocent confusion in her voice. Cruz must have trained her well. The two were probably lovers.

For some reason the image hit him hard and left him angry.

"You want to leave this island? It won't happen until you start talking."

"I'm here because of engine failure. We crashed. You saw the plane."

"Crashes can be arranged."

"Are you *nuts?*"

She sounded entirely believable in her outrage, but that was no surprise to Max.

"Where did you meet Cruz?"

"I don't *know* anyone named Crux."

"Cruz," Max repeated slowly, drawing out the word. He pulled off one glove, his eyes never leaving her face. "You're very good, Blondie. And you're lying." He looked down at Truman, who was still motionless, his head pointed toward Miki's right arm. "My good friend here doesn't ever lie."

"You mean that position is some kind of signal?" She

chewed her lip, and the more she chewed, the more worried she looked. "What is it supposed to mean?"

Her face was turning pale, her breathing irregular. No doubt she was worried that he'd seen through her cover story.

"I know you're involved, Miki. It will be far less painful for you if you give me the whole story now."

"You—you scum. I'm not afraid of you or your—"

Max caught her in mid-sentence. His bare fingers tightened, covering the pulse that throbbed at her neck. He opened his mind and dove down through the static the way he'd been trained, matching molecule names with chemical fragments registered by his sensitive fingers.

Surfactants.

Female sweat.

He touched her ear. *Sea salt. High octane engine fuel.*

And there—something else?

He ignored her flailing hands, moving lower, exploring the warm skin beneath her collarbone.

Her face filled with sudden color. "Stop. I'm not—"

His hand covered her mouth, cutting off her angry protest. The shock of skin-to-skin contact burned, stirring all of his finely honed senses. She was softer than he'd expected, warmer than was safe, a hint of perfume still lingering on her skin. She was throwing off all kinds of hormones, spiking cortisol and cytokines as her immune and stress responses piled up.

Max kept his focus tight but completely impersonal. Ruthlessly focused, he moved his fingers lower, settling at the warm hollow between her breasts. If Cruz had kissed her here, if he had left even a trace of saliva on her skin, Max would know it. Cruz hadn't been given details about his final surgery at Foxfire's lab. Ryker had ordered two chips implanted, chips that released a unique chemical formula into Cruz's bloodstream. The lab-engineered mix did not exist in nature as a precaution against false positives.

So the answer was clear. If Max found even a hint of that genetically engineered alkaloid on this woman's skin, he had full authority to treat her as a hostile and interrogate her by whatever means he deemed necessary.

He ignored her wriggling, her fear, the heat of her skin and the soft pressure of her hips cradling his thighs. Her softness and fear meant nothing to him. He had to find the marker formula.

He pressed her hard against the wall and pushed up the edge of her bra, his hand across her mouth. She was soft and full, her nipple pressing his callused palm. Despite his control, the slide of her breast against his bare skin tangled his senses, making his blood thick and hot with need.

He covered her breast with his hand and filtered out her muttering, fascinated by the heat of her skin and the way color flared through her face. He didn't care about her, he told himself. These feelings of his were strictly a reflex. This search was impersonal, no more than a way to gather clues.

But despite that, his hand tightened in reflex. Blood

pounded to his groin as his fingers opened, slow and gentle, claiming her breast with its perfect, dusky nipple.

He told himself all that mattered was finding Cruz's marker amid the layers of hormones sheening her skin. Desire was irrelevant and curiosity forbidden. There was no room for any emotion in his touch.

But his hand was hot where it lay against her skin. His nerves felt too sensitive, too volatile.

Pain stabbed beneath his left ear. Without warning dizziness struck him, and he swayed beneath a blast of sensory static.

She struggled ineffectually, her body twisting against his and her words muffled by his hand. Max saw her staring at a line of blood on his wrist.

Blood. His blood.

He had a nosebleed, and he never had nosebleeds. Max had no doubt that she had caused it somehow, probably part of Cruz's new skill set.

He felt sick at the sight of her, sick at the extent of Cruz's reach and the stench of his betrayal. "How much did he give you?" Waves of pain dug through his neck, and he felt fresh blood brush on his lip. "What's the going rate to sell out your country these days?"

She kicked him, biting down hard on his hand.

Even then something continued to tease him, shadowlike on her skin, a fragment that he couldn't identify despite all his training. Yet if Cruz had touched her, Max should have found the marker alkaloids immediately. There was also her concern for Truman, which had seemed entirely sincere.

She was his enemy, but the pieces simply didn't add up.

He released her arm, keeping his hand across her mouth, but the storm of her hormones pulled him in, overwhelming in their complexity. She hadn't had sex for quite a while, Max noted. Her body was responding to his touch, even amid her fury.

Fury. Not fear. She wasn't afraid of him.

Another piece of the puzzle that didn't fit.

He took a deep breath and straightened her shirt, trying to ignore the heat of her skin and the need that her body had aroused. He wanted to strip all the barriers between them. He wanted his hands free, moving over her like sunlight. He wanted to take her here and now, hard and fast against the wall while she moaned his name and came blindly in his arms.

The dizziness was worse, pounding behind his eyes. He couldn't hear.

Her face bright with color, she fought him, but there was no calculation, no cold cunning there, and for a moment Max wondered if Truman could have made a mistake.

He felt more blood on his lip. Something had happened when he touched her, bringing waves of dizziness and pain, and he had to find out why.

She tried to kick him again, biting at his wrist. He saw a line of bruises on her cheek, probably from her fall on the cliff. When he tugged her sideways, trying to get a better look, she fought hard, and her movements slammed her arm against the ship's metal wall.

She went rigid, her eyes wide and startled. Breath hissed from her mouth. And then she simply crumpled in his arms.

A drop of his fresh blood fell on her Hawaiian shirt, mixing into the bright colors. Everything about her was bright and clean, full of restless energy, Max thought. It was so long since he could remember feeling young or clean or innocent.

Yes, he could understand why she had caught Cruz's eye.

Pain stabbed at his ear as he set her on the rusted metal floor. He touched the inside of her wrist, picking up more of her stress hormones. Her face was pale and cool.

Her faint was no act.

Anxious, he touched her neck. Only when he felt the steady drum of her pulse did he relax. But his emotions were anything but calm.

He raised her hand, studying the angry scar above her elbow and trying to reconstruct the accident. Kneeling, he touched one edge of the wound gently.

Something jumped, racing like a spark up his arm and into his head, knocking him backward. In that blurred moment of pain Max felt completely drained yet in some way connected to her, fused in nerve and muscle.

He took a deep breath, and then touched the edge of her scar again. Another white jolt of light drilled through him, making his ears ring and his muscles clench.

The effect was definitely connected with her scar, he thought grimly. She had done something that day—or something had been done to *her.* Now it was affecting both of them.

She tossed restlessly beside him. Her eyelids fluttered and she murmured something that sounded like *race,* which made no sense.

Her beauty was unavoidable, but it was her energy that stirred his senses, making Max's hand curve gently over her cheek. Hunger made his blood pound. He wanted her fire and stubbornness, here and now. He needed to—

Stop.

He pulled his hand away. Slowly he stood up.

Everything was wrong, he thought. His feelings never drove him like this. He *never* lost control.

He looked down at his bare hand. She had been solicitous about Dutch, hotly protective about Truman. She had even worried about his embarrassment over his scars.

Nothing about it added up.

Except that she stirred his senses and made his body come alive in a way he had never experienced. For long seconds something hot and reckless had shimmered between them. Already Max knew that neither of them would emerge unchanged from that contact.

If it didn't short circuit him completely.

More blood trickled onto his lip, and he brushed it away in grim silence.

Anything that affected him this deeply was a matter

of national security. Ryker would need an update immediately.

Max stared at her white face, at the angry scar on her arm, turning the pieces over and over in his head. After making certain that she was stable and breathing normally, he left Truman on guard and climbed up to the deck. By the time he reached the water his dizziness was gone and the whine in his ears had faded.

Who was she? he thought angrily. *What* was she?

FIFTEEN MINUTES LATER MAX stood on a lower deck of the rusting derelict gunboat beyond the reef. "I'm sure," he said tersely to Izzy. "There was no question. Touching her triggered some kind of…weakness. We should be checking her medical records to research that scar."

"No records for anyone named Miki or Michelle. Not on any flights to or from Bora Bora in the last week." Keys clicked quietly at a keyboard. "How's that dizziness you experienced?"

"Completely gone now."

"Any other effects?"

Max didn't mention the inexplicable sense of bonding he'd felt. He needed to understand that better before he tried to describe it to Izzy or Ryker. "There was pain below my right ear. A small nosebleed, too."

The computer keys stopped clicking. "Small? You ever get nosebleeds?"

"Never," Max said curtly. "Not until today."

Papers rustled. "Describe the scar on her arm again."

Max repeated the details for the second time, watching a line of gray clouds race across the horizon. "She kept saying something that sounded like *race,* but it makes no sense."

"Let me play with it," Izzy said tightly. "What else can you give me?"

"She told me that a man spilled hot coffee on her arm. The shop was called the Java Express."

"Give me that again."

"Java Express."

"With luck, it won't be a chain," Izzy said. Computer keys tapped as fast as a weapon burst. "What else?"

"She was able to give an excellent description of the man who bumped her. Heavy tan. Red hair going gray, a small mole above his left eyebrow. But we still don't have any names."

Izzy's voice took on an edge of excitement. "I can crosscheck the store name with local E.R. reports for burns in the last sixty days, which would be the usual time frame for second-degree wound healing. We may find a record for the man's treatment. I'll get right on it."

Max rubbed his neck. "I'd better get back. Truman is guarding the upper deck, but I don't like taking risks in case she decides to run again."

"I'll report to the big man. Meanwhile, get me a picture of her scar."

"Will do."

"Any idea how she spells her name?"

Max shoved supplies into his waterproof tactical

vest. "The usual way, I guess, with an *i-e*." He stared at the darkening line of the horizon. "What's the radar showing for that storm?"

"Winds at twenty knots. We're calculating landfall around 2100 hours."

"Understood. Latest location of our friend's tracking chip?" Max was careful not to mention Cruz by name.

"Sporadic. The last coordinates we picked up were in Thailand, assuming it wasn't another malfunction." A chair creaked. "Hold on."

Max heard muffled voices and the sound of papers rustling.

"Listen up. We just got a new fix on that GPS chip you mentioned. The signal faded almost immediately, but my team managed to fix the location first. It's one mile away from your current position. I repeat, the target is in your vicinity, due southwest. Coordinates following."

"Roger that," Max said tensely. With Cruz in the area, he had to backtrack to the island immediately.

"One last thing. We've had reports of maritime hijackers operating in your area. They use speedboats with deck-mounted machine guns, and they are all-around bad news. Watch your six out there."

Great, Max thought grimly. Another complication he could do without. "They'll be on my radar. Thanks for the tip. Signing off now."

He didn't waste energy on questions or curses. After

memorizing the coordinates Izzy had given, he flipped off the radio, hid his equipment inside a rusted wall and secured his vest.

Two minutes later he was in the water.

LLOYD RYKER WAS STARING at the newest report from Izzy Teague and nursing a stomach-scouring cup of coffee when he heard a knock at his door. He barely had time to slide two papers off to the side of his desk before the door opened.

Wolfe Houston, the current Foxfire team leader, looked cool and calm, but after months of working together Ryker knew that the more tense the situation, the more cool Houston appeared. It was the mark of a good operative, but it made the man hard as hell to read.

"Something wrong, Houston?"

"Permission to speak with you, sir."

"Of course. Have a seat. I'd offer you some coffee, but the stuff I make will kill you." As Houston sat down, Ryker managed to spill his coffee over the open file on his desk. "Shit. Too much coffee in the last twenty-four hours has got me on edge." Ryker grabbed a handful of napkins and blotted the top-secret report that was now buried, out of Houston's line of vision. "What did you want to talk about, Lieutenant?"

"Preston's op, sir. Izzy Teague tells me things are heating up."

"Nothing that we didn't expect. Is there a problem I'm not seeing?"

"I just wanted to be sure everything was on target, sir." Houston's eyes were cool as they locked on Ryker's face. "And that there aren't any new developments you may have forgotten to mention."

Was there a warning in that question? If so Ryker would discipline Houston as soon as the mission was completed. He wouldn't tolerate insubordination or questioning of command judgment. "I don't follow you, Houston."

The tall SEAL sat back in his chair and steepled his fingers. "You updated me about the training Cruz was receiving before his flight from the secure facility. You mentioned a new chip that appeared to malfunction in the field. I wanted to be sure there weren't any other... modifications that you might have forgotten." Houston let the words hang. "Sir," he added calmly.

Ryker felt the muscles clench at the back of his shoulders. The question wasn't insubordinate but it was damned close. He'd have to keep Houston on a short leash from now on. "Modifications as in training and chips, Lieutenant. You think I'm keeping secrets from you?"

"I have no idea, sir. I simply want to be fully briefed to protect my man in the field."

"Perfectly understandable. And the answer to your question is no. To my knowledge Cruz had no additional training in process at the time of his escape."

Houston's eyes narrowed slightly. "'To my knowledge'? Is it a possibility, sir?"

"You know what I know, Lieutenant." Ryker decided

the conversation had gone on long enough. It was always a bad idea to let subordinates see a crack in your armor. He sat back and casually pushed his PDA over the file he had been reading when Houston entered. "You have the full resources of this project at your disposal to find Cruz. What else do you need?"

"Nothing, sir. Preston's a good man. He'll finish the mission as planned."

"That's exactly what I wanted to hear." Ryker studied a pile of government forms on the corner of his desk. "While you're here, I should mention that I'm considering your request for personal time...and marriage to Kit O'Halloran. You know my feelings about personal involvements."

Houston simply nodded, his face unreadable.

"Still, some rules are meant to be relaxed. I have the possibility under advisement." There, the tantalizing offer was now raised openly. Ryker snapped his briefcase shut and stood up. "Anything else, Houston?"

"No, sir. That's all. Izzy Teague has briefed me. The team is ready to deploy at your command."

"Stay ready, Lieutenant. I don't need to tell you what Cruz is capable of. You saw him in action."

"It's nothing something I'm likely to forget, sir." Houston stood up and picked up a wet napkin that had fallen from Ryker's desk. "I'll put those in the garbage for you, sir."

"No need. I clean up my own messes, Lieutenant." Ryker wondered how much Houston had seen in that first moment of entering the room. The man had superb memory, and one glance would have been enough.

No, that was impossible. The man was good, but no one was that fast.

"I'm leaving this to you, Houston. Take down Cruz. I want this problem dealt with."

"Count on it, sir."

When the door closed, Ryker pulled the wet napkins away from the top-secret file. Lab 21 had been a mistake from the start, but the possibility of success had been too great to ignore.

One day Houston and the others would know the full extent of Ryker's vision and the power it would create for all of them. But first they had to track down a traitor. Enrique Cruz was a time bomb that could send the whole Foxfire project up in smoke with two words.

Lab 21.

CHAPTER TWELVE

MIKI CAME AROUND SLOWLY, aware of a splitting headache and a taste like shoe leather in her mouth. Something bad had happened, and as she sat up, she remembered what it was.

He'd watched her, first curious and gentle. Then his face had hardened. She knew that something in the dog's reaction had been the trigger. After that, Max had turned cold and distant, staring at her but not really seeing her. Then he'd caught her against the wall and touched her as if he was looking for something specific, hidden on her skin.

Cruz. He'd asked her about someone named Cruz.

Crazy.

Miki took an angry little breath that caught in a hiccup. Slowly she stood up, trying to understand. She was in deep water here, and good and bad might not be where she expected them. She was almost certain that Max worked for the government and he was here under orders of secrecy.

She looked out the room's old, warped porthole, suddenly exhausted. She was out of her league, with no idea where to turn. Right now no one else even knew she was here. There would be no cavalry and no rescue teams charging in as saviors. She was on her own.

The sky was gunmetal under a blotchy sky. Miki watched a school of dolphins crest suddenly, leap in exuberant arcs and then vanish, and for a moment there seemed to be a message there.

But she didn't know what it was. She was cold and hungry and her arm throbbed badly. She wanted to be home, surrounded by mountains and the clear light of the high desert. She closed her eyes on another hiccup. Stress, she thought.

Focusing, she took deep breaths and willed away her panic. The hiccups vanished shortly after that and she watched angular birds walk clumsily on the beach, digging in the sand and calling hoarsely.

There was something wrong with her scar. It burned in a way it never had before. Her forearm was swollen, too. Somehow Max was involved in this though she didn't understand how that was possible.

Standing at the warped old porthole, Miki thought of all the reasons she wanted to live and all the things she was determined to accomplish. She felt the blood pump through her heart and squeeze through her veins and the cool brush of metal at her forehead where it pressed on the porthole and Miki thought it was good to be alive. If the pain and exhaustion were part of the price, then she welcomed them, too.

She refused to die.

With one finger she traced a line in the rust covering the metal wall. She could try to run again, but where would she go? Maybe she could find another cave, another bunker, but then what? More hiding and more running.

No, she was going to stand her ground. She would have to trust Max and work with him for the moment even though it went against every instinct. He was her only way out.

A gust of wind raced up from the ocean, shaking the old boat and something crashed behind her. She swung around and saw a dark head with a gaping mouth and bulging eyes rolling toward her.

She was on the edge of a scream when she realized that the thing on the floor was a World War II gas mask slung over an old nylon parachute. Twisted together on the floor, they looked like a figure straight out of hell.

She closed her eyes and took a deep, rasping breath. "Time to calm down," she said tensely. "Don't be an idiot. You're alone and you're breathing, so it could be a lot worse." And the jerk in the black wetsuit—okay, the gorgeous jerk with the buns of steel and abs of solid platinum—was nowhere to be seen now.

Miki looked around the dusty cabin. She was still confused by what he'd done and even more confused by his sudden nosebleed. And he hadn't seemed *personally* interested in her body. His eyes had been cold and focused, almost as if he was involved in a science project.

But *she* was the science project, and it had something

to do with the man named Cruz, who had done some seriously bad things, judging by the way Max said his name.

And he thought she was involved?

Miki made a nasty comment, rolling her eyes. No way would she ever sell out her country. Hard on the heels of that thought came another. If this man Max was tracking a traitor, that meant he was definitely one of the good guys. No matter *how* furious she was, she had to find a way to help him. After all, Truman was gorgeous and smart and wonderful, so how could his owner be all bad?

She took a wobbly step, wishing she had some of the water from Max's canteen. A quart of Starbucks premium espresso ice cream would have been nice, too.

But what she really needed to do was figure out the lay of the land. After that she would find a way to help him—even if she had to beat him to a pulp to convince him she was on *his* side.

She tried the wooden door to the companionway and wasn't surprised to find it locked. He had locked her up again. No doubt he would insist it was all for her own safety.

Half a dozen hard thumps with the weight of her body proved fruitless. Another thing that didn't surprise her.

Ignoring a wave of hunger, Miki studied the room, which appeared to be some kind of storage area. Old cardboard boxes and empty tins of food were shoved in a corner, surrounded by animal droppings and the small skeleton of what appeared to have been a rat.

Ugh. Rats again. She hated rats. Shuddering, Miki opened a rickety crate and checked inside.

Empty.

Wincing, she sat down on the crate and rubbed her arm, feeling another stab of pain along her scar, which was aching viciously. Her eyes flickered over the darkened room, taking in the gas mask and the old parachute. She wasn't sure what made her drag the mask and the torn nylon across to the door. She had never been very good at long-term career planning or financial strategies—the flat-broke state of her bank account was proof of that. She had always been a seat-of-the-pants, follow-your-bliss kind of person, but survival meant taking advantage of any tools you stumbled upon.

With awkward movements Miki pushed the heavy mask up against the wall and dropped the parachute on top of it, then searched the rest of the room. The cardboard boxes were empty. The food was all eaten. Only a rusty metal locker stood with its door askew across from the dented porthole.

Hardly promising. What would Lara Croft do now?

Miki's arm throbbed as she sat down on the empty crate. When she rolled up her sleeve, she saw a small line of blood and prayed the wound wasn't infected.

She was trying to relax when something skittered overhead like dry leaves. Metal creaked and the rustling came again, moving across the deck.

Miki grabbed the gas mask and parachute and sank against the wall next to the companionway door. The skittering had stopped, but something about that one sound made her uneasy.

A seabird cried in the distance.

The door latch rattled sharply and Miki's fingers trembled as she leaned against the wall, waiting, listening to the pump of her heart.

Something heavy shifted out in the corridor. The door slowly opened, and an arm appeared, hidden beneath a black rubber wetsuit.

So Max had returned. Yet something kept her rigid, watching the edge of the wetsuit. The figure's furtiveness didn't feel right.

Her heart lurched when she saw a serrated knife gripped in the gloved fingers. The face above the knife belonged to a stranger.

In sheer terror Miki swung the gas mask with all her might, knocking the man in the side of the head as she let it fly. He staggered against the wall, shook his head, then swung back to face her, blood streaming from his forehead. Flat, cold eyes narrowed on her face.

The big knife pointed directly at her heart. Miki knew she couldn't surprise him a second time, and even if she could, the gas mask was out of reach, halfway across the floor.

She took a gasping breath, fighting panic, then feinted right, made a run for the mask and shoved the metal crate between them. Because her attacker was right-handed, he was forced to change sides, but before he could reach her, Miki threw the parachute up in the air over his head, his knife slashing wildly as the nylon canopied out and dropped over his eyes. While the man was blind beneath the dusty fabric, she grabbed the gas mask and slammed him in the head again. He swayed, striking furiously and the blade's wicked teeth ripped through the nylon and slashed deep into her arm.

Tears blurred her vision, but she swung the gas mask yet again, knocking the knife free. The big blade clattered across the floor and her attacker cursed, then pitched forward onto the floor, wrapped up neatly in white nylon.

Miki closed her eyes and dragged in air, shaking as panic hit her full bore. Was she *crazy?* Had she just gone mano-a-mano with a mercenary wielding the biggest freaking knife she'd ever seen? Who did she think she was?

When her shaking stopped, she stood up slowly. Blood oozed from the long cut on her arm, and she felt oddly disjointed, separate from her own body. Shock, she thought.

I am going to throw up any second now.

When she turned around, Max was standing in the doorway, the big knife gripped in his right hand. He looked entirely comfortable holding it.

"What the hell happened?"

Miki stared at him in confusion, caught by terror and fury. "All of a sudden he was there, holding that knife. He tried to—he almost—" Her voice shook.

Dark and fierce, Max's eyes locked on her arm. "He

hurt you." He pulled her against him and shoved back her sleeve, frowning. "Pretty damned deep, too. I'll clean it up."

Miki swayed, fighting the pain burning down her arm. The wound felt as if it was directly over her scar, tearing open the fragile tissue all over again.

Sometimes life sucked.

Her knees buckled a little and she felt Max's arm brace her shoulder as he gently cleaned the wound. "Lean on me."

"Not allowed." She gave a shaky laugh. "I don't lean on anyone. By the way, if you're ever planning to kill me, do it fast, because I'm not very good with pain."

Miki thought she saw his lips curve slightly. "Looks to me like you're pretty damned tough, Blondie."

His hand at her shoulder was surprisingly gentle and Miki leaned on him just a little as he placed a bandage over the slash.

Then there was a noise behind her. The man on the floor came to life and made a swift jab with his foot. Max parried, hit him twice and sent him toppling back to the floor.

All she could do was stare, too tired to move. She didn't want to die. There were too many places she hadn't seen, too many pictures she hadn't taken. She looked down at the blood on her arm, oozing over her jeans. Now the denim was slashed at both knees. "Damn," she whispered. "These used to be my favorite. Do you have any idea how hard it is to find a pair of jeans that really f-fit?"

"Afraid I don't. I'm not into clothes." Max took a white cloth from his inside his vest, softly brushed back her hair and studied her face. "You're a mess, honey."

"What about *him?*"

"He won't be getting up for a while."

"Is he…dead?" Miki heard the words echo as if she was moving through a tunnel.

"He would have killed you."

No arguing with that. "Who is he?"

"Someone who plays for keeps," Max said grimly.

Miki took a tight breath. "Will there be more of them?"

"More than likely. That's why Truman is keeping watch up top. He's the one who saw that you had company. Sorry I wasn't here sooner."

"No problem. I took c-care of him."

"You sure did, honey."

"And this has something to do with that guy Cruz you mentioned?"

Max's eyes hardened. "More than likely," he said again, folding the cloth and pressing it gently to her upper lip.

"I don't understand any of this." Miki squared her shoulders. "But I can handle myself." Her nose was running and she wiped it on her shirt. "I took care of Creepy over there by myself, didn't I?"

"Yeah, I noticed." Max's lips curved again.

He had a nice smile, Miki realized. It was just a little awkward, as if he didn't use it much, but that made it all the more interesting.

"You're some kind of hard-ass, aren't you?" He refolded the cloth and replaced it against her top lip. "A hard-ass with a nosebleed that's not stopping," he said grimly.

He was wearing the gloves again, she noticed. They almost seemed like they belonged on him. "Me? You're the one who gets nosebleeds."

He didn't answer.

"I've never had a nosebleed in my life. Okay, once when I jumped out of a cottonwood tree on a bet with Kit's brother, but that was it. What the heck is happening to me?"

As he examined her face carefully, Miki felt more blood well up.

"Take deep breaths and try to relax."

Right, like she could really relax sitting with G.I. Joe on a rusty battleship in the middle of nowhere. It was going to take more than a few cleansing yoga breaths to deal with this nightmare.

"Breathe, damn it. Come on, honey. Don't faint on me."

"I n-never faint," she said raggedly, feeling the floor sway.

"Who's Kit? You mentioned her just now." His fingers traced her lip, wiping away blood with a fresh cloth.

"My best friend. She's Trace's sister."

He didn't seem to hear, busy pulling something out of his vest pocket.

"I have to get back to Dutch," Miki said hoarsely.

Max was too close, too gentle and suddenly she wanted to close her eyes and let him hold her. She wanted to lean, to touch. Very tempting. Very dangerous.

She tried to pull away, only to feel his hands tighten.

"Don't rush it, Blondie. Take a few more deep breaths while I look at your arm."

"I want to leave." Miki winced as he moved her hand. "You can check me out after you take care of Dutch."

He stared at her in silence as he zipped up his black tactical vest. "Dutch is lucky to have you watching over him." The words were so quiet, she wondered if she'd imagined them. "Take it slow. Lean on me if you need to."

His voice was low and husky. For some reason the rough tone made heat swirl into Miki's face as she thought about sliding her arm around his waist, her thigh pressed against his.

She cleared her throat. "What about Creepy over there?"

"Don't worry about him. He's going nowhere." Max's cold, professional stare was back. "No more noise until we're back in the bunker, understand?"

For a moment there had been something dark and hungry in his eyes. There had even been respect in his smile. Now both were gone. Miki had seen that same kind of closed expression on the face of Kit's brother, a Navy SEAL with a very hush-hush unit. "Are you in the Navy?"

His eyes cut back to her, cold and focused. "What makes you think that?"

"Your control. The way you watch things around you and say as little as possible. Nothing seems to upset you."

"Why would that make me Navy?"

She shrugged. Her arm was burning, but she tried to ignore it. "My friend swears SEALs are the best of the best. Of course, she's biased because she's going to marry one. Her brother's a SEAL, too." She studied Max's face, noting the hard jaw and the keen eyes. "Watching people is part of my job as a photographer. I'm good at it," she said with sudden pride. "If my last job had worked out… Never mind."

"The calendar you were shooting, right? *Best Beaches of the World?*"

She laughed tightly. "My big break that turned into my big disaster. Plane crash, cameras ruined, boss dead." She concentrated on stepping over the tangled parachute. "But, hey, I'm alive." Her voice hardened.

Her nose itched and she swiped at it again. Blood covered her fingers, making her feel sick. She looked away, staring through the rusted porthole. "I want to go."

He tightened the straps on his vest and nodded. "You'd better take that parachute. We might need it." He picked up the man from the floor and tossed him over one shoulder with no apparent effort. "Maintain a positive outlook. It influences tactical outcome."

The man was definitely military, Miki thought. She tried to feel positive, but all she could see was blood—hers and her attacker's, dark against the rusting floor. "What if more men come back?"

"No need to worry." He gave another faint smile. "I'm a hard-ass, too."

"Let me tell you—you have a great ass."

Something came and went in his eyes. "A compliment, ma'am?"

"Definitely. Your abs are pretty buff, too." It was the least she could do since he'd saved her life—*again.* Her smile turned shaky.

But Max didn't hear because he was busy locking Creepy in a small room at the bottom of the stairs.

Miki followed slowly. She was trying to stay upbeat like he said, but it was pretty hard when you had someone else's blood on your arm and you felt like throwing up.

Why did paradise always come with thorns?

CHAPTER THIRTEEN

RAGGED CLOUDS COVERED the sky and there was a hint of rain in the air as they crossed the beach. Max tapped Miki's arm, directing her through two rocks half-hidden by thick hibiscus bushes. He saw her eyes widen when he pushed aside the heavy branches and pointed out stone steps descending between the rocks.

Max took point, blooms dropping like bright rain as he followed the moss-covered steps underground. An earlier reconnaissance team had found a dozen tunnels scattered over the island, and this one would lead them back very close to Dutch's resting place. Once they were underground, Max restored the wall of greenery to its original appearance and waited for Miki to pass. He didn't miss her slow step and occasional clumsiness.

It was his job to assess field situations and evaluate threats. Where people were concerned he had an innate skepticism that had been heavily reinforced by his military experiences. He had to remain suspicious until he had an explanation for Truman's alert, even if instinct told him she had been pulled in blind and had no knowledge of Cruz's stolen guidance system.

He couldn't risk being wrong.

If she made the slightest hostile move, he would immobilize her without a qualm.

Truman trotted ahead of them, sure-footed in spite of deep shadows. When Miki stumbled, Max raised his Mini Maglite to give her more light and took her good arm. Despite her obvious exhaustion, she managed a smile and plunged gamely after Truman.

Max took a deep breath. He had always liked women with guts.

Suddenly the Lab reappeared, shooting straight toward Max. He stopped short and sat down at Max's feet, head cocked.

Danger.

Something moved in the tunnel beyond them. Max tracked his light around the tunnel through dust that whirled up in random patterns. Small rodent eyes flashed across the floor. He felt Miki start and then draw back.

But Truman wouldn't signal for a few rats. Silently, Max eased out his .45 and thumbed off the safety, careful to keep the woman to his left, out of his range of fire. Well trained, Truman had already inched to the left for the same reason.

The faintest breeze whispered around them. Truman growled again, ears flat to his head, back tense. Max leveled the gun, focused on locating Cruz's energy signature.

A current of air brushed his cheek as something dropped from the ceiling, hitting his shoulders. Max had a quick impression of muscle and cold skin before he flung the thing against the stone wall. Shadows rippled, and a black snake with orange stripes tumbled to the floor.

"Stay back," he hissed to Miki. Then he patted his leg, signaling Truman to heel.

But the big dog stayed right where it was, in full defensive mode, trained to defend at any cost even when ordered back to safety. Max felt something tighten in his chest at the sight of the dog's unflinching loyalty.

Before he knew it, Miki pushed past him. The parachute flared out, shimmering ghostly white in the beam of his flashlight.

"What the hell are you—" Max stopped. A second black shape slid along the edge of the parachute, within striking distance of Truman. The snake raised its head, its tongue flickering as it tested the air.

"Truman, freeze." Max gave the low, harsh order as the dog growled loudly. The snake slithered across the tunnel floor and stopped within inches of the snarling Lab. The flat, triangular head weaved back and forth, poised to strike.

"Don't move, buddy." Max's voice was soothing. "Freeze," he repeated.

Truman stood frozen.

Finally the snake vanished under the nylon parachute. A muscle twitched at Max's jaw and he released a breath, flipping on the safety of his .45.

"Truman, heel."

The dog looked back, then turned toward the parachute, as if determined to defend against a further attack. Max patted his leg again. "Truman, *heel.*"

This time the Lab bounded closer. Once the dog was safely out of range, Max grabbed a stick and flipped the nylon closed, twisting the ends together in a knot so that the snakes were caught inside, writhing madly but safely out of range. In two minutes he had dumped them outside and carried the parachute back, while Miki watched him wide-eyed.

"Your dog is amazing," she said quietly. "He didn't back down even when you called him. He could have been killed—assuming that pair was poisonous."

"Definitely poisonous." Max leaned down to pat Truman's head. "Nice alert, buddy." He chuckled as Truman's tail banged his face.

Miki knelt, too, but kept her distance, avoiding Truman's eyes while speaking softly. It was exactly the way to approach an unfamiliar dog, and Max wondered how she knew the drill so well.

The big Lab approached slowly, sniffed her arm, then lapped at her hand. When Miki didn't move, he bumped her side and whimpered, licking her face.

"Good dog." Miki laughed, scratching the dog's ears until Truman huffed in pleasure. "Big, brave guy," she said huskily. "Nothing scares you, does it? How could I have been so stupid about you?"

Her voice was soft, her hands gentle and soothing.

Truman pressed against her leg, yawned and

scratched behind one ear, then trotted toward Max and waited, ears alert.

Max pointed and the dog shot forward into the shadows. Max pulled a spider web out of Miki's hair. "You could probably do without this. And thanks for picking up that other snake."

"It was blind luck," Miki whispered and Max heard the ragged edge of fear in her voice. "If I hadn't been looking at the ceiling, trying to figure out when this tunnel was built, I would never have seen the second one." She touched her face carefully. "Is my nose still bleeding?"

"Looks that way." He tracked his light over the tunnel floor. "How do you know so much about dogs?"

"I don't."

"You know what not to do and how to put Truman at ease. He's pretty damned picky about strangers, believe me."

She shrugged. "I told you, my friend trains service dogs. I've managed to pick up a few crumbs of wisdom over the years. Kit insists that dogs are smarter and kinder than most people."

Something slipped through Max's mind, but he couldn't pin it down. "She could be right," he muttered.

MIKI BRUSHED COLD, STRINGY cobwebs off her face and took a quick glance at Max. He was only a few feet away, but he might as well have been on Mars, his attention centered on the shadows around them.

In some subtle way, things had changed between them. She didn't trust Max completely yet. She would still grab the first chance to leave the island. She was hungry and exhausted and her knee throbbed, but in spite of all those things she owed her life to this hard man.

How far could she trust him when he continued to be suspicious of her? More to the point, how far could she trust *herself,* when she found herself more and more fascinated by his cool control, broken by elusive flashes of humor and vulnerability?

She frowned into the darkness, watching Truman pace alertly in front of them. Her arm throbbed savagely. "Is it much farther?"

"A few hundred yards." He glanced over at her, eyes narrowed. "Need some help?"

Miki shook her head. She *wasn't* a leaner. She was reckless, stubborn and clumsy, but never dependent.

Her foot hit a fallen rock and she stumbled, throwing out her arms with a gasp. Instantly a hand grasped her elbow, holding her steady in a firm grip like it was the most natural thing in the world. The feel of soft leather sliding across skin reminded her of those unusual gloves that he wore constantly. She didn't buy Max's story about chemical sensitivities.

Was it a scar or a deformity he wanted to hide? He didn't seem the kind of man who worried about his looks, which meant that the problem had to be very serious. There had been no time to see his hand when he'd removed the glove once before. Miki shivered a little, conjuring up pictures of old wounds and mangled fingers with all the graphic detail that came from being a photographer.

But he had saved her life. She was determined to force some kind of stalemate in their mutual suspicions. Without basic trust, they might not make their way out of this place alive.

She felt him release her arm and move ahead without a word, touching Truman gently. His bond with the dog was another strange thing. Her friend Kit raised service dogs back in Santa Fe, and her four current training animals were beyond amazing, but even she lacked this kind of taut, controlled communication with her dogs. Though Kit didn't talk about it, Miki knew her friend had been in some kind of trouble recently, and her dogs had been involved. But the trouble had brought a remarkable man into her life. Sometimes life worked that way, hardships bringing unexpected gifts.

Miki frowned, wondering if she, too, would find something positive in this nightmare.

"Yeah, right," she muttered.

Max looked back at her, one eyebrow raised. "Everything okay?"

"Sure," she lied.

She wasn't going to discuss her throbbing arm, her hunger or her confusion with him. She didn't lean.

When she looked up, they were facing a steep row of stone steps. Max pointed through the shadows. "The door is at the top of the stairs. From there, it's about twenty yards across the beach. Follow Truman. No noise, remember."

Miki realized his warning was real. Someone had tried to kill her and there could be more like him out there.

You didn't hide from the facts, even when they were unpleasant. Miki had learned that rule the hard way, after her mother's diagnosis of leukemia and four agonizing years spent watching her fade away moment by painful moment. She had hated the x-rays and the needles, the thermometers and taking blood. She had hated being helpless to make things better.

Grimly, she forced the memories away.

When she got to the top of the stairs, Max pointed past a row of bushes. Weak sunlight bathed the beach as the sun went down.

Just another day in paradise.

Beside her Truman sniffed the air, ears raised as he studied a group of boulders above the beach, shadowed beneath high palm trees.

Truman looked back at Max, who made a small gesture with his hand.

Instantly the dog trotted over the sand and vanished.

Another bunker, Miki thought. The island was probably covered with them. But for some reason, she couldn't move. The sand glinted, too open, too exposed. She half expected to hear another airplane or feel a hail of bullets.

The hand on her arm was firm and reassuring, and

Miki closed her eyes, wishing that just once she could relax and lean, letting herself go into those strong arms.

That would be another stupid move, and she wasn't going to be reckless or stupid ever again. She would follow the wonder dog and the inscrutable warrior and keep her emotions buried where they couldn't cause any trouble.

Her hands were clammy as she stepped into the fading sunlight. She felt exposed and painfully vulnerable, tensed for some kind of attack. But there was no sound except the wind brushing her face, cool and clean. Only the sea, washing and retreating in calm majesty.

Miki closed her eyes, struck with a sudden awareness of being alive, *really* alive, feeling every heartbeat, hearing the tiniest sound. She looked around, giddy, seeing colors that seemed brighter and outlines that looked impossibly sharp. For a photographer whose life was tied up in images, this kind of sharp clarity was nirvana, and she clutched every detail in her memory.

Behind her Max shifted impatiently and pointed at the rocks. Miki nodded at him and followed.

"MIKI—IS THAT YOU?" Dutch was twisting on the cot, trying to sit up. His face was pale, his eyes bloodshot. Max had brought him from the cave only minutes before, and the trip had left him agitated.

When Max leaned around her to reach for his medical kit, Dutch stared at him in confusion. "Who are you? Where the hell am I?"

There was a faint blue tinge to Dutch's lips that Miki hadn't noticed before, and the change seemed ominous. As Max focused his light, Miki noticed that the man's neck veins were distended. He tried again to sit up, but the movement left him wan and gasping for breath.

Miki took his shoulders and pushed him down gently. "Take it easy, Dutch. Max is a friend. He's going to help us."

"Help us how?" The pilot's fingers twisted, digging at the blanket Max had thrown over him. He didn't seemed to notice when Max took his pulse.

It seemed like an eternity before Max put his equipment back into the medical kit and offered the pilot water through a straw shoved into his canteen. Dutch drank deeply, then broke into harsh coughing that was painful to watch. Miki was certain that he wouldn't survive without drastic intervention. Even though Max seemed to have decent medical skills, how much could you do with a few basic drugs and a small set of tools? Major surgery was out of the question.

Miki knelt and took the pilot's cold hand in hers, talking quietly about the plane, their travels, sports and the weather. Dutch didn't seem to understand her words, but the sounds made him relax. Finally his eyes closed and he fell asleep again.

Miki stood up slowly. "He's worse," she whispered. "Isn't there something you can do for him?"

"Maybe." He stowed the medical kit and ran a hand

through his hair. "It won't be easy, I warn you. I'd need your help. But let's give it a few more hours."

"He needs to leave now," Miki hissed. "Get on your radio and call someone." Her hands shook, opening and closing with anger. "Otherwise, he's going to die."

"He isn't as bad as he looks." Max's voice was tight and cold. The subject was closed.

He didn't care, Miki thought. He was going to go right on with whatever had brought him to this island, and nothing was going to make him deviate from that goal.

"His face is white and his lips are turning blue. Even I can see that he's not getting enough oxygen. He's had a heart attack or maybe—"

"It's his lung," Max said quietly. "A pneumothorax, probably from the pressure of impact. The airplane crash separated part of his lung from the surrounding cavity, and now his lung is compressed."

"You knew that all along?"

"I wasn't sure before. Now I'd say that it's a high probability."

"Then *do* something. You have to—"

"I am doing something. I'm watching him carefully. When the time is right, I'll do what's best for him."

"That's it? You say something vague like that and expect me to say *sure, fine, whatever?*"

"Take it or leave it." He turned away abruptly and pulled off his vest. Miki realized that his movements were slow and awkward, probably because he was exhausted. But she refused to feel a shred of sympathy for him.

She watched him open his pack on the floor and remove a small digital camera with lenses different from any she had seen before. High zoom capability, she noted. Good for distance work. He reached into his medical kit and pulled out a thermometer for Dutch. There, lying next to iodine and gauze, nearly within reach of her hand, was a seven-inch surgical scalpel. One jab with that blade in a vulnerable spot and Max would be incapacitated. If she could find his radio, she could call for help

Impossible. She couldn't pull it off even if she wanted. With her luck, she'd fumble and end up burying the blade in her own arm.

So much for trying to escape.

She gave an irritated sigh. "Aren't you going to feed Truman? The poor guy must be hungry." She walked past Max and held out a piece of jerky, one of the last in her stash. "Here, honey. You can have this."

"He's fine. Keep that for yourself or Dutch." He didn't move, studying her face. "You don't add up."

"What do you mean?"

Max's gloved hands circled her shoulders. "The scalpel was there. You could have used it. Why didn't you?"

The scalpel.

Okay, she'd thought about it, and it would have been nice to have something to protect herself from another attacker, but the way things were going, she needed more than a scalpel. Mortar fire and a tank battalion came to mind.

Frankly, she wouldn't have known what to do with the thing anyway. Slash his neck? Drive it into his heart?

She felt nauseated at the thought. Throat slitting just wasn't in her repertoire. On the other hand, she didn't want to give him any undue advantage over her. "What scalpel?"

"The scalpel lying in plain sight on top of my medical kit," he said quietly. "You looked at it, and you could have reached it, but you didn't."

"Do you have eyes in the back of your head? How do you know what I was looking at?"

"The camera. I saw your reflection in the steel body."

It had been a cool, calculated test—and she hadn't suspected a thing. "I don't like being watched. Or manipulated." Miki crossed her arms. "If you keep pushing me, I may decide to use one of those scalpels next time." But she didn't meet his eyes and the words sounded flat. So she wasn't the toughest fighter in the world. This whole situation was pushing her *way* out of her comfort zone.

She watched him toss a roll of gauze between his gloved fingers. "You expected me to attack, didn't you? You really think I'm some kind of hostile agent?"

"The thought crossed my mind." The gauze kept moving, slapping softly against his gloves. There was something hypnotic about the unbroken rhythm. "I haven't scrapped the idea entirely," he added grimly.

"Because of what Truman did?" Miki was trying to approach the situation calmly and logically, but it wasn't easy.

"That and other things."

"Care to be more specific?"

He shook his head.

"If you don't trust me, why tell me now?"

"Because things just got a little more complicated." He stared down at the medical kit. "I'm going to need your help."

Miki realized the harsh lines on his face came from exhaustion. So he wasn't a superman after all.

He studied her for long moments and then unzipped the front of his wetsuit. As he moved, a muscle clenched at his jaw.

Something wasn't right here. "Is there a problem you're not telling me about? Is it Dutch?"

"He should pull through. I know what to watch for."

"Then *what?*"

Max pulled his wet suit down to his waist. His chest was ridged with rows of muscle above sculpted abs. The up-close view made fingers of heat jab at hidden parts of Miki's body.

Okay, he was built. No, that wasn't nearly strong enough. The man was major-league hot. With a body like that he could have sold gym equipment on late-night television and made a fortune. There wasn't a hint of fat on him anywhere. She kept physically active and liked to think she was in decent shape, but this body was completely out of her league.

Miki took a deep breath. Something happened when a woman looked at a body like that. It made her wonder how those muscles would feel naked under her in bed.

He turned away and tugged at his wetsuit, his shoulders tightening in a beautiful, sculpted line. Miki felt new heat swirl through her body. What was going on here? He was the *enemy,* sort of. She didn't give a damn how gorgeous his body was.

Yeah, right.

But when he turned back, Miki's breath caught in horror. A six-inch gash ran across his back, oozing fresh blood. "That happened when you were fighting?" Her voice was unsteady.

"Our pal was pretty good with a knife." Max's face was unreadable.

"And you didn't say anything until *now?*" Maybe he was Superman after all.

"I had other things on my mind." Max tossed her his medical kit.

She fumbled, but managed to catch it. "I don't understand." She wasn't good with blood. Whether her own or others, the sight of blood always made her feel faint. A therapist had told her it had to do with watching her mother die and all the blood tests that were done during treatment and after treatment, all of which had failed. Miki didn't know if that was true—he'd hit on her after the first appointment so she'd never gone back.

Small wonder she didn't trust people very much.

"I can't see behind me, Miki. You're going to have to clean the wound and then stitch me up. Everything you need is inside that medical kit." His voice hardened. "If you're thinking about stabbing me, now's your chance. There are six different blades in that kit, and I'm going to trust you with all of them. Do you have a problem with that?"

Perfect abs, Miki thought, feeling a little dizzy. She took a quick peek, her eyes slipping lower.

Perfect *everything.* With no hint of self-consciousness Max gave a final tug and kicked off the wetsuit.

Gorgeous wasn't nearly strong enough in the adjective department. Miki swallowed, unable to take her eyes away. The buff, naked body moved closer.

Life was stupid and unfair, she thought. Women obsessed about wearing a halter top, much less stripping down to the buff, but men like Max walked around commando and didn't bat an eye.

He stared at her over one shoulder, his back turned. "Aren't you going to take the scalpels out? I'm ready." Their eyes met, and Miki felt heat fill her cheeks as he turned around to face her.

That was when she really began to hyperventilate.

CHAPTER FOURTEEN

THE MAN WAS ABSOLUTELY SERIOUS, Miki realized.

He was inches away, completely commando, a sight pulled out of her most private fantasies. She felt a little zing of dizziness as his thighs flexed. "You think— I mean, you want me to—"

He looked down at her, a faint grin on his face. "Yeah, I do."

Okay, *this* was what real hypoxia felt like. She wasn't exactly prim. She'd had enough serious relationships to know her way around the male anatomy. But she had never seen prime material like this before. As her pulse hammered in her ears, Miki realized that she had never had such a physical reaction to any other man. Was it the stress? The adrenaline rush of danger?

Her palms were sweaty. Her body was alive and restless, flushed with heat. She was seriously *aware* of him, sensing him with every nerve in her body. A little voice urged her to get closer, but she managed to ignore it.

Clearing her throat, she looked away.

This isn't happening, she thought.

Breathe, she thought.

Breathe before you pass out.

Except Miki had a feeling that any second her body was going to hit the red zone and she would do something crazy—like reach out and grab those amazing abs for the sheer pleasure of it.

What was she thinking? This man was her enemy, or at least still harboring hostile feelings for her, despite their awkward and very temporary truce. She couldn't afford to be swayed by a little skin.

She was smart.

She was tough.

She was also having a hell of a time keeping her gaze on his chest when it insisted on slipping lower. But all of that was going to stop right now, Miki swore. "You can put the swimsuit back on," she snapped. "Going full commando isn't required."

His eyes narrowed. He looked surprised. Miki realized he didn't understand her embarrassment.

She *hated* men who were completely self-confident about their bodies. It just wasn't fair. "Well?" She put her hands on her hips, glaring at him. "Get dressed." If you could call wearing a little scrap of black nylon dressed, she thought grimly.

He shook his head slowly. As his lips twitched, Miki realized that he was enjoying her discomfort.

The jerk.

She waved a hand in the general direction of his lower body. "I mean it. No clothes, no stitching." And how in heaven she was going to find the strength to face a knife wound was beyond her.

"Seeing my body really bothers you?" His brow rose. There was something unreadable in his eyes.

Miki felt heat torch her cheeks. "It's nothing I can't deal with," she snapped. "But it may be uncomfortable for you to get dressed after I stitch you up." A clumsy explanation, but it was the best she could do with her brain caught in a serious state of oxygen deprivation.

He smiled faintly, as if she hadn't fooled him for a second. "I'll survive. It's best to make an aseptic environment near the wound."

Aseptic, Miki thought dimly. Her brain bought the idea, but the rest of her body wasn't handling it so well.

"Look, I'd do this myself but I can't," Max went on. "I need you to stay calm and clean the wound, then put in eight stitches."

Eight stitches? She waved her hand. "No. Not even a microscopic chance. I can't. Sorry. Impossible," she said hoarsely.

His fingers cupped her chin. "Do you want to tell me why?"

"You're naked," she rasped.

"I can still talk," he said quietly. "So let's have it. Just clear the air."

"Air?" Miki didn't want to talk. She was unbearably aware of his lean, dangerous body within hand's reach, and *talking* wasn't anywhere near the top of her agenda. She cleared her throat. "It's personal."

"I'd say we've gotten past being strangers, wouldn't you?"

Miki closed her eyes, which was the only way to keep her restless gaze north of the danger zone. "I don't want to have this conversation." She was perilously close to blurting out the details of her mother's long illness, the months of dealing with the fragile skin and deteriorating veins that came from complex cancer treatments. Miki had never told anyone about her fears or the residual pain, and she wasn't about to start now.

She glanced over her shoulder, relieved to see that Dutch was asleep. "There has to be some other way. Maybe if I hold a mirror for you or—"

"There's no other way." He cut off her vague proposal. "If this wound gets infected, it could be dangerous." He gripped her shoulders. "I need you, Miki."

The rough sound of his voice made the little hairs stand up along the back of her neck. When had a man ever said that to her and meant it?

"Breathe," he ordered quietly. "I'll talk you through it."

"What about the pain? I'll have to give you something for that."

He shook his head. "Not necessary."

There it was, the tough-guy factor again. But there was no point wallowing in fear and uncertainty because she figured Max was right. He needed help and she was the only one available.

Looking down, she saw that she was clutching the medical kit. "What am I supposed to do?"

"Describe the wound to me. If the cut isn't clean, you'll have to recut the surface at a ninety-degree angle." He turned his back to her. "Look closely. Tell me if the wound is clean or jagged."

He had the most amazing butt, Miki thought grimly. She took a few seconds to enjoy the sight of his lean, tanned thighs, girding herself for the shock of the wound.

She took a deep breath, horrified by the bloody, jagged skin. "No, it's not straight. He must have jerked the knife." She heard the words echo hollowly in her ears. "I'll have to clean it before I can tell you anything more."

"Sterile gauze wraps are packed in the medical kit. You'll find a small bottle of Betadine there, too. Better clean your hands first."

After she'd washed with Betadine, Miki splashed some of the dark antiseptic onto a piece of gauze. Once the gash was clean, she could see the full depth of the incision. How had he managed to stay mobile all this time without a painkiller?

Max touched her shoulder. "How does it look?"

Awful. "Jagged."

"How deep?"

"Maybe half an inch."

"Can you see bone?"

Bone? Miki shuddered. "No." *Thank God.* More blood welled up and she brushed it away with fresh gauze. "What do I do now?"

"Take the number fifteen scalpel. That's the one with the long, curving blade. Do you see it?"

Miki found the blade and removed the scalpel from its sterile wrapping. "Ready."

"Good. Now you're going to stretch the skin tight because that's the only way to make a clean incision." His voice was as cool and impersonal as if he was talking about someone else's body.

"Shouldn't I give you something to numb the site? This can't feel good."

"I need to feel what you're doing in case you go too deep."

Miki's hands began to shake more than ever. How could he possibly do this? For that matter, how could *she?*

"Tell me how," she rasped.

"Squeeze the skin between your thumb and forefinger and look at the wrinkles. That will tell you the cross lines. Do it now."

"Okay. I see them."

"You're going to cut at a ninety-degree angle to those lines. You have to grip the tissue tightly so you don't slip. Take your time. Do it right. Forget about me and everything else."

Miki felt dizzy. She couldn't do this. He was crazy. They were both crazy if they thought she could.

As she hesitated, Max looked back at her and smiled crookedly. "You're doing fine, honey. Take a deep breath and look at me. Come on, breathe."

His voice sounded tinny, but the deep breath worked and her nerves settled. "You're certain you don't want some kind of anesthetic?"

He shook his head. "Take your time. I trust you. You'll get it right."

Her eyes snapped to his face in surprise. He *trusted* her?

Biting her lip, she shoved everything out of her mind but the task in front of her. "I'm going to cut now. If you need to…curse or anything, that's fine."

His husky chuckle echoed in the quiet air. Miki realized he was laughing.

"Honey, I've been through a whole lot worse than a few stitches. You don't have to worry about me screaming. You should get started now."

There was a sense of unreality about the whole experience as Miki tugged on a pair of sterile surgical gloves, trying not to think about the last time she had worn gloves like these, only a few days before her mother's death. Even now, the memories were still raw.

Following Max's calm directions, she pulled the skin, positioned the scalpel and cut outside the jagged edges, forcing herself to forget she was cutting living flesh. Instead she pretended she was working on an elaborate high school science project.

Blood welled up inside the wound, and she ripped open a new package of gauze. Then there was more blood. A new wave of dizziness hit her. She swayed and felt Max's arm slip around her waist, steadying her.

"You're doing great. Hold on."

She tottered on the edge of hysterical laughter. He was the one serving as a living pincushion, but he was reassuring *her*.

She forced herself to focus, shutting out everything else. "What next?"

"There's no sign of gushing blood, I take it. If an artery or vein were hit, you'd see it."

She shook her head and muttered, "No."

"That's good. Before you close the wound, you need to check it carefully. Use the scalpel and be certain that there's no foreign matter, no dirt or cloth present."

The calm instructions helped her clear her mind, and she probed the wound from one end to the other. "It's clean, but it's bleeding."

"A little blood flow is good to help clean things out. Since the wound is less than six hours old, we can do a direct suture. You'll need to drape the wound to make a sterile barrier before you start. Truman, bring the bag."

The Lab looked up. Without hesitation, he pulled a black nylon duffel bag out of the corner and carried it across to Max, who unzipped an inner pocket and pulled out a plastic pack with sterile paper towels.

Almost over, Miki told herself. It wasn't as if he was going to die from this.

He handed her the closed plastic bag. "Drape the wound and then put on new gloves. I'll hand you the needle." As he spoke, Max stretched out on the cot, turning onto his side in a smooth movement.

Despite her panic attack, Miki was still a woman, and she had to savor the sight of all those rippling muscles just once more. "I'm ready."

"Use a square knot, and try to keep the stitches even.

You want both edges to meet, with no overlapping skin. No spaces. either. Any open places become a playground for bacteria."

"Okay." Miki swallowed hard. Stitches? She *couldn't* do this. "What else do I have to know?"

His voice was husky. "That you're damn brave, Blondie. You can cut me up anytime. Only next time you have to get naked, too."

Her eyes cut to his face. His words were like a dark caress, spurring a wave of hot, sexual images. But she wasn't going to think about how those hard hands would feel sliding over her heated skin.

Breathe, idiot. Gritting her lips, Miki took the curved needle he offered her. If he could be cool, so could she.

"Focus on the suture tension. Try to keep everything even, and don't pull too tight. How do you feel?"

Like shit. "Fine," she lied. She took a jerky breath and felt Max's hand open, gripping her thigh.

"It's going to be fine. You can do it."

"I can do it," she repeated, and as she said the words something bleak and heavy lifted from her shoulders. She stood a little straighter, breathed a little deeper. "Damned right I can. I've got the idea." She gritted her teeth. "Bombs away." She felt sweat bead her forehead as she pushed the needle cleanly through both sides of the wound. Time seemed to stretch out in a nauseating blur.

Finally her first suture was in place. With fierce

concentration, she finished two more stitches. "Are you okay?"

"Fine. You're doing great."

She put in five more stitches, smeared antibiotic cream around the wound and taped a fresh gauze pad firmly in place. "Done. Everything is clean and the stitches look even. At least I think they are." As she sat back, bile filled her throat and she tried to speak, but no words would come out.

"Take it easy." Max turned, grabbed her shoulder and pushed her forward. "Head down. Deep breaths. You'll be fine."

Miki hunched over, feeling blood fill her face while the world slowly came back into focus around her.

She realized she'd lumbered her way through, despite the painful memories of her mother. She sat up and smiled at Max crookedly. "I may not throw up after all."

"Always good to hear that." He brushed a strand of hair from her cheek, his eyes narrowing. "Still dizzy?"

Whatever it was, the bout was over. She managed a smile. "I guess not. Are you ready for that anesthetic? Me, I'd be begging for hard drugs by now."

"Not quite yet." His eyes darkened. "Because there's something else I've been wanting for a hell of a long time." His hands slipped around her shoulders.

Before Miki could brace herself, he was kissing her and it was the real deal, full contact, hot and expert.

CHAPTER FIFTEEN

MIKI COULDN'T MOVE. Her skin was on fire, her head pounding. It was the dizziness that got her, she thought. Dizziness and stress could make you do strange things, couldn't they?

Like kissing him back.

His hands opened, lifted her face.

Miki felt pulled toward him, gripped by curiosity and need in a primitive way that would have scared her if she'd been calm enough to think straight. But the last thing she wanted was for this moment to end before she knew exactly where it was heading.

"You're not screaming yet." His eyes were dark and focused. "You're not calling me a bastard and trying to knee me in the groin."

"No," she whispered.

She wasn't doing any of those things, not even thinking about them. There was an odd whine in her head and her pulse sounded too loud. They were strangers, she thought. Her mind told her to back off.

But her body had other ideas. And right now, her body seemed to be calling the shots.

"What is it about you?" He pressed his mouth against the pulse that hammered at her wrist. "Something about how you drive your hands through your hair." His tongue nuzzled the sensitive base of her throat, slow and searching.

God, the man was like a drug. He made her breath back up in her throat, made her forget all the reasons that this was not wonderful, but a very dangerous thing to do.

"That perfume of yours is driving me crazy."

What did he mean? she wondered. All her perfume was gone, washed off in the ocean, and the scent from the broken bottle in her purse had long since evaporated. How could he smell anything but seawater on her skin? Miki meant to ask him that, but he was biting her ear, drawing the tender skin against his mouth and then she couldn't think of anything but how it would feel if he touched her in other places with the same slow, delicious torture.

Her pulse played a rackety bass in her ears and she saw his arm clench, hard muscles perfectly outlined. She resisted the urge to glance lower and see how the rest of his body was reacting.

But she didn't need to see because suddenly she could feel him clearly. And he was still wearing the damn gloves. It was too odd—but she didn't care. Her knees were putty, she couldn't think straight and she was praying he wouldn't stop.

"There's baby oil," he said roughly. "I can smell it on your throat and right here behind your ear. Fresh and a little sweet—very sexy."

"Massage." Miki's mouth didn't seem to be working right. "At the hotel. The night before we left." It was hard for her to remember back that far. Everything about her life before the crash had morphed into a gray blur. "How could you know that?"

He ignored the question. "They added some sort of ginger to the oil." His mouth grazed the tender skin behind her ear while her brain shouted that this was reckless and stupid and she had to stop *immediately.*

But her body sighed and turned off the volume, immersed in the pure ache of his hands and mouth. How did he make her feel so greedy? She wasn't sure that the answer mattered, of course. She was too lost in sensation to care.

He leaned closer, kissing the curve of her shoulder. "More baby oil. Sexy as hell." He pulled her onto the cot beside him and opened the top button of her shirt.

"How did you know about the baby oil?" she rasped.

"Already told you. I'm very sensitive to chemicals." He traced the line of her jaw and turned up her face, kissing her slowly while Miki's toes curled. Every muscle turned to mush, and her brain along with them.

"Your cut—you shouldn't be moving around." She swallowed as his mouth brushed her collarbone.

Two more buttons slid open. His tongue feathered along the top of her lace bra.

"I'm fine. You did a great job." He pulled her back into his arms and suddenly Miki was caught up by the power and heat and absolute control of his body against hers.

This had to be wrong, a quiet voice whispered. This could get her into a *whole* lot of trouble.

But Miki didn't listen. Some deep restlessness made her turn her head until they were face-to-face, only inches apart, his breath stirring her hair. Her nipples felt hot and tight as he opened another button on her blouse.

"Nice bra." He traced the front clasp. Something hard filled his eyes. "You could run away, you know. You could even tell me to stop." His hand was warm between her breasts. "In fact, it might be a better idea if you did."

"I bet you say that to all the girls." With a man like this, there had to be dozens of women. Miki needed to remember that, to keep in mind that this was an illusion, a blip of insanity and nothing more.

Not that this was *personal.* He was a tough, amazing man and what woman wouldn't want to feel that hard body against hers?

"No woman has ever stitched me up before, honey. Not too many have argued to make me put *on* my clothes, either," he said wryly.

"So you've got a great body and you know it."

His mouth brushed the hollow between her breasts. Miki's palms went damp and her hands moved, sliding through his hair.

"*Your* body is what counts." His tongue slid beneath the edge of her bra and she felt a sharp, ruthless tug of desire. "Trust me, it's spectacular. And I owe you, so name your payment. Whatever you want, honey."

Miki's heart fluttered.

You, against the wall. No words, no promises, just more of this dark, shifting pleasure wrapped around me and within me while you turn me inside out.

"You—you don't have to pay me back." Her breath caught. His mouth cruised down one breast. There was only a flimsy layer of lace between her aching skin and his hot, searching mouth, and her body melted, wanting everything and wanting it *now.*

His lips curved as he studied her flushed and very aroused skin. "So you're turning down my offer?"

No! "Yeah." She took a ragged breath. "Not that it isn't— Look, forget it, Max."

Lace shifted.

His tongue brushed across one tight nipple and Miki bit back a moan of pleasure. She needed to stop him because if he did much more, she was going to come apart in his hands.

And he hadn't even taken off her bra.

His warm breath touched her skin. "You're amazingly sensitive right here." His thumb slid along her nipple, flexing the clasp of her bra. But he stopped short of the movement that would free her flushed skin. "Do I keep going?"

Did he? Did she trust him—or herself for that matter?

How had things gotten so dangerous and out of control? With her next ragged breath she decided she didn't really care. His eyes were hot and focused, but his hand shook slightly as he opened the last button on her blouse. And that single movement toppled Miki over the edge.

Tough as he was, Max was no more in control than she was.

She circled his hand—and instead of pushing him away, she gently bit the skin at the edge of his glove. "Take it off," she ordered.

"I can't," he said grimly.

Miki's fingers tightened in his hair. She was struck by a sharp wave of loss. She didn't want any barriers, not when touching and being touched by him was as natural as breathing. But there were going to be some conditions and the gloves were number one on her list. "The gloves go."

"Not happening."

"Because?"

Something flashed through his eyes. "Because I said no."

"Not good enough," Miki said tightly, pulling away. She began to button her blouse, only to feel his hands close around her wrists.

"Why does it matter? Trust me, honey, you're going to enjoy yourself either way. I'll see to that."

She shook her head. "You keep saying I have to trust you. But that works two ways. You'll have to trust me, too. I haven't touched any makeup or perfume since the crash, so there's no reason for you to keep the gloves." She gnawed at her lip thoughtfully. "If you have scars you want to hide, don't worry. They won't send me screaming into the night. I spent nearly two years in the hospital when…someone close to me was sick. Trust me, there's very little in the way of scars that I didn't see then."

Max's jaw hardened. "It isn't about scars, Miki."

"No? Then what is it about?" She glared at him. "The only answer is trust—and you don't have it." She turned away and finished buttoning her blouse. "Which means this conversation is over."

He muttered a short curse. When Miki stood up, he followed her. The man was oblivious to being naked, but he wouldn't consider ditching his gloves? She shook her head.

A moment later he was backing her out into a connecting tunnel, away from Dutch. His eyes were unreadable as he pinned her against the wall.

One glove dropped. Then the other.

Miki couldn't look away. Somehow this gesture was more intimate than sex itself. The naked desire on his face made her heart jackknife.

The wall, she thought blindly.

She wanted him against her, inside her. Her hands dug at his shoulders. "Max."

A muscle flashed at his jaw. Somehow she had known it would. "This is a bad idea, honey." His voice was harsh.

"Like hell it is." Miki pushed him back against the cool stone and her hands slid into his hair. Her leg moved of its own accord to wrap around his hard thighs.

He muttered a low curse, flipped open her bra and watched her breasts spill into his bare hands. A shudder ran through him as her fingers tightened in his hair. Miki heard him take a hoarse breath. "You're ripping out my guts here, honey."

It wasn't smooth or poetic, but bluntly honest, and her body responded in a way that was shockingly wet and reckless.

She had *never* wanted a man like this.

Never even close, she thought dimly. Why now? Why him?

Then thinking was forgotten as she pressed him closer to the wall and bit his shoulders, feeling a surge of primitive delight when he cursed softly, his hands locked at the waist of her jeans. Denim hissed and parted, sliding over her hips.

One sheer layer of lace separated their locked thighs.

Miki closed her eyes, memorizing the feel of his body, stunned by the odd sense of safety she felt in his arms. But when his mouth closed, hot and wet, tugging at her taut nipple, *safe* was the last thing she felt. Dimly she sensed him turn and press her back against the cold rock. His hand trailed across her stomach, calluses scraping the sensitive skin.

When she shuddered, he slanted his mouth over hers and muttered her name as if it was an answer, not a question.

His fingers opened across her stomach, toying with the lace and then slipping underneath. Miki wriggled restlessly, trying to slide out of her last piece of clothing, but Max didn't let her. "Take them off," she rasped. "Hurry."

"Like hell, I will."

He sounded awed, which made no sense at all. Miki was too different, too tall, too awkward. She might turn heads occasionally, but it was because she was so—unexpected. Not cute or petite. Not soft or feminine.

And Miki had learned very young that *different* frightened the heck out of most people.

So there was no reason for him to look overwhelmed. "Why are you—" Her breath caught as he brushed her mouth and crooked one finger around the edge of her panties. His tongue slid over hers, perfectly textured to the movements of his finger.

She squirmed with need.

"Hurry," she said again, her voice ragged. She felt his smile against her lips and then the lace shifted. She felt him slowly work the fabric down her hips. When her last shred of clothing pooled at her feet, the force of his eyes was almost tangible.

He took a hard breath. "Sweet God." His fingers circled her waist and he slid his palm down her stomach, watching her body quiver. When she tried to move, his fingers tightened. "No, don't move. Hell, you're—gorgeous." Then his hand opened, slid lower, molded against her hot, damp curls.

Miki closed her eyes, lost in sensation.

He spread her sleek skin and caught her moan against his mouth. "Closer," he said hoarsely. "Lean against me." She quivered as he slid one finger inside her. "Beautiful," he whispered. And she slipped over an edge she couldn't see and didn't expect, every nerve tuned to unbearable clarity. When he slid another finger inside her, Miki felt her breath stop, her heart catch and then she was tossed into a place that felt like magic. Trusting him completely, she moaned his name when the first hot wave took her by surprise and she came, shuddering against his careful fingers.

They were strangers bound by something that felt achingly familiar.

There was no time for awkward awareness because he drove her up again, this time kneeling and running his tongue over her until she forgot everything but the hot friction of his mouth doing things no man should be clever enough to do.

There shouldn't have been more, Miki thought blindly. She shouldn't have felt her body move again, desire coursing in a new haze of madness until she whimpered and dug her nails into his shoulders, coming against him again.

Her knees buckled. Dimly she felt him rise and catch her, pinning her against the wall with his body.

With his gorgeously aroused body, she realized.

When she looked into his eyes, she swallowed. "What *was* that? I mean how did you—" She shivered as he tugged at her taut nipples.

"It's not usually so fast for you?" There was something dark and possessive in his gaze. "You don't come like this every time?"

Heat filled her cheeks. She wasn't used to discussing her climax with incredibly sexy men who were still clearly aroused. "How about we drop this subject?"

"I need to know." His fingers shifted inside her, slow and deep, and desire filled her like warm honey, making her body quiver all over again.

"I—" She swayed, giving a husky moan. "No." The man didn't really expect *details,* did he?

"And this…thing between us. The immediacy of it," he said roughly. "You felt that, too?"

Miki nodded and focused on his face, trying to bite back a moan as he eased another finger inside her.

"Because it's important. Something is going on here." His eyes darkened. "Something beyond good sex."

Make that *fantastic* sex, she thought. *Astounding* sex. But he was too controlled and Miki decided it was time to turn the tables. She feathered one hand over his hard stomach and traced his erection. "Do you mind?"

"Mind what?"

"Taking your hand out of—that place where it is." Her voice was hoarse. "Doing that thing you're doing."

"You mean this thing?" His lips curved and his hand opened and he did something slow and amazingly erotic inside her that made her eyes cross.

"*That.* Cut it out." She pressed one palm against his chest. "You're too good at this. I need to think." It was her turn to touch and goad and watch him lose control.

"Forget about thinking." He worked her bottom lip between his teeth and frowned as if he was concentrating on something. Then he bent his head once more to her stomach.

And he was liking what he saw.

His hands circled her legs. His mouth opened, sliding over her in a way that made Miki forget about pride and everything else. "You taste like sex and sea," he said harshly.

The hot friction of his tongue made her shudder and she raked her nails across his shoulders, caught in another wave of blinding pleasure.

Dimly she felt him holding her up. Slowly the world came back into focus and she sank against the wall, boneless and sated. Her throat was dry, her heart pounding.

"Help," she said weakly.

"Anytime you want," Max rasped. His fingers speared through her wet curls and he licked her gently. "Like right now."

From a distance Miki heard a rattling noise, followed by Max's gruff curse.

When she opened her eyes, he drew away slowly, his eyes hard. "We're going to finish this later, honey. Whatever the hell it is," he added roughly.

"How about finishing it now?"

"Can't."

She made a low sound of protest as his hand moved away from her. He draped her blouse around her shoulders and shoved two buttons closed. "I'll be back as soon as I can."

"Why?"

Reality was charging back, and Miki didn't like the sound of it. She was naked, still shivering from toe-curling sex and now she was supposed to dress docilely, swallow her questions and vanish? No way. "Max, talk to me."

"Later." His face was shuttered. "That sound came from the pager I took from our pal with the knife."

Miki looked down and saw the pager vibrating in Max's hand. "So he's getting a message? Well, what does it say? Let me see—"

"Don't bother. It's in code," he said grimly.

Max studied the LED intently, turning the device over on his palm. She had to wonder what was so important about holding the pager.

He slid his hand along the row of buttons. "Hell," he whispered.

"What is it?" Miki stopped in the middle of zipping her jeans.

He didn't answer.

"Max, what's wrong?" She had the odd feeling that he had forgotten about her.

When the vibration started again, he pressed a button on the side of the unit and read the small, backlit screen.

"What do they want?" Miki's throat tightened. Things were happening too fast, and it was getting harder and harder to stay calm.

"I have to go." Turning off the pager, Max slid it into his pocket. "Whatever happens, don't go outside. You'll be fine here, but I can't guarantee your safety anywhere else. Remember that."

Miki knew he was right, even if she didn't like the fact. "I understand."

Max pulled a revolver out of a pocket on his vest. "Can you use one of these?"

"I've done some plinking." She hesitated and then took the gun. The metal grip was cold in her fingers. By habit she flipped open the chamber and checked to be sure there were no bullets loaded and none in the barrel.

"Always good to check, but it's empty now." Max held out a box of .45 bullets. "Keep these with you. Truman will be up above on watch. Everything's going to be fine."

Like hell it would, Miki thought. What had he seen on that pager?

Hiding her anxiety, she turned away, buttoning her jeans. "What if Dutch gets worse? How can I reach you?"

When she turned around, she was talking to dead air. Max was gone.

CHAPTER SIXTEEN

"FIVE TEN. Probably 190 pounds. Brown eyes and a small tattoo of a red scorpion surrounded by three diamonds in the middle of his left wrist." Max paced the lower deck of the gunboat, talking quietly into his encrypted satellite phone. "See what you can get on this creep, Izzy."

"I'm on it. Tell me about that pager you found."

"Some kind of new model, nothing I've ever seen before. It's got a big self-contained power source, but I can't tell what kind without opening the unit. The message was brief. *Tango-12-Bravo-97.* After that a string of numbers."

"Read them to me," Izzy said.

Max recited the number string, which he had already committed to memory. "The same text scrolled through twice."

"They'll be expecting an answer. When they don't get one..." A chair squeaked. "Let me work on it. I'll check our database on that tattoo while I'm at it, but I'm not too hopeful. What's his current status?"

"He'll be out for at least six more hours. I gave him two shots of your special Thorazine cocktail."

"That'll do it," Izzy said dryly. "Anything useful in his pack?"

"Compass, water purification tablets and two more knives. A nice preban silenced AK-47, too," Max added grimly. "Everything for your well-equipped, garden-variety terrorist. All well maintained and packed in waterproof bags. Our friend was loaded for bear."

"Would you expect anything less? Cruz doesn't fool around. We know he makes very few mistakes."

"Ryker was a good teacher."

"Any feedback from those motion-activated sensors you buried along the beach?"

"Nothing yet. None of my energy sweeps have revealed any definite signs of Cruz, either."

"The coordinates we picked up might have been a chip malfunction. Either that or he's managed some new set of tricks. We know his skills are growing."

It wasn't what Max wanted to hear, but he never let his emotions cloud his field planning. You surveyed your terrain, targeted the enemy and set up a defensive net in accordance with the facts, not what you wanted to be true. Good intel and detailed preparation had kept Max alive too often to count, while emotions interfered with capability and tactical response. He had been trained to keep his emotions locked up tight, where they couldn't cloud his judgment.

All that had changed thanks to one shadowed moment in a cool tunnel with a woman whose body was hot silk. She shot through his control the way no woman ever had, driving him right to the edge. Responsive and hungry, she had stolen right out of his darkest fantasies.

Only now it was over. It had to be over.

Do the job.

Forget the rest.

"Anything on those thermal images I uploaded?" Irritated, Max checked his supplies and tested the blade on his knife.

"No significant anomalies. Nothing to suggest where they could be storing the guidance system. To protect the electronics, they'll need a top-notch cooling system, but I've seen no hint of that. I've still got sixty or so images to check. The camera I gave you is almost too sensitive, and I have to rule out thermal bleed from adjacent rocks and solar pooling. Even with my new processors it's like crawling through wet cement. Once all of this is over, I'll program a better system, but that's no help now."

Max crossed to the porthole and scanned the water, but there was no sign of a boat anywhere. "What about that storm you mentioned?"

"Rolling in, right on schedule. It's going to be nasty."

That could be useful, Max thought. Anything that slowed his search would also conceal his presence on the island. "Tonight I'll check the third quadrant. Map coordinates 9.21 to 11.02."

"The woman?"

"She'll stay underground." Somehow he'd have to convince her it was necessary.

"How can you be sure of that?"

"We've reached an…understanding," he said coolly.

"What about Truman?"

"He'll be right beside me."

"Be damned sure that he is. You're good, but Truman can hear a cricket drop at rush hour."

Max knew from firsthand experience how good the dog was. "Copy that, Izzy."

"What's that noise?"

"I'm going through her camera case. I brought it out here my last trip but I haven't had time for a closer look." Max pulled out two new Nikon digital cameras in plastic bags that had torn open on impact from the crash. "I doubt any of this stuff will ever work again. Nikon body. Lenses, filters. The usual."

"Anything to make an ID?"

"Wallet's gone. She had a bottle of perfume, but I disposed of it after it disabled Truman." Max rummaged deeper in the bag. "Beef jerky sticks. Nail file. Mascara. Something lacy."

Something short and *sheer* and lacy. Tiny white straps slid through Max's fingers, making his throat go dry. The top would slip low and tease unmercifully, leaving a man crazy to remove it.

"Max? I asked if there was anything else?"

"Just some clothes." Opening a plastic bag, Max pulled out a pink lace thong with pink satin bows. As the narrow lace band pooled through his fingers, he pictured Miki inside it. Then he imagined taking it off her slowly and savoring her flushed skin.

Focus, fool.

He dug deeper in the bag. "Wait, there's something else." He pulled out two smooth wooden sticks with points at both ends. Beneath them was a ball of damp yarn. "False alarm. It's just her knitting needles and some yarn. There are notes here, as if she was working on some kind of top."

A *skimpy* top, Max thought. A narrow string around the neck was the only thing holding it up. He would have given a million dollars to see her wearing that and nothing else.

He felt a bead of sweat on his brow. Stifling a curse, he stuffed the pink thong, the notes and the knitting gear back in the camera case. "Nothing helpful here, Izzy. Knitting is a hobby, photography is a passion and she's pretty good with dogs. Even Truman took a shine to her. She told me that her best friend Kit is convinced dogs are smarter than most people."

"Come again." A chair creaked sharply. "Say that last thing again."

"I said that Truman likes her."

"No, the other part. Tell me about her friend."

"Her name is Kit. Miki said she raises dogs."

"Right. That part." Izzy sounded tense. "Kit who raises dogs." He whispered the words as papers ruffled, and then silence fell. "This can't be happening." A book snapped shut. "What's her friend's last name?"

"She didn't say."

"Stay where you are."

The line went silent. Against his better judgment, Max pulled out the lace top again. Though it was crazy, he slipped off one glove and ran his fingers over the sheer edge.

She'd worn it recently. He picked up traces of sweat and caffeine. Hormones, stress, excitement and high energy bled into his sensitive hand to create a picture of a restless, vibrant woman who threw her soul into work that she loved. He imagined the sexy sway of her breasts beneath the lace and the tight fit of the thong, snuggled against warm skin.

Hell. This was torture he didn't need.

With a curse, Max dropped the soft lace back in its bag, but the images were harder to escape. He could almost taste the faint layer of sweat that clung to her breasts and he knew exactly how she'd feel when he pushed her against the wall and filled her, fast and deep, while they both lost their minds in the kind of sex that didn't happen often. After their experience in the tunnel, Max had no doubt that taking her would be unforgettable.

But that was never going to happen. He couldn't afford distractions and meltdowns. The job always came first.

He tried to get her out of his mind. She was mouthy and stubborn, but she'd stood up to a man probably twice her strength wielding a knife. She wouldn't be easy to ignore.

The thought irritated him as he tugged his gloves back on. Women *weren't* long-term. Not in his life. Not ever.

Izzy came back on the line. "I don't believe this. You're sure she said her friend's name was Kit?"

"Not a doubt. She clammed up after that."

"Describe her to me again."

Max ran through the basic facts, then frowned. "Her eyes are the color of the sky. Sort of like after it rains in the mountains."

"You mean they're blue?" Izzy said dryly.

"No, they're more on the gray side. But there's a hint of blue. Maybe even some green. Something cool and soft." Max cleared his throat. "Gray-blue with green, call it."

The chair squeaked again. "I'm looking at a receipt for two Nikon digitals and the models match the numbers you gave me. These babies aren't cheap and they don't get sold by the thousands in a mall camera store." Izzy sounded resigned.

"So?"

Computer keys tapped like gunfire, and Izzy made a disgusted sound. "Your mystery woman is no hostile. I even met her after that mess we had in Santa Fe, but I didn't connect her with the crash. Hell, I should have thought of her sooner, but who would have figured the odds?"

"Who *is* she, Teague?"

"Her friend's last name is O'Halloran."

"You mean she knows Trace O'Halloran's baby sister?"

"That's right."

Max rubbed his neck, stunned. So Miki wasn't working with Cruz. She had nothing at all to do with this mission, other than blind bad luck. His instinct to trust her finally made sense.

"Here it is, *Best Beaches of the World.* It's already presold half a million copies, according to the file I just hacked into. Apparently the production staff was lax about posting their local flight plans. The office manager in L.A. took off to Catalina for a four-day vacation and just now realized the plane hadn't returned."

So Miki was family—or nearly as good as family. In Foxfire the boundaries tended to get blurred. Her friend Kit O'Halloran was engaged to marry Wolfe Houston, the SEAL who had become Foxfire's new leader.

Hell.

"Trust me, Houston's going to be seriously pissed off if anything happens to his fiancée's best friend."

"I'll see to it that doesn't happen." Max zipped up his vest. "Anything else?"

"Just one question. If she's truly out of all this, why did Truman alert for Cruz so clearly?"

That same question had been bothering Max. "Maybe there's something we don't know about Miki. Someone she's met, something she's bought or someplace she's been. It could be that her shoes or even one of her cameras have a scent trail to Cruz or someone very close to him."

"You think Cruz's people passed her something without her knowledge?"

"It's a possibility."

"How in hell can I trace something like that? We're all connected, if we go back five steps, at least that's what the sociology wonks keep saying." Izzy sounded irritated.

"Sorry, can't help you there. You're the techno go-to guy." Max glanced at the luminous dial of his watch. "I'd better move. Two cliff scans to finish as soon as it's dark."

"Keep your ammo dry."

As Max stared out through the uncertain light, he saw something cut through the choppy water to the south.

"Shit," he snapped. "We've got company."

CHAPTER SEVENTEEN

MIKI YAWNED. Her watch was ruined from seawater and she couldn't be certain of the time. Five o'clock. Maybe six?

She looked over at Dutch. For about ten minutes he had struggled for breath, tossing restlessly, but now he was snoring quietly again.

Miki stretched out on the floor, pillowed Max's sweatshirt under her head and tried to sleep, too, but she kept seeing the stone-cold eyes of the man who had tried to kill her.

Muttering, she rolled over and pulled the worn sweatshirt over her head. Worrying was pointless. If she hoped to have any energy left, she needed to sleep. She *definitely* wasn't going to think about having sex with Max. She wasn't used to that kind of raw physical intimacy and her wild response frightened her. She knew that stress broke down barriers, but stress alone didn't explain her reaction. The thought of his hands and expert mouth still made her heart lurch.

No, she wouldn't go there. It was just sex. By the time he came back, the whole encounter would be forgotten. With that thought firmly in mind, she tried to relax, wriggling on the cold ground. But the instant her eyes closed, she found herself thinking of Max again.

Wondering where he was. Wondering what he was doing. Hoping he was safe.

Even Max had been shocked by their instant sensory bond. His blunt questions had left no doubt that the intensity was unusual for him and he wasn't used to women going off like roman candles in his arms. Miki couldn't figure out if that was a good thing or a bad thing.

New heat brushed her face as memories crowded into her mind. There was no avoiding the truth. Some dark, physical bond had been forged between them. First both of them had been hit with unusual nosebleeds, and Miki wondered if that was one more symptom of whatever was affecting both of them so strangely.

Not that she was complaining about the whole physical thing that was happening. Only a fool would have a problem with a gorgeous man who appeared to be fascinated by every detail of her body. For a crazy moment, she had almost thought he had been reading her mind.

Irritated, Miki rolled over, forgetting she was on the floor. She knocked her forehead against the wall of the bunker and winced.

Some adventure.

Closing her eyes, she focused on relaxing, breath by breath. What she needed now was a distraction. Something to calm her down.

She could think of *one* kind of distraction, but she'd already done that with Max and it had made matters worse.

Miki opened her eyes and sat up. Photography was her passion and lifeblood, but when she was keyed up and needed to recharge her creativity there was only one answer.

Her eyes narrowed. She picked up Max's tool kit and the pile of dried branches near the door and went to work.

ONLY A KNITTER UNDERSTOOD the addictive solace of a pair of smooth needles with buttery yarn that slid over your fingers, making big problems shrink and small problems vanish. Something to do with repetitive motions and brain chemistry, Miki had read somewhere. Since the science was unimportant, she hadn't paid much attention. The effect spoke louder than any set of dry explanations.

She'd begun to knit the summer her mother had been hospitalized and her world fell apart. One of the intensive care nurses, a restful woman with intelligent eyes and gentle hands had given Miki her first pair of needles. They were cheap plastic, an ugly orange.

She had never loved anything more.

Her first few attempts had reduced her to sputtering, furious idiocy, but somewhere around day five muscle memory kicked in and she stopped thinking. First it happened for only a moment here or there, but soon her thoughts quieted, her fears and worries cast aside for as long as her hands moved. Within days she had given her mother a set of needles in a reflection of the same gift that had been made to her.

But Miki had chosen smooth, fine-grained rosewood for her mother, and soon the two women were knitting in quiet companionship, sharing a sentence here and there, comparing yarns or stitch definitions.

But one day her mother was too weak to hold circular needles and bulky yarn. A month later she was too weak to knit at all.

Two days after that, she was dead.

Knitting had been Miki's solace during the long illness, and became her focus on the long journey back from loss. It wasn't something she discussed with people, and years later she was still uncomfortable knitting in public—KIP, as knitters called it.

Now she looked down at the two decent needles she had managed to carve with one of Max's surgical scalpels. She had sanded them on a grainy piece of limestone. For yarn, she had found a package with a smooth and surprisingly light fiber that looked like cotton but felt like silk. Intrigued, Miki ran the fiber through her fingers and wondered why she had never seen anything like it before. The stitches grew beneath her fingers in smooth, even rows that were dreamlike and almost effortless against her needles, which made her swear to locate the manufacturer just as soon as she got back to the States.

She tested the fiber, made a few more sample stitches, and then smiled. The pattern jumped into her head without any planning. Leaning back against the wall, yarn in her lap, she began to knit.

She had barely finished two rows when a sound echoed near the concealed entrance to the bunker. Shooting to her feet, she clutched the knitting needles in one hand and a scalpel in the other, but it was Truman who came bounding through the shadows toward her.

The dog raced past her and sniffed Dutch's hand, then returned and bumped Miki's leg in excitement.

"What is it, honey? What do you want?"

The dog turned in a tight circle and bumped her leg again.

"I'm having a little communication problem here, so help me out. Do you need something? Food or water? Or maybe you want something from Max's bag." Miki stroked the Lab's head. "Did he send you for something, big guy?"

Truman sniffed Miki's arm and then cocked his head, ears raised. This time Miki heard it, too.

A motor throbbed out beyond the breakers. But instead of feeling joy at the possibility of being rescued, she sat frozen. This could be a fishing boat or innocent tourists. On the other hand, it might be one of the hostiles Max had warned her about. She wasn't about to risk being wrong.

She gripped her needles tighter, listening to the rising drone of the motors. Truman pressed against her leg and licked her face, then turned back toward the entrance, his hackles rising.

"Truman, what is it?"

Before Miki knew it, he was gone.

Brushing aside a stab of panic, she raced after the dog, up the stone steps and back through the bushes that concealed the entrance. In the slanting afternoon sunlight she saw Truman stop again, head raised.

A gunshot cracked like thunder. Miki felt the force of it tighten her chest. Gunfire was a bad sign and she wanted nothing to do with it.

"Truman," she called softly. "Come back here with me."

The big dog didn't move, his head pointed toward the breakers where a sleek white speedboat with two decks was tossing up white foam in its race ashore. Miki noticed something about its main deck looked odd and asymmetrical.

Her throat went dry when she realized the thing she was looking at was a mounted machine gun. A man in a bright blue shirt was holding the gun, aiming at a man kneeling on the deck. She couldn't hear their voices, but the sense of threat was harsh and unmistakable.

"Truman," she rasped. "Come *here.*" The dog didn't turn back or register her command in any way, and as the big yacht came closer, the dog's tension grew.

Another burst of gunfire cracked the silence. The kneeling man fell.

Miki put her hand against a rock to steady herself as she watched a second man dragged out onto the deck. Now she was close enough to hear his wild, pleading cries.

She wanted to look away, but she couldn't. Truman was at the edge of the sand now. When the yacht came closer, the dog would be clearly visible from the beach, bound to attract curiosity.

"Truman."

When the dog didn't respond, Miki shot through the bushes and crouched behind the Lab, one hand stroking his head reassuringly. "Honey, we *have* to go. This is too dangerous."

Miki's hands were shaking and she couldn't seem to hold the leather collar. After two tries, she managed to hold tight and tugged hard, trying to get the Lab's attention. "Come back now. *You can't stay here.*"

The dog's eyes flickered toward her for a moment, then locked on the sleek boat again. The shrill cries from the deck made Miki's stomach churn. Suddenly there was a glint of metal and the man in the blue shirt swung around, raising binoculars from a strap around his neck.

He looked toward the beach.

Toward the spot where she and Truman were crouched, frozen.

She heard a shout. The machine gun swung around slowly, dipped, then pointed across the sand directly at Truman.

CHAPTER EIGHTEEN

SHOUTS FILLED THE AIR. Even as Miki dropped flat on the sand behind a flowering bush, she knew it was too late. They'd been spotted.

Excited cries echoed above the hiss and slam of the surf while Miki tried to pull Truman down beside her, but the big dog refused to leave his vantage point beside a line of rugged boulders on the beach.

The big man in the blue shirt turned slowly, scanning the whole beach with his binoculars. His hands chopped at the air as he shouted orders Miki couldn't hear. A loudspeaker thundered and two men ran across the deck, pointing at Truman.

Like hell she was coming out, Miki thought. But she had to find a way to draw Truman back out of sight. Her calls didn't work and her soft shoves were ignored.

Time to try something different.

Miki gave a little cry and flopped back down on the ground, her arms outstretched, her eyes closed. She heard sand crunch. Truman's wet nose bumped her face, but she didn't move.

Another bump.

Truman lapped her cheeks with his tongue, and she managed to stay still. Something nudged her jeans and the next thing she knew, Truman was dragging her across the sand, his teeth gripping her pants leg, saving her as he had been trained to do. As a precaution, Miki didn't respond until she felt the sand give way to stone beneath her back. Then she opened her eyes and faked a long moan.

Truman bumped her leg, sniffing her face with an intense curiosity. Ears alert, he was in full rescue mode, oblivious to the cries of the men on the approaching ship.

Just as Miki had hoped, the Lab nudged her back toward the stairs to the underground bunker and safety. But before they were out of range, a line of bullets cut across the sand barely two feet away from Truman. Miki responded by gut instinct, her heart pounding and her throat dry as she grabbed the dog's neck and pulled him low to the ground.

More bullets strafed the beach and Truman went flat, covering Miki with his body while sand shot up in clumps. As the bullets cut closer, Miki wiggled free and pulled Truman toward a gardenia bush. Something hit her wrist, making her wince, but she didn't release Truman's collar.

More gunfire drilled the sand, accompanied by shouted curses and Miki realized she was too late, their position blown, with no way to cross the beach in time to escape the bullets that were pounding closer from the deck-mounted machine gun.

This is how it happens, she thought. *I am going to die and it will be right here, in dirty jeans on a beach with no name. No one will even know what happened.* Against the scream of bullets, panic took hold, clouding her logic.

She hugged Truman, shaking.

Then she raised her head and looked in the dog's keen eyes and felt her fear slip, pulling free. She took a deep breath, finally able to think again, and saw the figures scattering over the deck of the ship, which was nearly through the surf. She and Truman would have to run for the trees above the beach. Anything was better than waiting, silent and craven, until they were shot or tortured.

Miki pulled vainly at the Lab's big collar, sick to her stomach, knowing she could never leave the dog behind, but Truman refused to budge.

His head lifted. The shots from the boat came closer and closer.

Something white drifted past the gardenia bush. Not sand. Not flower petals.

Miki frowned. She felt Truman's tail straighten as he stared out toward the horizon while the air began to fill with tiny flecks. Then the white flakes swirled and ran together into a pale cloud, blanketing first Miki's corner of the sand and then the whole beach.

Fog.

She watched the layers drift and thicken until the world blurred and vanished completely, until all she could see was fingers of white drifting past her feet, cool on her face. Then the bullets stopped. A strained silence fell, broken only by the sound of the surf.

Truman looked up at her and sneezed, his tail stiff. If a dog could grin, then his open mouth was set in a grin. He turned in a circle, tail wagging. Then he sat, raised one paw and stared at her.

Like a high five, Miki realized. Dogs didn't do that, did they?

But they weren't out of danger by a far cry, not with the shouts of anger and confusion that began coming from several directions through the fog.

The fog…

It was just like the other time, fog swirling up out of the ocean, and Miki was sure it wasn't from a simple act of nature.

Truman? No way. That had to be impossible. An animal couldn't…

The Lab sneezed, his tongue lolling. He whimpered softly and then sank against her.

"Tru?"

Whimpering softly, Truman blinked, his eyes unfocused. Then he sank against Miki's chest. Hard on the heels of his collapse, a figure appeared from the fog, bare-chested and barefooted. He was missing two teeth and cradled a sawed-off rifle, whispering into a headphone that probably connected him with the yacht.

Bad news. Way bad news.

He spun, peered through the heavy clouds, saw Miki.

And he smiled slowly, revealing another gap in his dirty teeth. The shotgun lowered. "You come here."

Miki scooted backward, clutching Truman, who barely moved. She'd forgotten Max's revolver in the bunker. That left only one weapon available to her.

Grimly, she palmed her hand-carved knitting needles, slipping them from her pocket into the waistband of her jeans. Ineffectual at long range, they could still do damage up close…assuming she didn't get blasted by the shotgun in the next three seconds.

Stall.

Miki released Truman, raised her hands and stood up slowly. "You want money?" she rasped. "I've got an iPod around here somewhere."

"IPod?" The man's eyes narrowed. "Nano or Shuffle? You got Bose headset, too?"

"Uh—sure." *Like hell.* "Right up there behind that rock. I'll show you where it—"

"You *stay.*" The man's voice was tight and uneasy. "I look." He smiled at her and rubbed his crotch idly. "You American, sure. I love Julia Roberts. You know her?"

Know Julia Roberts, as in personally? "Uh, I can't say—"

"Maybe Paris Hilton?" He kept on scratching, his eyes narrowed. "She make lots of movies. I see on Internet."

Miki clutched the knitting needles, her hands trembling. "Yeah, I've met Paris and Julia. Sure I have. Great people. Friendly, too."

The man with the gun sighed in pleasure. "You get

iPod for me. Then you come. Leave dog." He stared at Miki's legs and moved closer. "Take off shirt first."

"Pardon me."

The shotgun jerked sharply. "Shirt. Put it on sand. *Now.*"

Miki swallowed and stepped away from Truman, keeping him well out the line of fire as she reached for her top button. Her hands were shaking so hard she couldn't open the blouse, but she kept a big, silly smile on her face. "Sure. I can do that. Why not?"

One button.

She took another step sideways, still smiling. The fog swirled up between them and Miki calculated how far she would get before he cut her down.

Two buttons.

"Hurry up. You fast."

Three.

"Take off all. Then you get down on sand."

Uh-oh. Miki fought to hold the smile, opening the last button on her shirt and letting one shoulder slide free. She'd ditched her bra because it was gritty with sand, rubbing her skin raw. With luck she'd buy a little distraction time.

The man's shotgun tilted. He stared avidly as her shirt parted. "Faster. The others come soon. You hurry and maybe I help you when they come here."

Miki fought panic and slowly lowered the other side of her blouse, with the cotton clutched to her chest. Then she let it fall.

Her attacker's eyes darkened. He slipped the shotgun into a holster under his arm and fumbled with his zipper. "We do it now. Maybe then I help you."

Oh, sure you will, Miki thought grimly. But the needles were in the waistband of her jeans and if he got any closer, she'd have a weapon.

It would have to be the eyes, she thought. Then a blind dash through the fog. Except she couldn't leave Truman behind.

The man with the scarred chest shoved her onto the sand, staring at her hungrily. Miki gripped her needles in her right hand, smiling vapidly, waiting until he was close enough so that she wouldn't miss. His hands dug at her shoulder, pinched her neck and rubbed her breasts. His breath was hot, sour like spoiled meat, making her gag.

She pulled out the sharpened wooden needles.

And then he made a little gurgling sound and pitched sideways onto the beach, his shotgun falling with a hiss.

Max stood glaring down at him, his eyes dark with violence. "That should teach the shit." He grabbed the shotgun and a knife stuck in the man's belt, then looked at Miki. His eyes hardened as he saw the bruise on her breast. "Maybe I'll kill him after all," he said hoarsely.

"Let's g-go. Truman's sick."

Max shoved her attacker over, saw that he was out cold, and smiled grimly. He picked up Miki's shirt and slid it around her shoulders, gently closing the buttons. His body was hot, reassuring, and she fought back a shaky sob, wanting to lean against him, drawing heat and strength from those hard arms.

Instead she took a step back and knelt beside Truman, stroking his head. "The fog came again. Truman was acting so strange. I almost think that…"

"Tell me later," Max said tightly. "The others won't be far behind." He tossed her the shotgun and lifted Truman's motionless body, scanning the sand. "There's a spot just beyond the beach where we can hide."

Always prepared, Miki thought.

She followed him into the swirling white and noticed that it was beginning to fade. A shout came from somewhere to their left and Max grabbed her arm with his free hand, tugging her up the slope, urging her to go faster.

It was like coming awake from a nightmare, Miki thought. Her hand shook as she felt the points of her knitting needles dig into her palm. Dimly, she felt a pain near her elbow, but she was too confused, too focused on keeping up with Max to pay much attention.

Gunfire exploded behind them.

Max grabbed her shoulder and pressed her to the ground, his body across hers. A hero trained to protect, just like Truman.

Gunfire hammered over their heads and moved off to the right. Silently, Max pulled her to her feet and pointed to a wedge of ragged limestone up the slope. Only when Miki scrambled around a tree did she glimpse the shadow of another tunnel. She headed down, stopped and turned to look for Max.

"Go on," he whispered.

"Give me Truman then. Help me get him onto his feet and we'll manage from here. He's starting to look more energetic."

His smile was swift and hot, knocking the breath out of Miki's chest, heating her face and diving deep into the wary corners of her heart. His lips curved, rakish, smooth as sin itself. "You go, girl."

He waved her forward and then turned, vanishing into the fog.

CHAPTER NINETEEN

MIKI SAW A STREAK of blood across her arm. Hers or her attacker's? She decided she didn't really want to know.

The man was probably dead. It might just as easily have been her or Truman lying on the sand, bleeding out their last seconds of life.

Miki began to shiver. Fighting back panic, she leaned against Truman, helping the Lab down a row of steps to a shadowed space just like the other bunkers. The dog still hadn't moved when she set him on the floor.

How had things gotten so wrong, so far out of control? Her throat was raw as she closed her eyes, struck by a sudden, blinding need to be home in Santa Fe, wrapped in the beauty of the high desert. She thought of her friend Kit and her four wonderful dogs, smiling just a little. Then she thought about all the stupid, small, pleasant things that made up her day and how much she missed them.

Coffee. Checking her e-mail. Watering her plants and watching the sun rise over the rugged Sangre de Cristo Mountains.

Silence stretched out around her, magnifying the thunder of her pulse. Max was gone and the gunfire had stopped.

Her stomach twisted and she fought down an urge to gag. She had to help Truman, and as soon as possible, they'd have to find Dutch. Responsibility and fear made her hands shake.

Didn't Max know she wasn't good with planning and responsibility? Didn't he understand she wasn't the best person to trust with important things like saving lives and maybe even protecting her country?

Miki remembered his stern orders about dehydration. Though she could barely swallow, she forced down several gulps of water from the canteen he'd slid under her arm, and kept her gaze away from the shadows farther back in the tunnel.

If there were more rats hiding there, she didn't want to know about it. But suddenly the weight of death and violence was all around her. She sank down on the stone floor, thinking about Max's trunk and its neatly stacked clothes, rolled maps and zippered mesh pockets with papers inside.

Government work.

Her hands twitched.

Looking down, she saw that the knitting needles were digging into her palm, raising beads of blood. As she fingered the rough wood, Miki turned over the few explanations that Max had made to her. Who was this man Cruz and why had Max been so interested in the scar on her arm? Mostly she wondered how the strange fog had come out of nowhere two times, both when danger was present.

Hugging Truman close, she found the fiber she had begun to knit. Already it seemed like years had passed. When she sneezed, she gripped the last of Max's white fiber, light, yet warm against her fingers.

She spread it gently over Truman and then she sat in the darkness, too tired to move.

Too tortured to sleep.

JELLYFISH.

Max hated the damn things. They had been everywhere when he climbed out of the crashing surf. His wetsuit had been slashed in three places when unexpected currents had tossed him against the shelf of coral. Big surprise number one.

It was just Murphy's Law that they had to be the really nasty kind, capable of a virulent sting. He had encountered box jellyfish twice before in the South Pacific, and both times the stings had required medical intervention. Now his shoulder and neck were swelling, and he didn't need to see his face to know he was going to swell up again unless he got to Izzy's miracle mix.

But the jellyfish fix would have to wait. With fog trailing in faint wisps, he made his way from boulder to boulder until he was no more than twenty yards from the surf where the yacht rode at anchor. A man in a blue shirt shouted orders to his frightened crew in a snarl that sounded Indonesian or maybe Cambodian.

DAMNED MARITIME PIRATES, Max thought. The modern-day variety armed with cell phones and GPS and Swiss bank accounts. Men who would attack boats under contract and kidnap by pre-arranged e-mails.

He would have enjoyed cutting them down in one blitz, but staying out of sight and under the radar remained his mission priority. He wondered if Cruz had picked up their presence yet. If not, it would be soon.

While he waited behind the boulder, Max winced, feeling the burn of the jellyfish tentacles. He needed to irrigate the wound areas with Izzy's potent surfactants and apply a tight pressure wrap to prevent the spread of the neurotoxin.

But he didn't move.

At least Izzy had provided him with several doses of box jellyfish antivenin to be used in just this event.

Max gritted his teeth against the pain and grabbed the man who dashed behind the boulder. One blow sent him to the ground.

Two minutes later a second man appeared and Max took him out, too.

The captain was shouting on the yacht. Machine-gun fire raked the beach, and then the motors kicked in. The yacht sputtered, then roared out to sea.

Max glanced south, noting the outline of storm clouds that had built up in the last hour. Izzy's predicted storm was closing in fast.

Wincing at the burning pain at his shoulder and chest, he surveyed the rest of the beach. Two crabs scurried across the sand. A seabird fluttered its huge wings as it nested near the water. Otherwise the cove was empty.

He glanced at the luminous dial of his watch and rubbed his neck. He had been working straight for thirty-six hours. He was going to need to a nap soon, before his reflexes began to slow.

He looked over his shoulder, half expecting to hear Truman's soft footfalls any second. He frowned as he crossed the beach and up to the top of the slope. As a precaution he watched the yacht until it vanished at the horizon. Then he made his way along the cliff and pulled away the rocks disguising the tunnel entrance. The rope was right where he had left it.

Swinging down with one hand, he pulled branches back to cover the opening and descended into the darkness.

The dark shape at the side of the tunnel brought him up cold. There was no mistaking Truman's motionless length. Miki was holding him against her chest.

Her face was white, her body stiff. When she looked up, her eyes were tense. "Are they gone?"

Max nodded, already searching his vest.

"They were…" Her voice trailed away.

"Pirates. Damned nasty people."

She didn't seem to be hurt. Max saw that she was pale, but there was no sign of blood or bruises.

"What happened?"

"Truman heard them. He was guarding me and they saw him. Then that man with the missing teeth found us, even in the fog. He—" She took a deep breath, her face lined with exhaustion as she lost her balance and swayed.

"Take it easy." Max sank down beside her, bracing her back. "Everything's going to be fine." He smiled faintly when he saw the carved sticks on the ground beside her. "Chopsticks?"

"Knitting needles," she rasped.

"What were you going to do, knit him a pair of Fair Isle socks?"

She took a shaky breath. "I was going to blind him. Hit his throat if I had to." She shuddered, then tried to pull away from Max.

He wouldn't let her move, not even an inch. "Are you hurt?"

"I don't think so."

Max pulled off his shirt and covered Truman. The dog's pulse was weak but steady as Max squeezed some of Izzy's supercondensed gel into Truman's mouth.

The Lab's eyes opened and his tail wagged once.

"Take it easy, ace. Enough good work for one day."

Truman licked Miki's face and then bumped his head against Max's shoulder. Weak as he was, he went from one to the other, three times. Then he sneezed and fell asleep.

"He's amazing," Miki said softly.

"You're telling me. Can you handle him for a few minutes more?"

"He's fine right here."

Max sat on the floor, pulled off his vest and then

stripped back his wet suit. The sooner he applied Izzy's antivenin, the better.

He heard Miki gasp.

"What *happened* to you, Max?"

"I ran into a few jellyfish." A whole damned school of them, Max thought grimly. "Not one of my better days." He dug out his medical kit, feeling Miki's eyes on him as he filled a syringe and injected the muscle of his upper arm. After that there was nothing more to do but wait. He needed to make another patrol on the beach and then find Dutch, but exhaustion was finally catching up with him.

He stifled a yawn. "How was Dutch doing?"

"About the same. Sometimes his breathing was worse, but a few minutes later he seemed to calm down."

Max nodded. The details seemed fairly standard for a lung injury of this sort. He dropped his vest and tugged at his wetsuit. "I need to get a nap. An hour should do it."

"Only an hour? And what about those welts? They have got to hurt."

"I'll survive. The medicine should kick in soon." Max had weathered far worse than this.

Miki looked away.

She was giving him privacy to change, Max realized. But he didn't have the slightest bit of self-consciousness as he stripped off the tight black rubber suit and changed into dry clothes from his vest.

"What about the man on the beach?" Miki's voice was shaky.

Max shrugged.

"I'm tired, Max. And I'm tired of being in the dark." Her fingers tightened in Truman's hair. "This is no ordinary dog and you're no everyday soldier. Don't you think I'm entitled to know *something?*"

Max looked at her for a long time. "No." He rubbed his neck, desperately needing to sleep. "I can't talk about this. You're going to have to trust me, Miki."

Her jaw hardened.

Given the fact that her life appeared to have gone straight to hell in the last twenty-four hours, Max couldn't blame her.

"Did you call your team…your people?"

He nodded.

"And?"

"And they'll do what they can."

Max stretched slightly, wincing as pain lanced through his shoulder. He hadn't told her a lie. He had equipment for communication with the Foxfire team in the event that they had to deploy on the island.

Right now, that didn't appear likely.

"What does *that* mean? Truman needs help. So does Dutch."

Max gave a little shrug. He reached into the medical kit and took out a topical analgesic for his neck. Reaching over his shoulder was painful, but it had to be done.

"Stop." She sounded irritated and worried at the same time. "Let me do that for you."

"I don't need—"

"Lie down and shut up, Max." She slid free of Truman and knelt beside Max, smoothing cream gently over his neck and shoulder. Every motion made him jumpy. Her breath skimmed his cheek and Max told himself the sharp, hot tension was strictly because he wasn't used to people taking care of him.

But that was a definite lie. He was far too aware of Miki's skin and scent and warmth. He caught the faint smell of her sweat and the heat of her body where she knelt behind him. Max knew that if he pulled off his gloves and touched her now, skin to bare skin, her emotions would flood into him, raw and unconstrained.

And some deep part of him demanded that contact. On some level things had already gone too far to turn back.

"That's good enough." His voice was curt. It was getting harder and harder to keep his eyes open, but he managed to lean down and scratch Truman's head gently, then remove his harness. He poured some water from his canteen into the dog's mouth, but in his exhaustion, the canteen nearly slipped from his fingers.

"Idiot." Miki grabbed his gloved hand, her fingers locking around his while she replaced the cap. "You're dead on your feet."

No kidding, Max thought grimly.

"Go to sleep." She ran a hand through her hair, then squared her shoulders as if she had come to some kind of decision. She glanced at his watch. "If you want me to wake you up, I'll need your watch."

Max tried to undo his watch, but his fingers were stiff. In the end, he simply held out his arm and watched her remove the heavy strap. She slid it onto her hand, pulled the strap tight, and put one hand on his chest.

"Go to sleep," she ordered again. Trying not to smile and failing. "I'll wake you in an hour."

That one small smile with her light and casual touch still packed the force of a punch. Max had to work to concentrate on what she was saying, instead of how she felt and smelled and how much he wanted to feel her body pressed against his.

Simply the effect of working thirty-six hours without a break? Or was it something more insidious?

"I trust you. Heaven knows why." She shook her head and then pushed him back down onto the ground and rolling his vest into a pillow.

She looked at him intently. "I saw some photos in your trunk. They were thermal images."

Her words were tinny. Max could barely hear her. "So?"

She looked defensive. Max wanted to tell her not to bother, that he understood. He was slipping into sleep, his body finally starting to relax, and he wanted to tell her that he liked the way she smelled, liked the way her hair spiked around her cheeks.

Sexy, he thought.

Strong and yet vulnerable.

"Just photos," he repeated. "Nothing important."

But that was a lie. The thermal images were crucial to his search.

"They looked important to me," she said thoughtfully. "Whoever took them had to climb some rugged cliffs, according to what I saw. They went to a lot of trouble. I think they were looking for something up there."

"Talk later." Max yawned, curling onto his side, trying to find a comfortable position despite the pain burning through his shoulder and neck. "Have to sleep now…"

She started to say something more, but stopped, shaking her head. "You're right. This can wait. I'll be quiet so I don't wake you."

"No need. I can sleep through anything," Max muttered. "Part of the job." He stretched, rolling his shoulders. "Only one hour, remember? I set the alarm in my watch. I'll hear it anyway."

"Are you always this bossy?"

Max smiled, half asleep. "Not always. Not when I'm in bed with a beautiful woman and I'm busy getting her naked. Not when I've got my mouth exactly where I want it. I figure you know where that is." He hadn't meant for that last part to slip out, but by the time he realized what he'd said he was already slipping down into sleep.

He didn't hear her quiet laugh. He didn't feel her bend close and smooth the blanket across his chest. But in some strange and very unfamiliar way, while he slept, he felt the odd sensation of being safe and well guarded.

HE DREAMED OF TURQUOISE water, bordered by white sand beaches. He drifted in bloodred dawns that burned up out of the South China Sea. In those dreaming waters he swam effortlessly, surrounded by ever changing schools of flashing fish. Gold faded into bright blue and green shimmered into neon red.

But something was wrong with the sea around him. Nets of black tangled around him, turning the water cold.

The dream was a message, Max thought dimly, a warning he couldn't unravel. He felt weightless, trapped inside huge bubbles, chasing a shadow that stayed always out of reach.

CHAPTER TWENTY

MIKI SAT IN THE DARKNESS, listening to Max's slow, steady breathing. A glance at his shoulder convinced her his pain was worse than he would admit. His resources and his reserve were greater than any man she had met, but even he couldn't hide his exhaustion any longer. And how could he hope to recover with only one hour of sleep?

Because he was different.

She closed her eyes, going through the details of all she had seen inside his trunk, the papers, tools and weapons that showed a hard-eyed professional at work.

The truth was, she had enjoyed rummaging, enjoyed the chance to touch Max's clothes and pick up the faint scent of man and soap and sweat. When she was done with her search, she was convinced there was something strange about one of the photographs she had seen pushed beneath his clothes. Something about the heat signatures seemed off somehow.

But Miki was no expert in thermal photography. She could be wrong about her assessment. Meanwhile, the fatigue on Max's face convinced her to table any discussion until he awoke.

With Truman beside her, she sat staring at Max's watch. He had saved her life on the beach, a silent and lethal protector appearing out of the fog. She didn't want to consider what might have happened otherwise.

Above her head, thunder rumbled. In a crazy way, Miki felt a sense of belonging here, even though she was thousands of miles from home in the company of near strangers. As she scratched Truman's head, she listened to Max sleep, shocked by how responsible she felt for this man, his dog and for the pilot who had saved her life in the crash. The small stuffy room felt like the true world, while everything else shrank to pale irrelevance. Miki had read enough to know the effect had to do with stress and captivity, a mixture guaranteed to play havoc with normal outlook. Logic warned her this was a dangerous illusion and her emotional bonds would evaporate as soon as she left the island. Without this life and death situation to keep them together, she and Max would forget each other.

The thought left a lingering sadness.

MAX WOKE ABRUPTLY, peering into darkness.

He didn't move, one hand wrapped around the automatic he kept under his head when he slept. Instantly awake, he listened to the small sounds in the darkness, letting the sense of movement take on location and meaning.

Rats, most likely. Nothing big.

It had been an hour since he fell asleep, he was

certain of that. He had always had the ability to set a mental clock, even when he was exhausted. "Miki?" he whispered.

There was no answer.

Something moved nearby, and a cold nose nudged his face. Laughing, Max smoothed Truman's fur. "That's one question settled. Glad to have you back, ace. Nice job out there on the beach. We'll have to do some damage control later, and Izzy will want to track our nasty friends, too." As Max sat up, the dog caught the edge of his shirt. "Where's Miki gone?"

Truman tugged hard to the right, and Max heard the drum of thunder marking the storm that Izzy had predicted. But another sound echoed off the stone walls, and the muffled hiss pulled him to his feet, gun in hand.

He followed the noise through the darkness toward a line of restless light. Beyond the light a shadow separated from the darkness, tossed against the bunker's stone walls.

Max didn't move, his senses sharp and focused. There was a freshness to the air that was new, and he heard a steady rustling over his head.

Rain. Falling hard.

In the dim light, he saw Miki standing beneath a current of water channeled down from the ceiling. Her hands raised, stripped down to her underwear, she was singing softly and very off key.

Taking a shower.

It was the most erotic thing Max had ever seen.

His throat tightened as he drank in the sight of her. With his eyes dark-adapted, he had no trouble picking up the pale outline of her skin, slim and strong beneath the coursing water. All she wore was a set of damp lace underwear that might as well have been invisible.

Max felt his pulse spike unnaturally, and the perception wasn't idle. He was trained to read his basic body functions, and what he was feeling now went beyond normal male reaction into something hard and gut wrenching.

Something that felt dangerously *personal.*

She was doing it to him again, twisting him up in tiny knots, messing up his world. Max was pretty sure he felt sweat covering his face. What was it about the woman that dug under his skin and played havoc with his control?

Hell if he knew. How could he know, when it had never happened to him before?

She was humming a little tune, running her hands through her hair as the water beat down on her shoulders. Max didn't recognize the song, but it was making her swing her hips from side to side, rocking in time to some remembered hit from the past.

His throat went bone dry. All he could think about was having her, deep and hard, right against the stone wall.

He watched her body sway and sensed the drum of her pulse, though he was fifteen feet away. He still couldn't place the song, but that didn't surprise him. He'd spent most of his boyhood in foster homes, where there had been no time or opportunity for privacy or relaxation. Music was just sound you caught from someone else's open windows.

As an adult, none of that had changed. All his energy had gone into his work and his constantly upgraded training. Max had never regretted the sacrifices he had made since joining the Navy. The way he looked at it, he'd been given far more than he'd lost. But right now, he couldn't get Miki's voice and her husky little tune out of his mind, which made him obsess about the words.

Something about dark summer nights. About feelings that were too fast, too hot. All of it was unfamiliar to Max, one more example of how different their futures would be and how disparate their pasts.

But thinking about his past reminded him of all the reasons why he shouldn't be here. What he was feeling was too intense, breaking every rule of his Foxfire training. In spite of that, his feet kept moving through the shadows, driven by a tortured need he couldn't explain. There was no permanency, no future for them, but whatever happened here would be enough. Her body was a landscape of secrets and dreams, and Max meant to find his way along every inch of her before they finished. The certainty of that knowledge drummed in his blood, tightened every muscle.

Something bound them. He couldn't deny that knowledge any longer. He didn't believe in fate and he wasn't sure he believed in religion, but he did believe in the sight of Miki and the husky tone of her voice as her body teased him in the darkness, offering him things he couldn't name, things he hadn't realized he'd been missing.

As a boy he hadn't known how to dream. As a man, there had never been time to try. But now, looking at her, he knew what it felt like to dream. To want.

To mate. Max wasn't sure where that thought came from; all he knew was that it was true. His logical mind was losing ground to his primitive side, the part of him that hunted silently and without mercy. As he felt himself moving deeper into that primal world, the pale trappings of civilization fell away and instinct took control.

He couldn't tear his eyes from Miki's body.

She fed his need until he hungered to claim her, to mark her as his own just as she had marked him with her bravery and laughter. Some part of him wanted to shove her against the wall without a thought for her wishes, taking his own release without preliminaries.

He knew how she'd feel, slick and warm against him.

His hands tightened and his blood took on a heavy, pulsing beat that mirrored the drum of the rain. Though they hadn't touched yet, Max knew the cool curves of her skin and the unexpected strength of her hands. With all his senses stirred, he caught layers of a dozen hormones scattered warm and rich across her skin.

The force was so strong, so unexpected that he took a deep breath, fighting a need to dominate and overwhelm her. The pounding in his blood warned him there was danger here, danger from his mind and from his strength, but nothing mattered beyond physical completion, her body opening to his, driven to him by shared hunger. As a man it was his right to command and he would start now.

Now.

He stopped walking. His hands closed into fists.

This wasn't him. He didn't ever lose his edge of control. His planning and organization had been legendary from the first day he joined the SEALs. But that control seemed to be crumbling, destroyed by the simple magic of a woman's off-key voice and the shimmer of her slender body beneath a restless veil of water.

Was he crazy or was she?

Pain dug at Max's neck. She still hadn't seen him, her eyes closed against the water, the sound of her voice and the thunder overhead masking his quiet approach. Distantly, he noted the growing hammer of his pulse and wondered if this was the prelude to another nosebleed. There was no mistaking that something happened when he was around her. He didn't believe in coincidence, and his instincts still whispered that Cruz was involved, though there was no reason to distrust Miki now that Izzy had identified her.

Her threat to him came as a woman, not as a hostile agent, and he wanted—no, *needed*—to understand the nature of that threat.

He slipped off his tactical vest. His black t-shirt went flying beside it. The movement finally caught her attention.

She spun around, her face sheet-white, one of her knitting needles leveled like a weapon. Max saw the moment she recognized him, saw the instant fear changed into uncertainty and then something else that mirrored his own dark hunger.

She started to speak, but he reached through the cool sheet of water and touched her mouth with one finger, silencing her as he took the knitting needle from her unsteady hand. There were questions to be explored, but Max knew that words weren't clear enough for the answers he needed. Only skin would do. Only in the most intimate of touches could he read the shifting tides of her body through the language of a potent chemistry.

His awareness of her was almost painful, her movements so quick and full of life that they hit him like a dangerous magic. The cold soldier in him insisted that he turn away.

The hot-blooded man in him didn't listen.

She stared at him, close enough that he felt the warmth rise from her skin. "Don't you need more sleep?"

"I'll get by. No need to use your needles on me," Max said.

"I thought you were…" Her voice tightened.

"I know." His foot hit something sharp and he bent down, picking up her second needle. "Where did you get these?"

"I used one of the scalpels you left and made them. I was restless and knitting always helps me think."

Max stored that information away, surprised at her ingenuity. He didn't understand how two sticks and a string could make you relax. Trying to knit would have made him crazy. "I have ways to help you relax," he whispered, aware that he was about to break the first rule of his training. But he had to have true contact, skin to skin and nothing held back.

Just once.

Over their heads lightning cracked. Electricity seemed to dance along Max's skin, gathering in Miki's hair. Slowly he slipped off his gloves.

"What are you doing?"

"Touching you. I can't seem to think of anything else."

Miki moved first, brushing his mouth with unsteady fingers. In that moment of contact he felt her need and uncertainty laid out naked on her skin.

"You need to understand something first. This won't be sweet or tender." He forced out the gruff words. "It won't be all the things it should be." That much Max was certain of. His control was fading and his blood was on fire. She had to know how he was affected—and the risks she took.

She slid her fingers through his hair. "You'll hurt me, you mean?"

"Not if I can help it." His muscles locked as she leaned closer and stared hungrily at his mouth.

Her tongue brushed his lip. "I don't want sweet or tender. And what if I hurt you?"

"Honey, you're welcome to try."

The sudden nip of her teeth made him curse. Though her hands on his chest were torment, her sensual challenge made Max smile faintly.

"So what are we waiting for?"

He shuddered, feeling a trace of her saliva on his tongue. The taste of her was strong and complex, and he could pick out the notes of her body the way a wine connoisseur read tannins, oak and fruit signatures. Her body was slick and strong, and his control took another hit. He wanted to hear her cries of pleasure echoing through the darkness. He wanted her naked, lost in his arms. Foxfire's icy civilian project manager would have told him to plunge ahead and treat this like a medical experiment to be carefully studied.

But there would be no reports or analysis because Max would never mention this to Ryker or anyone else. Tonight was between Miki and him, a stolen moment of forbidden contact, never to be repeated. There was sudden pain in that thought.

Never forget that you're different, Max thought.

But tonight he didn't want to be different.

"You're wearing too many clothes." She gripped his head and slowly drew his face down to hers while he stood just beyond the water's spray. She scissored her wet mouth across his dry lips, giving him her moist, slick tongue until his senses screamed for him to take her violently and completely, pinned against the stone wall while he hammered deep and spent himself inside her.

Some thread of sanity remained, holding him still. Control and logic had become dim memories, but he recognized the trust that shimmered in her eyes.

He wanted—*needed* to be closer, to wrap himself up

in the deep trust he saw there. He could withstand torture, betrayal and uncertainty, but this simple trust was his undoing.

How long since a woman had trusted him rather than used him?

He smoothed his fingers over her wet hair and tongued the hollow at her shoulder, her soft moan an explosion against his senses. With one arm he dragged her out of the water. She shivered, staring at him helplessly, her skin growing cool to his touch.

Too cool, Max thought. He sensed her shudder before he felt it, the nuances of her emotions brushing his skin like fog. He rubbed her back and shoulders, then dried her hair with quick strokes of his shirt. Only then did he catch her face and kiss her slowly, drawing out a whimper. She rose onto her toes, her hands at his neck, her body shifting restlessly against him.

Hunger like a knife. Need like the beat of a heart.

Desire stripped them both bare.

Max pulled away, yanked off his pants and kicked them into the pile with the rest of his belongings while desire hammered through him. He closed his eyes and ran one hand over her slick skin, drinking in the hot cloud of her response, read clearly on his fingertips.

Sweat and confusion.

Need and excitement. Even her smell had changed, dusky with sex and pheromones.

The mix hit him like a blow. He hooked his fingers around the lace of her bikini pants, trying to clear his head.

Her body strained toward him. “This is crazy,” she whispered. “I’m out of control. It’s too strong.”

“You’re the doing the same to me, honey.” Max brushed her breasts, smiling when he felt her nipples harden. “We don’t have much time.” The words were rough, muttered as he cupped her breasts, leaning to pull one tight nipple between his teeth.

“Then hurry.” She whimpered, her nails raking his back. “I’m burning up for you, Max.”

“That makes two of us,” he said grimly. He gripped her waist, pulling her against him. “Tell me where you want me, honey. Otherwise, I’m going to take you now and I’ll make my own choices.”

But Max found that he didn’t need her words. Under his hands, her body sang, damp and urgent. Every bead of sweat answered his question, clueing him by the nimbus of her arousal.

Here, he felt. Where her breasts met his tongue. *There,* where his fingers slid under lace, buried in warm, tangled curls until she gasped, rubbing her hips against him in unmistakable response.

Heat and need.

No hiding.

No lies.

A woman could never lie when he held her like this, tapping the secrets carried in her body’s arousal. And those secrets, now bared, left him awash in primitive instincts, his blood drumming with the need to control and claim. He had a dark vision of her legs wrapped around his waist as he slammed home inside her, again and again. One vision became two, and two became ten.

He wanted her hot against his mouth. He wanted to hear her moan when he worked three fingers inside her and pressed his tongue to her heat, intimately tuned to her orgasm as he pleasured her, worked her slick skin with unerring precision.

Max knew his rules weren't fair. He couldn't fail to read her emotions when his skills gave him that advantage. But he could never tell her that.

He bit her shoulder, pulled off the damp lace at her thighs, every touch fueling his own need. There were no casual social contacts for the men of Foxfire. Security precautions meant that women were arranged at necessary intervals. Sex was fast and impersonal, with no messy emotions and no questions asked.

But Miki was nothing like any of those women. She made him smile and then made him curse in the next breath. She wasn't weak and she definitely wasn't compliant—and the mix was driving Max crazy. Their encounters were raw and personal, and he realized things were probably going to get messy fast. Worst of all, he didn't care if they did.

He scowled, driving away all thoughts about their future. Whatever happened here had to end here. There would be no quiet bonding, no gentle laughter, no white picket fences. This was scream-out-loud, screw-your-brains-out sex and nothing more.

Not that Miki appeared to mind. Her eyes were wide,

her body restless and wet like a quicksilver fish he could never hope to hold. She ran her fingers through the soft hair on his chest and watched his face as her hand slid down, curving over his hard stomach.

And then lower, sliding cool and damp to cup his out-of-control erection until Max had to grind his teeth and force her to stop.

Because he wanted more, because he craved softness as much as force, he denied himself and denied her, hardening his face and making his voice cold. "Don't look for a future here, Miki. Don't ask me for anything but what's happening right now."

"You have a name for this?" she rasped. "I'd love to know it if you do."

There had to be words, but Max couldn't remember them. There had to be definitions and calm descriptions. But he wasn't aware of anything beyond her damp skin, warm hands, urgent eyes.

He frowned at her. "Look, Miki, I—"

She pulled his head down and bit his mouth, drawing a bead of blood. "Do it. It's all I can think about." She was panting when he gripped her shoulders, drove her body back against the wall, came inside her hard.

Her hands seared him, urging him to take what they both wanted. Awash in new sensations, Max fought for control when there was a real possibility that he might hurt her badly. He forced himself back from the edge as their bodies brushed, separated, then brushed again. Her foot traced his calf, her mouth restless, her nails impatient.

Shaken by the pounding force of his feelings, Max tried to pull back.

Miki wouldn't let him. She gripped his hair and watched it slide through her fingers. "Did I tell you that you have great hair? Wonderful arms. And a *really* amazing butt."

Max shook his head. "Afraid you take all honors there, honey. I could have gutted that bastard when I found him frightening you, touching you." He traced a tiny bruise at her breast and cursed.

"Hey, I wasn't frightened." She smiled crookedly. "Not too frightened to fight back, at least. I was just about to use my needles on him."

"Isn't knitting supposed to be a quiet and gentle hobby?"

"Not the way I do it," Miki said proudly.

Smiling, Max looked down at the floor. Her bra and panties were dropped on top of his discarded vest, looking completely out of place, sheer lace against ballistic nylon. Just like the two of them, he thought grimly. This shouldn't be happening, according to the rules.

Damn the rules. He wasn't about to stop until he'd had one taste of her pleasure. She shuddered when he kissed the tips of her breasts, her body arching in his arms. The sight of her made his touch turn rough.

It seemed that her heart hammered inside his chest, her blood churned in his veins. Something linked them, bound them, while Max traveled deep through the storm of her aroused senses.

"You want it slow?" he rasped. "Because that isn't happening, honey. Not this time." Not that there would be a *next* time.

The sound she made was part whimper, part wild laugh. "Stop trying to frighten me. It's not going to work. I know exactly what I want." She rose to her toes and caught his lower lip in her teeth. Smiling, she smoothed her hands along his locked thighs, teasing the heavy weight of his erection. "Whether you know it or not, you're pretty unforgettable. Now if you're done trying to make me change my mind, I'd really like to feel you all the way inside me."

Miki had wedged a little penlight between two stones on the wall. In the faint light he could see her eyes, dark and urgent, but with the hint of a smile.

"Prepare to get yourself screwed into oblivion, honey."

"Is that a promise?"

Max turned her sharply and pressed her hands against the stone wall, holding her in place with his body while his heavy erection rode against her tight, perfect butt.

With one hand he found the warm triangle of curls and stroked her apart. When his callused fingers played over her, she moaned and tried to turn in his arms, but he nipped her shoulder and worked his fingers deeper inside, past slick barriers that tightened at his touch.

She wedged her hips against him, wiggling madly. "Max, I need—"

He realized she would have been furious if she hadn't been so lost, already on the edge of her first climax. So he pushed her over, capturing her breasts in his hand and stroking her damp, sexy mound until her body tensed and he felt the slam of her release. He didn't wait, spinning her around and driving her up again, voracious as he took in her breathless cries and the whisper of his name like a soft plea.

The sound shocked him.

His name. This wasn't distant and impersonal, and Max wondered if he'd ever escape her pull—or if he wanted to. The intimacy seduced him and suddenly he had to hear his name again, given blindly in her passion. He needed that affirmation of contact and humanity more than he needed breath. Kneeling with the rain on his back, he savored the taste of her stomach and then inched open her wet heat, exploring with his mouth and tongue until he found the faint throb of her pulse through the delicate folds of her skin.

She smelled like sex and his deepest, unknown dreams. Her husky cry cut through the silence as she gripped his shoulders, swaying while Max held her upright with one arm at her waist, working his mouth over her, bringing her up once more.

Her nails scored his neck.

"Can't." Her voice was breathless as she sank back against the wall, trembling. "There can't be—more."

"Like hell there can't," Max said grimly. He slid two fingers inside her and heard her gasp as a new wave of pleasure broke over her. And then while she hung suspended, her heart pounding, he kicked away the clothes at his feet and pulled her hard against his thighs.

Need seemed to solidify, dancing in ghostlike fingers of electricity around them. He had trouble finding the edge of his senses—and the beginning of hers. Damned weird energy here, he thought. He'd have to figure out exactly what was going on. Later. In an hour, he might actually be able to hold two thoughts in his head.

"No protection," he gritted, aware that pregnancy would never be an issue, not after the genetic work that had come with his military selection. But Miki wouldn't know about that.

"What?" She stared at him blindly, took a sharp breath.

"Protection. I don't have any, honey."

She pulled him closer and slowly savored his mouth, her dark eyes focused on his face. "I should care, but I don't. We could be dead tomorrow, Max. Tonight I want everything, and I want it fast. Get my message?"

He couldn't miss it. Not when her hand slipped down to cup his length and his vision took on an electric haze, like a circuit board that was overheating.

She teased him with both warm hands, and Max bit back a curse. "You're too damned good at that, honey." He caught her wrist and moved it to his thigh, where it would be marginally less dangerous.

"Hey, let *go* of me. It's not fair. That's one great body you've got, and it's not the kind of thing I'm likely to see again. I want a shot at it."

Max muttered a string of choice phrases. "Forget it, Blondie."

"No, now." Her chin angled up. "Otherwise everything stops here."

Max felt the slam of her heart, the spike in her stress hormones. She was serious. "How about we compromise with later?" *Never,* he thought. Because there wouldn't be anything later for them.

So this encounter was going to play out by *his* rules. No woman had ever tried to fine-tune his lovemaking before. If she had, he wouldn't have cared.

But he cared now, damn it. He wanted to do this right for her.

Miki considered the compromise, then frowned. "I'm out of here. Not interested. Halt." She hissed the words as Max pulled her around to face him. His thighs rode against her damp softness. With one hand pressed to her heart, he read her body's response.

Pulse kicking. Stress levels up. The woman was lying through her teeth. She was as interested as he was and just as committed. "I'd say you're lying, honey."

"What makes you so sure?"

"Let's say that I'm good at reading the signs."

"No way. No one can—"

Smiling grimly, Max lifted her leg across his thigh and entered her with a deep, slow thrust that brought half his length inside her.

She whimpered and closed her eyes.

He thrust again.

"I hate you." She bit his lower lip, sighing. "I wanted more time so I could drive you crazy, but I couldn't, could I? There's some part of you that never relaxes. You're always ready, always prepared for something bad to happen."

He wasn't thinking too much now. Max groaned as she opened sweetly to his strokes, then sucked in a breath as he felt her teeth nip at his jaw.

He watched her face as he stroked deeper. In the same moment he leaned down to kiss her, savoring the metallic taste of her saliva on his lips. Dozens of chemicals and body markers filled his mind, the rich complexity of her making him smile possessively.

Life with her will never be boring.

Max froze. He did a mental freeze frame and went back over that last thought. He had to be crazy even to imagine there would be time together for them. This was it, all they would ever have.

He tried to forget the image of her body in his bed at night, her sleepy face on his pillow at dawn as he brought her awake with his mouth and tongue.

"What's w-wrong?" She pressed closer, wriggling to draw him deeper inside her, her face dazed and urgent.

"Absolutely nothing."

But everything was wrong. This was sex and nothing more. It was simple, dead-perfect screwing. Period.

His mind knew that. The cool voice in his head swore it was true.

But his reckless body and pounding heart had a whole different take on the situation, dragging him into dangerous, unknown places where his emotions colored every movement, every breath. He fought the pull of her sigh, her skin, but nothing worked.

He *wanted* a future with her, damn it.

He wanted more time. But he wouldn't have either.

So he shoved away his useless hopes like cold cobwebs. His breath was raw as he drove away everything but reading her heartbeat while his hands tightened in her hair, cushioning her head against the wall as he pushed home, as deep as he could go.

Once and then again. So slick and so beautiful. Tighter than he had expected, Max thought dimly. She looked dazed by her response, which meant that this kind of pleasure was new to her, too.

The thought fisted in his chest in a way that was dark and primitive. He wanted to feel her naked need. He had to know she'd carry this memory of him always.

His slow withdrawal made her nails dig into his back. She hissed a protest, then sighed when he caught her hips and stroked deeper, stretching her until she took him inch by inch.

Her body tightened. She gasped his name, and he drank in every raw sensation, lifting her up onto a narrow ledge in the wall, pulling her legs around his waist while he watched her slow return to full awareness.

When her eyes opened, he whispered dark praise in a voice that sounded like a stranger's and he took her there, every pounding stroke driving her against the cool stone wall until they were both sweating, both frenzied. Until there was no separation and no holding back.

Their hands met, fingers locked. Skin to skin with no barriers.

The air was charged around them and time seemed to shimmer. Then Miki's body convulsed again, and this time she dragged him along with her, her voice low and urgent. In that moment Max was warrior and protector. His blind mating drove him deep, hot and thick inside her.

He was careful not to call it love.

CHAPTER TWENTY-ONE

TWO MINUTES PASSED. Neither one had the energy to move.

A few lifetimes later, Max ran one hand down her back. When he pressed against her, his desire was unmistakable.

Miki stared at him. "You *can't* be ready to do that again."

His smile belonged on the face of a jungle predator. "Of course I can."

Miki stared at him blindly. Her legs hurt. Her body was on fire.

And she had never felt so good. Memories of Max's hands and the slick friction of their wet bodies made something dark stir inside her, making her want more. She locked her legs and drove her body against his, the hard wall at her back and his harder muscles beneath her legs. The man was huge and *built,* with a sculpted body that left her throat dry. He was big everywhere, and she was dazed by his intensity, dazed by the slick, stroking fingers that shot her up again, into a blinding release.

Dimly, she realized he'd lifted her onto some kind of ledge while his mouth skimmed hers. She tilted her head and sighed when their tongues met in hot, delicious friction. He muttered when she tightened her muscles around him. Sweat dotted his skin when she pushed her body against his, rewarded by deep, pounding contact.

This time she was too stunned, too lost, to cry his name, but it rang through her thoughts as they fell together, hands locked, his eyes on her face as if some unspoken question had finally been answered.

EXHAUSTION.

Bliss.

Complete insanity.

Miki winced as a piece of stone dug into her back. Moving would have been a good idea, but her muscles refused to respond.

She wouldn't call it surrender. The experience had been less and far more, a bonding of blood and heart born of sweat and sex and honesty. She'd never felt anything like it before. He was stronger than any man she'd ever met, but he had been careful and protective, cushioning her hips with his open palms and her back with his arm. He'd made her feel protected and at the same time possessed. If the whole experience hadn't been so overwhelming, Miki would have been irritated that he had read her so well.

As it was, she was too tired to smile and too sated from sex to argue with him about anything.

Rough fingers cradled her neck. Slowly they opened over her cheek. "Anyone here among the living?"

"Jury's still out on that."

"Any broken bones or torn ligaments to report?"

Miki assumed he was joking, but she realized there was uncertainty in his voice. She slitted open one eye, trying to focus despite her exhaustion. "I'm fine. Just as fine as I can be without any functioning muscles. Give me a few centuries to catch my breath."

He brushed a strand of hair from her forehead. "As long as you don't try to move. I want to feel you against me."

Miki flushed as she savored the intimate friction of their cooling skin. There was no mistaking the way his body tightened in response to every movement she made. "I've never been touched like that," she said unsteadily. "I didn't think it was possible to feel so much. I doubt that makes any sense."

He didn't answer her.

"Are you agreeing with me or disagreeing?"

Still no answer.

"Max, there are things we need to discuss. I don't know anything about you."

His mouth hitched in a crooked smile. "You seem to know all the important things."

She winced a little, trying to pull away, her hand braced against his chest. "I'm not complaining about the sex." She swallowed, feeling the brush of his body inside her, the heat beginning to build again. "Max?"

His smile was slow and predatory.

"No way, not again. That was it. I am beyond dead. Let's forget this."

But she couldn't hold back a sigh when he ran his

fingers over her tight nipples. Where did the man get his skills? He was a menace to women everywhere.

"I could get you into the mood." His hand slid down, teasing the slick folds hidden beneath damp curls. He feathered over her until she closed her eyes on a low sigh. "It would be my pleasure."

As sanity returned, Miki glared at him, one hand planted in the middle of his chest. She'd never had sex remotely this good, and he was ready to do it to her all over again.

So why was she stopping him?

Shut up and let him screw you senseless a dozen more times. You can act tough and independent later, when you're both done with each other.

But too many questions sprung to mind, leaving her wary. He still hadn't explained why his big dog was so smart. He hadn't explained why he was really here, because a petrochemical engineer this man was *not.*

Most of all, he'd never answered her questions about that strange way he had of touching her skin, almost as if he could see inside her.

"Any particular reason you're glaring at me?" His voice was rough as he caught the tender curve of her ear in his teeth.

Fire shot to all the wet places Miki was trying to forget. In spite of her resolution, her hand opened and brushed the soft hair covering his chest.

If she dropped her fingers just a few inches, she could recall what velvet felt like, wrapped around forged steel.

No. Where was her willpower, her dignity?

"Okay, let's stop here." Her voice cracked a little. "We need to talk."

He moved her backward against the wall. "Stop what? This?" His fingers teased, slipping in and out of her until she was wet and panting. "I never can stop with one dessert." His fingers slid inside her.

Miki's eyes fogged over. She thought her jaw might have dropped. Meanwhile, his fingers stroked deeper and his palm opened, kneading her until she moaned.

Somehow he knew what she was feeling, Miki thought. He knew where her skin burned and where her nerves ached for release.

He knew, even though it was impossible.

"No." She stared at him, eyes wide. "I don't believe it."

"Believe what?" His eyes darkened. "I'll stop anytime you want me to, honey, even though I'm ready to drive you up against the wall a dozen more times. But if you want me to stop, I suggest you quit moving your gorgeous butt and pushing against me. I suggest that you stop raking my chest with your nails, too."

"I am so *not*," Miki rasped.

But she was. When she looked down, she saw exactly what he'd described. "Get out of my head, will you? Stop—stop *reading* me. I can't think when you touch me this way."

Something flared in his eyes, and then it was gone, his face showing nothing but cool control. "It seemed to me that you were as hungry as I was to do this all over again." He eased away from her, the movement careful but unmistakable. "Apparently, I misread the situation."

Miki wanted to grab him and pull him back. Her body felt painfully cold without his.

All the more reason to wise up and stop this invitation-to-disaster sex. Even if it was the best sex she'd ever had—or was likely to have—it had to end.

She took a long breath and then looked around for her clothes. "I don't want you to think I do this...*this.* I mean, there have been men in my life. None of them like you, of course. But sometimes when things clicked, we—"

"You don't have to explain." His voice was rough. "We're not involved. What you do with your life and who you have sex with is entirely up to you."

"Then how come you make it sound like I'm *supposed* to explain? Believe me, I *don't* do this and I didn't plan for this to happen." Her voice broke. "I don't know if we'll ever get out of this damned, moldy place or off this little island alive. Maybe one of those creepy commando types will come back with his friends and finish us the hell off in our sleep. And I mean for real this time."

"That's not going to happen."

"Just because you say it can't?" Miki spun around, furious at herself. She wasn't going to whine and she wasn't letting her heart get involved. Too many heartbreaks in her past had convinced her there was no point in getting serious.

"You're absolutely right," she said tightly. "We're

not involved and I *don't* have to explain anything to you. I will definitely have sex with whoever I want."

He sighed, and she thought he muttered something that sounded like *women.*

Instead of arguing, he bundled her into his arms, tucked her head beneath his chin and held her—just held her, not saying a word.

There was too much comfort in being held snug against his powerful body, guarded and cherished.

She had never learned how to lean; she wasn't docile and she didn't trust lightly. Yet though his face told her nothing, she trusted him, certain that he would protect her with all his strength and skill.

She twisted in his arms, feeling his pulse pound against her chest when she pulled his head down and kissed him. If she was going to die tomorrow she wanted reckless sex to be the last thing she remembered.

He muttered something that sounded like *too late,* but he didn't stop what she'd begun. He pinned her to the wall, her wrists spread as he pushed inside her, slow and hot, until Miki forgot her uncertainty in the drum of their joined heartbeats. Shuddering, she drove her hands into his hair, telling him what she wanted.

His jaw hardened as he gave it to her, without questions or reservation.

Everything fell away, her body caught in pleasure so fierce that there were no words left and thought became a dim memory.

CHAPTER TWENTY-TWO

THERE WAS SEX—AND THERE was *sex,* Miki thought.

Miki had never learned to trust easily, yet here she was, putting her life into his strong hands. Hell, she had put her body into those strong hands, and the results had been spectacular, even if she was a little achy from the workout.

It beat being hacked into little pieces by a man with a serrated knife and rattlesnake eyes. She knew clear to her bones that Max would never let that happen to her. He took his promises seriously.

So this was what a hero looked like. A lot of men claimed to be heroes and swaggered through the role, but Max didn't swagger or bluster, and if he made a promise, he kept it.

Miki frowned at his muscled chest. Promises were dangerous. A keeper meant long-term commitment—and responsibility. She didn't believe in breathless vows of loyalty or forever. She'd seen her own parents start out happy before they took a sharp slide into armed aggression. One day they were discussing paint samples for their adobe garage, and the next her dad was chasing her mother around the back yard with a pair of gardening shears. After that he'd packed up and vanished.

She was nine years old at the time, and Miki hadn't heard from him since, but she didn't miss him in her life. She had written him out of her script the day he threatened her mother.

And men had fulfilled her low expectations ever since.

Until *now.*

"Something wrong, Blondie?"

"I never liked that name."

His fingers traced her mouth. "Too bad. It definitely suits you. You're sharp and funny, full of guts, and you take shit from no one. I'm glad to have you watching my back, Blondie."

She blinked at him. He thought that about her? He actually thought she was brave? Heat melted into the dark corners of her chest despite her resolve to keep things cold and impersonal for both their sakes. She was smart enough to know that his job was highly classified and extremely important, which meant he wouldn't hang around and let the dust settle after they found a way out of this place. This time was all they had.

A wave of heat, a spike of insanity and some unforgettable sex.

Miki told herself she could live with that. There was no point in believing there would be more. She'd learned to be tough, guarding her heart behind sharp wit and cool laughter. She'd force herself to do that again to protect herself from Max and to keep him from feeling guilty when he left.

She wiggled a toe and sighed at the tug of unused muscles throughout her sated body. She had to admit, the man was a walking advertisement for hair-curling sex. After that kind of earth-shaking response, how was anyone else going to stack up?

She was curled against his chest as he leaned forward, his hands braced against the wall while he held her up. The jerk wasn't even breathing hard, while her whole system was nearing cardiac arrest. Miki flushed at the long welts her nails had left on his chest. *She* had done that during their wild sex? She didn't remember that at all.

The marks didn't seem to bother Max. In fact, nothing seemed to bother him. He was always cool, always prepared for any threat or challenge. She wondered if he enjoyed taking risks because it kept life from becoming boring.

She frowned, forcing her mind back on track. She needed him to know that she wouldn't hold him or try to plan for a future that was impossible. "Now that we've finished whatever *that* insanity was, we should talk."

He wrapped her gleaming hair around his fist and let it slide over his wrist. "That *thing* we just had was stupendous sex, honey. There was nothing insane about it. I'd say that was once-in-a-lifetime stuff."

Miki kept her eyes on his chest. "Whatever." She wasn't going to fall apart and turn emotional. Putty wasn't her style, unless it was a hair product. She cleared her throat, looking away from the lean, naked body that still mesmerized her. "I made something for you." She pointed to a white shape on top of their fallen clothes. "There was some fiber in your big pack and I figured you could use a second pair of gloves, given your…situation. The sensitivities, I mean. Your black pair is getting a little worn."

Max's eyes darkened. "You knitted something for me?" He lifted the half-completed glove and ran it slowly through his fingers. "I don't know what to say."

"Don't look so bowled over. Hasn't anyone ever made you a gift before?"

His jaw tightened as he touched the rows of neat, even stitches. "No," he said after a long silence. "You're the first."

"Didn't your family ever do that kind of thing? I mean, bake cookies, build pots, hammer crooked bookshelves that broke the first time you used them?"

"No." He was staring into the darkness, his eyes hard. "I was adopted. Mostly I spent my time in foster homes, one step ahead of trouble."

Miki felt a stab of pain at the cool, flat way he spoke about what must have been horrible memories. "Max, I—I'm sorry."

"For what? I got food and clothes and a roof over my head. I had no reason to complain."

Miki held his face between her hands. "It takes more than food and a roof to make a child happy." Her voice was fierce and she couldn't help hating the parents who had left him to face a world of strangers. "I wish I'd known you then. We could have gotten into trouble together," she said, smiling gently.

"You and me together at fifteen would have started a forest fire, honey. Just as well that we didn't meet until we were grown. I doubt that I could have resisted your smile and your body." He frowned as he stared at his watch on the floor. "I'm having a hell of a time resisting you now. So what was it you wanted to discuss?"

He seemed uneasy talking about himself or his past and Miki didn't push him. She sensed he had already told her more than he'd intended.

She tried to ignore his body, but he was seducing her again. When she reached for her clothes, she was stopped by his arm draped across her shoulders.

Their eyes met.

"Leave the clothes. We've got a little time left."

Miki took a deep breath and focused. "It's about those photos in your trunk. They're thermal images, infrared to be exact, and they were taken with a damn good camera."

Max didn't move. He'd been sliding his hand back and forth across the unfinished glove made of mystery yarn, but now he stopped. "What about them?"

"All I know is, the third one in the pile was wrong. I saw it because of the heat outline of the palm tree. I've done infrared photography for a few commercial firms so I'm familiar with the color layout. This one was off."

"Say that again." All emotion left his face.

"The third one down was off, I said."

"Tell me how."

Miki was still having trouble concentrating after what they'd just done. She looked at him blankly and then frowned. "I tried to tell you before you went to sleep, but you were exhausted and I figured it could wait."

"You were wrong." A muscle flashed at Max's jaw. "We were both wrong." Bending down, he tossed her underwear in a perfect arc without looking up. "Get dressed. We've got work to do." He was already pulling on his t-shirt and dark pants. "I need you to point out exactly what you saw in those images."

"They're important, aren't they?" Miki slipped on her underwear quickly. "Who *are* you?"

"Someone you can trust."

She felt the force of his words slip deep and lock in. "I know that now, but I don't know anything else—like who you work for."

"We don't have time for that now. I need answers."

She heard the urgency in his voice, but her hands didn't work the way they should have. All her coordination seemed to be off. Apparently insane lovemaking did that to you.

She felt as if she was watching a movie with a damaged sound track, words and images out of synch. Max had changed in the space of seconds, all emotion put away, and he expected her to do the same.

She couldn't, but she tried to pretend only her body

was involved in the unforgettable sex they had shared. Right now she needed to be cool and distant like Max.

How could she, though, when he had touched her heart with his unspoken pain and his ironclad sense of duty? How could she deny that he had cherished her and made her feel safe, in spite of any threat?

Miki closed her eyes and faced the frightening truth. She had fallen and fallen hard. She had given her heart to a virtual stranger, and there was no going back.

"Miki, are you listening?"

She managed to nod, but her hands were cold with the force of her realization. *This is the one*, a quiet voice said.

"We have to hurry."

She swallowed hard and looked at the possibilities, then made the hardest decision of her life. She'd let him go, let her future go, because it was necessary. She refused to create emotions or guilt that might distract him at a crucial moment and get him killed.

"What's wrong?"

"N-nothing. I'm just a little dizzy, I guess." She forced a smile. "Show me what you need."

He studied her face for long seconds. "You're sure there's nothing wrong?"

"Absolutely."

Max pulled her down the corridor toward the bunker's main room and spread a stack of photos on the floor, fanning them out in a row. "Show me which one."

Struggling to hide her emotions, Miki pointed to a pair of palm trees on what appeared to be a rocky promontory. "The tree on the right. The heat outline for the roots and lower trunk is wrong."

"How would you recognize something like that? Have you had professional training with infrared?"

"At first, I experimented on my own. After that, I did some predictive diagnostic work for a commercial real estate company. We checked roof insulation, sub-floor water pipes and electrical fuses for maintenance problems with infrared photographs. You can map temperatures via color chart, so it's handy for predicting equipment failure. One of our clients put in about a thousand palm trees, and most of them developed problems because of irrigation pipes that were buried in the wrong places. When you look at about a hundred thermal images of a palm tree, you start to recognize what's normal and what's not."

"Give me details. Is it too hot, too cold? Is the temperature stable or erratic?"

"None of those things," she said quietly. She wanted to touch his face, but she didn't. There was no room left for emotions. "It's the shape of the tree. The trunk is wrong, and there's no significant heat difference between the tree and its roots. That's impossible for a real palm tree."

Max nodded slowly. "Okay. I can use that." His hands tightened as he yanked on his gloves, smoothing the black leather over his fingers.

Back to normal, Miki thought. Everything calm and impersonal.

But not for her. She was changed beyond recognition, unable to find her way back to her old, easy cynicism. Now that she needed those protective walls so badly, they were gone. All she wanted to do was touch him again.

"I asked what you thought." Max was staring at her. "Are you certain the tree is a fake?"

The edge to his voice told Miki that the question was not to be answered lightly, and she ran her fingers through her hair, taking her time before answering. "I'm not an expert in infrared technology or horticulture, so I can't be totally certain. But based on what I've seen, I'd say yes. That palm tree is probably fake, made of some kind of resin that gives a consistent infrared output from trunk to roots."

Max turned and packed his vest. "I've got to go."

"But what's so important about that tree?"

"I can't tell you that."

She had expected this answer, but it cut deep just the same. "I know you're going back out there. If you took me with you, I could pinpoint the problem."

"Not happening." Max stared down at the photos, his eyes narrowed. "But you can help me with this." He pulled a map out of his trunk and spread it out nearby. Truman trotted up, looked over his shoulder and licked Max's face.

"Gotta get your two cents in, don't you, champ?" As he scratched the dog's head, Max held the map open. "Give me any suggestions you have." He tapped one corner of the map. "I'll be coming in this way, from the water." He pointed at what appeared to be a high ridge. "It's a sheer drop of three hundred feet."

She sucked in a breath. "You're going to climb *that?*"

"No one will expect an intruder coming from the cliffs on that side of the island. It will buy me valuable time beneath the radar."

Miki turned the map slowly, weighing every word. "Go in just before dawn."

"Why then?"

"Look at this ridge." She traced the area he planned to climb. "The other cliff faces east, and you'll be climbing behind it. When the sun comes up, it will cast this whole slope into shadow." She tapped the topography lines on the map. "Vance wanted me to do a shoot like this back in Tahiti, and it was a real challenge because the cameras were set in the wrong direction. I can tell you from experience that if you time this right, they won't even suspect you're there. Not unless they're alerted in advance," she said grimly. "So no singing, please."

"I never could carry a tune. Any more suggestions?"

"You won't have much light to climb." She studied the map, aware that every detail could save his life. "It will be tricky finding handholds on the ascent. Try to be in place on your cliff about half an hour before dawn, just before the light begins to change."

"I didn't think about the light falling through those two mountain ridges at dawn. It's a good tip." Max pointed to a different corner of the map, placing an infrared photo off to one side. "This is my target point.

See the heat disparity between the two sections of terrain?" He tapped the picture of the fake palm tree. "Is there anything else you can tell me? Think hard. This is as important as it gets."

Her shoulders tensed. "I've screwed up a lot of jobs in the last five years, Max. Some people might say that I'm a major failure." She crossed her arms tightly across her chest. "But photography is what I know, so I'm sure about this."

"I believe you then."

"You're sure I can't go along to help?"

Max's voice was tight. "You're staying here. If I'm worrying about you, it will slow my reaction time and put us both in danger."

Miki looked away. New rules, she thought. She had to forget about her feelings. "In that case, I guess there's something else you should know." She crossed her arms, looking at him defensively. "There's…someone else. He travels a lot, but we're involved. In fact, we're getting married this fall."

The map closed with a snap. "Married." Max looked down at his vest. "Nice of you to mention it."

"I thought you should know, just in case you were expecting anything…more." She took a tight breath. "Because it isn't going to happen. You should forget about me."

Max tightened the straps on his vest. "Good advice. I'll try to take it. Any other revelations before I go?" His voice was grim.

Miki saw that her fingers were locked together, and she forced them to relax. "No. It was good, but now it's over. That's all I wanted to tell you." She was surprised at how calm she sounded when her heart was being torn in little pieces.

"Understood. But there's one thing I need you to do." His voice was curt, and he didn't look at her face as he reached into his pocket. "It has to be done right. Can I trust you?"

She swallowed hard. "Of course you can."

He held out a radio transmitter. "I need you to send a short-burst signal as soon as I leave." He pressed the unit into her hand. "Hit the black button by your thumb six times with no delays. Count to twenty, then do it again. Can you remember that? It has to be done exactly the way I said."

Miki fought a chill. She was a klutz. She'd always *been* a klutz. And he trusted her with a top-secret communication?

She squared her shoulders. "Two short bursts of six, twenty seconds in between. I can do that."

He nodded as he attached a full canteen to his vest using a carabiner clip. "There are MREs against the wall. You've got water and you've got a weapon there, too. Stay safe, and don't be afraid to use the gun if you have to. I don't know when I'll be back." His voice was cool and clipped. "Don't leave this area. Your life depends on it. If you believe nothing else, believe that."

"I'll be here. Max, about tonight—"

"Forget it. It's history."

She was dulled by the flatness of his voice. "I'd like to go through the rest of those photographs. I may be able to spot another anomaly—assuming that you still trust me."

Hs face locked down, without any expression. "Be my guest. You'll be safe here if you do what I say."

Miki didn't believe him. She had a feeling that things were about to get a whole lot worse, and her life wouldn't be simple ever again. She couldn't go back. Even if she never saw him again, this silent, hard man would always be part of her life.

Talk about colossal mistakes.

A cold voice whispered that taking risks was this man's job. Danger was his high, and death was part of his resume.

She didn't have any idea what kind of danger he was facing, and she might never know. She watched him shoulder his pack, her heart beating hard. It felt as if she lost a part of herself when he walked away.

He didn't look back, a shadow swallowed up by the night.

CHAPTER TWENTY-THREE

ISHMAEL TEAGUE WAS EATING a tuna fish sandwich with wasabi and organic bean sprouts when the signal came through. He dropped his sandwich and lunged for his radio receiver, listening intently.

Not that listening mattered. There was an automatic recorder in place so that nothing would be lost.

The signal was clear. Two bursts of six separated by a twenty-second pause, according to the pre-arranged code. *Probable weapon system sighting.*

Izzy played the short-burst message through five times, just to be sure. Each time was the same.

There was no mistake.

Max Preston was close to his target, and that would make Lloyd Ryker ecstatic. But something continued to nag at Izzy. He leaned forward and punched a string of commands into a keyboard, then sat back impatiently. As a security caution, he had entered speed and strength parameters for all incoming messages, and he had already input Max's movement and strength variables. Now he sat frowning, wasabi and bean sprouts forgotten as he waited for his computer to compare the two sets of data.

The computer finally gave an answer. The sender of the message was not Max Preston.

From what Max had said, the pilot was too sick to do anything. That left only the woman, Miki Fortune. Izzy sat back and steepled his fingers. Then he picked up his phone to call Ryker.

The Foxfire director was not going to be happy.

KIT O'HALLORAN WAS UP to her elbows in soapsuds, giving Baby a bath. The baby in question, an exuberant black Lab puppy, whimpered in pleasure as Kit scratched her soft ears. They had been out before dawn, practicing search and rescue procedures in the nearby mountains. After six hours of mixed work and play, Kit was bone tired.

Meanwhile, Baby and Kit's three other Labs were as fresh as they had been at dawn. Life wasn't fair, she thought wryly.

She smiled at the sound of paws charging over the patio behind her. All she had to do was think about Baby's three litter mates and they appeared an instant later. Right on schedule, Diesel, Butch and Sundance raced through a bar of sunlight and skidded to a stop at her feet.

In the middle of the big copper tub, surrounded by soap foam, Baby glanced down imperiously, every inch the leader of this canine team. As Kit ran an expert eye along the puppies' lustrous fur, she was pleased by what she saw. Her newest feed mix was working better than she'd hoped.

She couldn't resist a small surge of pride for these four special dogs. All the service dogs she trained showed exceptional curiosity, loyalty and stamina, but these four had skills that went right off the charts.

No one in the government would give her too many details about the dogs' bloodlines, since they came out of a classified government program, and Kit accepted the possibility that she might never know. Even Wolfe Houston, the Navy SEAL she was going to marry—as soon as he stopped flying around the world on top-secret missions—could add little additional information. But Kit didn't need government files or medical reports. She had trained her first dog when she was nine years old, and she knew a champion when she saw one.

These four were *all* champions.

She leaned over to scratch Diesel's head. "Aunt Miki says that I spoil you guys and she's probably right." She turned away to look for a brush and Diesel shot away. When the dog returned, he was carrying a red Hawaiian shirt in his teeth.

The shirt belonged to Miki, who had left it behind after her last visit to Kit's ranch.

Was this another coincidence, or did Diesel truly understand more than Kit realized? All four dogs had a range of comprehension that was astounding, and their knowledge grew every day. Even more surprising was their ability to work, think and plan as a team, something Kit had never seen in her years as a trainer. That ability had saved her life several months earlier, and Kit knew that with the right training, the dogs would go on to handle any kind of challenge the government could throw at them.

She didn't want to think about the dangers they would face. She didn't want to imagine the day they would leave her care. Kit knew perfectly well that she couldn't keep the dogs forever, playing and training on the sunny slopes of her mountain ranch north of Santa Fe. But oh, how she wished she could. The day they left she would feel as if her heart had been torn out.

But life meant transitions. Wolfe always said that changes were good, but it usually took time and perspective to see that.

Her husband-to-be, the philosopher-warrior.

A sudsy Baby shot forward in the water, licking Kit's face eagerly, and soap went flying across the sunny patio. Kit didn't mind a bit. The dogs were her life as much as her career. At least now she had a man to share that life with.

Kit had loved Wolfe Houston as a teenager when he came to live with her family. She loved him now as a woman, with no reservations and no regrets. If the man would just stop crisscrossing the globe, saving civilization as they knew it, she was going to haul him down to the local courthouse and marry him. Miki had volunteered to take the wedding photos, and Kit was already dreaming of an uninterrupted honeymoon spent in her family's isolated cabin north of Chama.

She didn't think they'd make it out of bed once.

But the world was an unsafe place, and her fiancé seemed busier than ever keeping it safe. With a pang of loneliness Kit closed her eyes, wondering where Wolfe was at that moment. A training mission in Thailand? Surveillance in the Middle East?

She worried about him every minute of every day, but she kept her fear in perspective through sheer effort of will. He'd come back when he could, and when he came, she would make up for all the lost hours. They might even have time for a quick stop at the courthouse on his next visit. She ran a hand through her hair, smiling crookedly at the thought of Wolfe's reaction to her wedding dress.

Miki had found it first, of course. Because she was a photographer, Miki followed fashion with the detached but expert eye that could separate trends from keepers. The dress she'd found hugged Kit's body in a slim column of antique white lace, drifting gracefully when she walked, and the back was cut well below the waist. Talk about sexy.

Kit hoped that Wolfe's first glimpse hit him like a jackhammer. She had loved him for too many years to take the thought of their marriage lightly. It was only fair that he should be as hot and bothered as she was by the reality.

Sunlight streamed over the patio, dancing off the smooth surface of the pool as Kit dreamed about specific—and highly graphic—ways she would drive Wolfe crazy in bed. Suddenly Baby shot to her feet in the tub, tail wagging. Diesel barked once, then sat down alertly next to Kit while the other two dogs moved in wary circles through the grass.

Had they sensed some new threat? It seemed like a lifetime ago that Kit had faced down a ruthless killer here. Now she wondered if that old danger had come back to stalk her.

Baby rested her paws on the side of the metal tub, her tail wagging wildly. In one movement she kicked hard, sailing onto the flagstones in a blur of wet fur.

"Baby, stop. Your bath isn't finished."

Diesel shot past.

"Diesel, stay. Baby, *heel*."

Furry bodies raced in circles around her. Though young, the puppies were already well trained, and they usually responded to Kit's commands instantly.

But not this time. Something was definitely wrong. The dogs were quivering with excitement, staring toward the adobe fence that circled the side of the house.

Wind played over the back of Kit's neck, tossing leaves through the sunlight. The dogs didn't move, listening to something that Kit couldn't hear. Another cougar?

Suddenly Baby shot across the yard, grabbed a well-chewed stick between her teeth, and bulleted back to the patio, as if the threat had vanished. Kit took the stick and sighed in relief. These four were better than any alarm system, though Wolfe had insisted on installing one on his last visit. "Baby, let me finish brushing you, honey. Then we can play fetch."

Baby's tail banged on the wet bricks. The puppy

gave a single high-pitched bark and then tugged the stick out of Kit's fingers, racing off to join her littermates. The four of them sat panting in a neat row, their eyes on the adobe wall. Thinking and acting like a team, Kit thought.

Suddenly, a black duffel bag came flying through the air, followed by a Frisbee. A second later Wolfe Houston climbed nimbly over the top of the wall and dropped lightly onto the patio.

Wolfe?

Kit ran an unsteady hand through her hair and tried to brush foam off her chest and cheeks. Typical of a man to give her no warning. Typical of *her* to look like she'd been rolling around with the puppies.

Which she had.

She was surprised that the dogs hadn't rocketed across the yard and mobbed him. There was generally a canine riot whenever he appeared. But this time Wolfe was watching the dogs, a little smile on his face, and if Kit hadn't known better, she would have thought the five of them were having a silent conversation, which was beyond crazy, of course.

Then every other thought was forgotten as Wolfe sprinted toward her and caught her in his arms. "Forget about the suds and the water all over your jeans, honey. You'd look good enough to eat soaked in mud and crude oil." His eyes narrowed. "Now there's a kinky thought. Maybe we should try that sometime."

Before he could say anything more, Kit wrapped her

arms around his neck and pulled him down for a fierce, searching kiss, fueled by memories of their last night together a month earlier. When she finally ran out of breath and pulled away, Wolfe was sweating and his eyes were dark.

"How about we ditch this lunatic crew and find somewhere private so I can really say hello?"

Baby threaded her body between his legs while Diesel pushed his nose in expectantly. Then Butch and Sundance shoved their way between the other dogs until Wolfe and Kit were surrounded.

"Outflanked and outgunned before we took one step," Kit said, laughing. "I think they're as glad to see you as I am." She bit his lips, her fingers trailing along his chest. "Almost as glad."

Wolfe cleared his throat. "I'm dying here, honey. I may not have a lot of time, so—"

As he took a step back, Baby shot under his feet. Seconds later he and Kit plunged backwards into the swimming pool. When they came up for air, Wolfe pulled her into his arms and swept damp hair out of her face. "I think we just got suckered."

"No doubt about it." Kit blinked, brushing water out of her eyes. "Sometimes I can't believe what they do. Yesterday I was ready to drive into town, but Baby kept running around to the back of my truck, jumping up on the fender. I finally realized she had her paws on the gas tank." Kit hesitated. "You're not going to believe this."

"Try me, honey."

"I was nearly out of gas. How she sensed a thing like that is beyond me." Kit frowned. "Do you think it was a coincidence?"

Wolfe watched Baby cavort over the yarn. "Maybe she figured out that the gasoline smell wasn't as intense as usual. I don't have to tell you how sharp their olfactory sense is." He watched Baby lean over the edge of the pool and drop the Frisbee in Kit's lap.

"I think they want to play." There was an edge of uncertainty in Kit's voice as she studied his face. "Will you be here long?"

"I'm afraid not. I needed to meet someone in town, and I carved out a little time first." Something dark filled Wolfe's eyes. "They'll pick me up in two hours." He ran his fingers through her hair. "It's the most I could manage. Things are a little…complicated right now."

Kit forced herself not to ask about her brother, a member of Wolfe's unit. The rules of their dangerous work demanded absolute secrecy, and she knew she was lucky he'd told her anything.

"Have you heard anything from your friend Miki?"

"I had a postcard ten days ago, postmarked from Maui. Otherwise, nothing. Funny, she was supposed to e-mail me from Tahiti." Kit's eyes narrowed. "Why do you ask?"

Wolfe raised his hands protectively. "I'm not allowed to ask an idle question?"

"I'm not sure." Kit wrapped her hand around his collar and pulled him through the water toward the edge of the pool, her eyes full of challenge. "But we don't have time for chitchat. I think we'll start in the kitchen."

"Why? I'm not hungry," Wolfe said hoarsely.

"Who said anything about eating?" Kit yanked off his shirt and ran her fingers along his chest. "The kitchen table will be good. After that, there's the sheepskin rug in front of the fireplace. With luck, we might even make it upstairs to the bedroom before you collapse."

"Who's going to collapse?" Wolfe shoved down the zipper on her sweatshirt while Kit vainly tried to reach his belt. They left a trail of wet footprints and scattered clothes as they made their way across the patio.

Behind them in the afternoon sunlight the four dogs sat in a watchful row, ears alert, sensitive to every movement. As the low laughter faded upstairs, Baby shot across the patio, tail wagging. The black puppy bumped noses with Diesel in what had to be the canine equivalent of a high-five. Then the four dogs took up their posts at each corner of the yard.

Keeping watch over the two people they loved most.

KIT RAN HER HAND ALONG Wolfe's gorgeous chest and sighed lazily. "I can't move."

Wolfe slid his arm around her protectively. He had come damn close to losing her several months earlier, when Enrique Cruz had made his break from a secret

Foxfire facility near Los Alamos. Wolfe's work had put Kit in grave danger, and it was hard for him to live with that guilt. Yet he knew what Kit did not: her four special dogs made her risk even greater. After a lengthy argument, Lloyd Ryker had agreed to install a high-tech surveillance system at Kit's ranch, constantly monitored from the Foxfire command center. Between the surveillance system and what he had seen of her dogs' growing skills, Wolfe knew that Kit was in excellent hands.

Or excellent paws, to be exact.

He rolled onto his back, pulling her on top of him, staring at the bruise on her rib. "What happened here?"

"We were practicing jumps in the wash and a boulder slipped. I fell a few feet."

Wolfe traced the bruise, frowning. "You need to be more careful."

"Explain that to my dogs." Kit's eyes narrowed. "I hope you aren't telling me how to do my job."

Wolfe cupped her hips, sliding her against his hard thighs. After a moment he sighed. "Point taken. I'll shut up."

"Good. Let's forget about my bruise. I notice you've got a few new ones yourself." When Wolfe nudged open her legs, Kit's voice became a husky croak. "How do you do this? You're grinning like the Cheshire cat, ready to start all over again." She closed her eyes, sighing as she felt the intimate brush of his hands. "Don't you ever get tired?"

"Not where you're concerned." Wolfe's eyes were

dark with need. He wanted her again, hard and fast. He would never have enough of her.

Kit seemed to have the same thing in mind. Laughing, she drove her heels into the scattered quilts, twisted to her side and pulled him on top of her.

Sunlight spilled through her hair, danced over her shoulders, reflected in her vibrant eyes. Wolfe had never seen anything more beautiful. Their bodies met, teased, and desire flared back to life, even though they had made love in three different locations before they'd made their way to Kit's bedroom.

He knew how much it cost her not to ask questions about her brother. He also suspected that she and her friend Miki were cooking up some kind of plan. The last time he'd been here, Miki had shoved something white into a big box and pushed it back out of sight in the closet.

Wolfe was almost positive it had been a wedding dress.

He couldn't think of anything he wanted more. He'd marry Kit in a heartbeat, except for one small problem.

Foxfire.

The oath of loyalty he had made to his country meant that all personal relationships had to undergo scrutiny of the team, and Ryker had met Wolfe's first request with stony silence. Over the days that followed, Ryker had said nothing more, neither agreeing nor disagreeing. Wolfe had already decided to press for an answer when he returned. But marriage meant potential security risks and emotional complications, things that Ryker was determined to avoid at all cost.

In spite of that, Wolfe couldn't see any real reason that two sane, mature people couldn't tie the knot. Maintaining a long-distance marriage wouldn't be easy, but Wolfe was determined to make it work.

Kit's nails raked his back. "Daydreaming, Navy? You must get bored fast. Here I am, naked and available, and you're thinking about tactical training manuals."

"Not a chance." Wolfe's hands tightened on her shoulders. He leaned down, nipping a wet path over her stomach until Kit squirmed. She wrapped her legs around his waist, driving their bodies together while Wolfe tried to keep his mind in one piece.

A dull whine came from the middle of the bedroom floor.

He cursed softly.

It was his beeper, vibrating in the back pocket of his jeans. Disappointment swirled through Kit's eyes. Without a word she wiggled free, stood up and reached for his pants, then tossed him the beeper that was still vibrating loudly.

After that she walked out of the room without a backward glance.

No questions, no anger, no protests. She was one hell of a woman. She didn't like it by half, but she knew it came with the job.

Wolfe pressed a button on the encrypted pager. A terse message ordered him outside to the gravel road in front of Kit's house. A chopper would be there to pick him up shortly.

Wolfe glanced at his watch and cursed. He had less than five minutes to dress and say his goodbyes.

Join the Navy, see the world.

KIT WAS DOWNSTAIRS, fully dressed, her face calm. Baby pressed against her right leg, nuzzling her hand while her three other puppies watched the stairs.

When Wolfe came down, they shot toward him, then sat down abruptly. For a moment, Wolfe wondered if Kit might have been crying, since her head was turned away.

She pressed his duffel bag into his hands. "Be careful." There was no mistaking the raw emotion in her voice or the telltale shimmer of her tears. "I hate this part," she whispered. "I hate not knowing where you are or what you're doing. So—damn it, just be *careful*."

Wolfe closed his eyes, dragging in the faint citrus scent of her shampoo, pulling her warm body against his. "Count on it, honey. You're not getting rid of me ever again." Down the hill he heard the drone of motors, moving fast.

"They sent a chopper for you, didn't they?"

Wolfe nodded, scratching Baby's head with one hand and Diesel's back with the other. All the dogs were huddled close now, pressing Wolfe and Kit between their warm bodies. "I have to go, Kit."

Kit looked down at Baby and took a deep breath. "I know you do. You've got the world to save and I've got puppies to train."

Something bumped Wolfe's leg. Baby was shoving

something against his hand, and Wolfe realized it was the red training leash that Kit always used to mark the transition from play to focused work time.

Baby was telling him that she wanted to go along, that playtime was over and she wanted to work, too.

Something burned at the back of his eyes. There seemed to be no limit to these dogs' intelligence. Any soldier would be lucky to have their help.

But Baby wasn't going anywhere. The puppies were far too valuable, and it would be months before they were experienced enough to be tested on their first field assignment. Ryker wasn't going to risk another attack from Cruz.

A black speck appeared on the horizon and the motors drummed closer. Kit made a small sound, slid her arms around Wolfe's neck and kissed him, locking her body against his. A shiver ran through her. "Something's wrong," she whispered. "He's out there, Wolfe."

Cruz. Only one person could make Kit feel this kind of panic.

Abruptly she stepped away, staring out at the black helicopter sweeping over the mountains. She looked angry. "Do you think he'll come back here?"

"Not likely. Cruz is a fast learner. He's looking for different prey now. But I'll have two men watching the ranch just in case," he said grimly. He traced her cheek, committing her face to memory, aware that it could be months before he saw her again.

A sense of loss hung between them, so bitter he could

taste it. But Wolfe had made a promise when he joined Foxfire, and duty wasn't a responsibility you could toss away when your life changed.

Even if you'd found the love you'd never believed was possible.

He swung his duffel bag over one shoulder and scratched Baby's head, bending down to take her red training leash. "You guys stay close. Keep an eye on the boss here, okay? Work hard and don't give her any guff." Baby gave a small growl and shot forward, licking his face thoroughly, while the other three dogs pushed closer.

The helicopter roared along the gravel road toward the house, and the dogs turned sharply, running to the front door, bodies tense. In full protection mode, Wolfe realized.

He felt Kit's hand touch his shoulder, just for a second.

"Get moving, Navy. We'll be fine. Just...don't get yourself shot."

The emotion behind her words slid into the dark places of Wolfe's heart.

He gripped her hands for a second, his touch saying all the things that words couldn't while the blades of the helicopter churned and hammered, sending up a vortex of dust and sage twigs. Then he opened the door and walked across the front yard.

He didn't look back.

KIT STOOD IN THE QUIET house, her heart pounding.

Damn it, she *wasn't* going to pieces. He was tough

and smart. He'd come back. When he did, she'd make him crazy and they'd get around to that wedding.

Something bumped her hand.

When she looked down, Baby had a box of tissues in her mouth, holding it up to Kit. She gave a watery laugh. Around these dogs, there were absolutely no secrets.

The helicopter lifted off, banked sharply, and headed west. Kit's eyes followed it every foot of the way.

WHEN WOLFE SLID INTO his seat, Lloyd Ryker's aide was holding out a file. "Teague just sent us an update. He's received an encrypted short-burst message in code. Probable weapon sighting at the island."

Wolfe stared at the horizon as the chopper thundered west toward a military cargo plane less than half an hour away. In less than five hours, he'd be back with the rest of the team in the Pacific, and he'd be carrying new hardware to deactivate the stolen guidance system.

"Any news on that storm?"

"It's holding right on course. Teague says it's going to be nasty."

Wolfe pictured the sky over the island, methodically running through the details of his last briefing. Max Preston was a fine solider, highly decorated before he was selected to join Foxfire. Thanks to his bio-enhancements, he had become even more formidable. He knew what Cruz was capable of and his new sensory skills would take him as close to the weapon system as humanly possible. Ryker had planned every detail of the mission carefully.

But once you dropped out of a plane and hit the ground, Wolfe knew, plans usually went awry.

He patted his front pocket, which held documents from the current investigation of Cruz's actions in Santa Fe. Ryker wanted Wolfe's scrutiny in the hope that some detail might have escaped their notice. Now, thanks to Miki Fortune's detailed description of the man who had spilled coffee on her, they had a possible target under surveillance.

The net was closing, Wolfe thought, as the chopper headed west. The only question was whether it was closing fast enough.

CHAPTER TWENTY-FOUR

MAX TIGHTENED HIS CARABINER and squinted through the rain. He was hanging from a wall of sheer granite with rain whipping his face and visibility next to nil. The sea was two hundred feet below him. It would have been nice to be doing this on a dry, sunny day, he thought, instead of during the final hours before a hurricane. Grimly he rechecked the placement of his carabiners, leaned away from the rock face and pulled himself up to the next handhold, fighting the cold wind that drove in from the ocean.

He'd told Miki that this was going to be a rough ascent. That had been a serious understatement.

A bird soared past, brushing his shoulder, and Max locked his fingers into a crack in the cliff face, swaying.

Stupid birds.

He took a deep breath and stretched his shoulders. He had one hundred feet more to climb and it was thirty minutes before dawn, which put him exactly within the time frame Miki had suggested.

Max's hands tightened. He wasn't going to think about her cool announcement of upcoming marriage, since killing the groom probably wasn't an option. The force of his emotions continued to surprise him, but Miki was right. Best if he forgot her.

He was going to start right now.

He paused, recalculating his route. With one stretch, hand over hand, he pulled up slowly and then clipped his safety rope into a new carabiner anchored on the cliff face. And thought about Miki's hair sliding over his fingers.

Damn her and damn the memories.

Max felt a slight burn at his calf muscles. He was starting to sweat despite the cool air. One of his new chips allowed long-distance monitoring of his body and he could picture the Foxfire scientists huddled over a computer screen, muttering about the spike in Max's vital signs. Thanks to Miki's transmission they would soon know that he was closing in on the stolen weapon system.

Max tested his rope and took another fluid step, swinging his body out into space to wedge his foot into a crack. Each new position demanded complete focus and perfect footwork, a kind of Zen meditation in mass and movement while the wind gusted, driving rain into his face.

When his view cleared, he saw the top of the cliff a foot away. He had been shielding his presence using standard Foxfire techniques. They wouldn't fool Cruz completely, but they should delay any detection—unless Cruz had developed new skills.

Squinting into the rain, he gripped a rock and pulled himself up until he was staring down at the center of the island. In that first second, he was hit by a wave of energy that seemed to coil along the highest ridge. Through the rain Max scanned the pre-dawn darkness and tracked the energy source to a ledge thirty feet down the far slope. He unclipped his climbing rope and dropped flat behind a row of boulders. Working quickly, he stripped off his right glove and pressed his fingers to the ground.

As he shoved his bare fingers into the dirt he picked up the layers of Cruz's bio marker. Either he was in the area now or he had been here recently.

Max's eyes hardened. He had to bring the rogue operative down before more lives were lost, and every instinct told him that he wouldn't have much time to do it.

To the east, a faint line of gray tinged the horizon. He had thirty, maybe forty minutes before dawn, and the rain would offer him additional concealment after first light. As he pulled a high-tech silk and nylon rope out of his tactical vest, he was barely aware of being soaked and cold.

So much for paradise.

He was about to take a closer look at the ledge below when he heard the faint crunch of gravel nearby. Silently, he crouched behind the boulders, reaching warily for Cruz's energy signature.

But nothing clicked. Whoever was on the narrow trail wasn't Cruz. Slowing his breath, Max closed down his thoughts, making himself fade into the landscape as the footsteps came closer. A heavy man with an Australian bush hat appeared above the rocks, an Uzi slung over one shoulder. Slow and methodical, he checked every corner of the trail, stopping at the top of the ridge where Max had tied off and discarded his climbing rope only minutes before.

As rain continued to sheet down, the man leaned forward, peered down at the ocean, then crouched to examine the dirt along the ridgeline. Max waited uneasily, certain he had swept all his prints clean, but the man at the ridge continued to study the ground. He rocked back slightly, looking east, his hand on the stock of the Uzi.

Max made his energy as smooth and still as a pond at dawn.

No danger.

No movement.

No one here.

Slowly, the man reached into his chest pocket and pulled out a walkie-talkie, but for long moments he didn't move, staring down at the water, squinting against the rain. Had Max missed some small detail?

Static hissed in a sudden burst. The man fingered a button, hunched over against the rain. "Malovich here." When he released the transmit button, more static crackled.

"Where are the hell are you, Malovich? The plane's due in thirty minutes and we have a shitload of cargo to finish unpacking before *he* gets here."

The man on the ridge crossed his arms, unmoving at the edge of the cliff. Max saw him frown as he picked up a handful of gravel, tossing it up and down in one hand.

Rain drummed and hissed on the granite slope. The man still didn't move, his shoulders tense. Max drew his energy even tighter, making a hole and pulling it in around him.

"Malovich?"

"*What?*" The man on the cliff pulled off his hat and scratched his head, then stood up. "I'm here. Checkpoint twenty-six. Situation stable."

"What the hell is taking you so long up there?"

"I'm not sure. There was something…" He shoved his hat back on his head and turned away from the wind, his words muffled. "Forget it. I'll take the short way back. I'll be at base in ten minutes."

"Move it." Static crackled like grease hitting a hot frying pan. "You know he'll be expecting a report."

"Copy that. On my way. Malovich out."

As the man disappeared down the slope, Max slowly let out his breath, then shouldered his pack, swept away his footprints and stood up.

Rain slammed into his face from a nearly horizontal wind. Izzy's hurricane was moving in right on schedule. That was the good news.

Of course, it was also the bad news.

THE LEDGE WAS FAR DEEPER than Max had suspected.

As he followed the trail down from the cliffs, he saw that the recess in the rock went back for at least ten feet, and it had been used recently, judging by the smudged footprints in a dry area protected by an overhang.

He pulled a pair of thermal imaging goggles out of his backpack and scanned the area. There were no hot spots or cold zones near the ledge. No anomalies near the trail, either.

When he turned a corner, Max saw the palm tree Miki had warned him about. With his goggles in place, there was no mistaking the heat disparity she had seen in the photos.

The stolen weapon guidance system had to stay cool to retain its effectiveness, so Max searched for signs of electricity and air-conditioning units. Now that he had a location, it was time to rely on his special tactile skills. He ran his bare palm along the rocky trail.

Fallen tobacco ash. Traces of melted rubber.

A tiny piece of waxed paper impregnated with soybean oil and spices.

Max sniffed the fallen piece of paper and frowned. A torn wrapper from an MRE, he thought. Fallen food items meant this was a popular route, part of regularly patrolled terrain. The guidance system should be fairly close. The more important an area was, the more closely it was watched.

He left the trail and circled across a row of boulders for a closer look. Within five steps he found what he had expected to see.

Trip wires dotted the edge of the slope. Two motion sensors were hidden beneath a flowering hibiscus bush. Touching the ground gently, Max picked up layers of human sweat, with markedly high level of stress hormones. As he rubbed the dirt between his fingers, the chemical layers filtered through his senses. Alcohol residues mixed with sizeable steroid and amphetamine markers. Was Cruz keeping his force wired on drugs?

Silently he continued his scan. In an open space beside two trails he saw Miki's false orchid. Just as they had expected, a wireless sensing device was hidden beneath the fragile pink leaves.

Hail hail, the gang's all here.

Max squatted in the rain, every sense alert. The location made perfect sense. There could be an underground entrance or a trap door hidden in the scattered boulders. Yet something didn't feel right. He couldn't shake the feeling that he had found this spot too easily.

Small, unformed details continued to bother him as he backed away from the tripwires and climbed out of sight above the trail. There was something wrong about his bunker, something different. As the impression grew stronger, he realized he had made a fatal mistake.

The mistake of trust.

Huddled in the rain, he stared at the horizon as the truth hit him like a blow. When he'd opened his medical kit to give Miki the scalpels, there had been three sets of pills inside.

But two hours ago one of those sets of pills had been gone.

The answer hit him with brutal force. It had been there in front of him all along, while Cruz had played them perfectly. Max's emotions had clouded his judgment, making him miss a clue that normally would have triggered his suspicions. The damage was done.

With steady hands, he pulled a waterproof bag of explosives and a detonation cord from his backpack. There was no more time for subtlety. Time to blow and go.

MIKI PACED THE UNDERGROUND tunnels, listening to the muted drum of rain above her head and trying not to think about Max. She had wanted adventure, excitement and a complete change in her life.

Be careful what you wish for.

In an effort at distraction, she folded a blanket on the ground and emptied out the contents of her camera bag, which Max had returned to her before leaving. It was a relief that he didn't suspect her of being some kind of hostile agent anymore. If he'd known the details of her screw-up past, he would have seen how laughable that idea was.

Miki's past was very much with her as she stared down at the sad remains of her life scattered over the cot. Waterlogged tube of lipstick. Dental floss. Old library card for books she never had time to read. Chewing gum and breath mints for Saturday night dates that had become nearly nonexistent. Knitting needles—rosewood double points. Okay, those weren't depressing. But the beef jerky, moldy after being soaked in seawater for hours, was definitely a downer.

Eww.

Depressed, Miki picked up the items one by one. She

had finally turned over a new leaf, gotten serious about her career and grabbed her first chance to show her skill, and where had it gotten her? Ditched from a seaplane in the middle of the ocean, caught in the middle of something that had top-secret military security written all over it. How could her luck possibly get any worse?

Bad question. She heard a small movement from somewhere in the nearby tunnel and froze. Low, skittering sounds filled the darkness.

Rats. The sooner she got out of this place the better. At least Max's first bunker on the beach had been clean and relatively spacious, unlike this place.

Restless, she listened to a dull scuffing sound above the shriek of the wind. When the sound came again, she climbed the narrow steps and listened intently and realized it was the scrape of paws on rock.

Truman.

Had something happened to Max?

She shoved open the door a crack. A second later Truman nosed past her, sniffing the air intently. Ears back, he shot down the tunnel.

Maybe he needed water. Maybe Max had sent him for supplies. She was running through all the possibilities when she heard Truman growl.

Miki froze. The big dog never growled. Noise discipline, or something like that. Max had been very firm about any noise.

She felt a stab of uneasiness. "Truman, what's wrong? Why—"

When she turned around, the dark shape in front of Miki wasn't Truman. The big dog was standing to her left, ears back, body rigid. It was Dutch, breathing heavily, his face white and pasty. In his hands was the gun Max had left for her.

"Forget the dog. I'm afraid the bad news is just starting, Blondie."

CHAPTER TWENTY-FIVE

"DUTCH, YOU SHOULDN'T BE standing up." Miki looked down at the pilot's unsteady hands, totally confused. "Where did you get that gun?"

"Same place I got the pain medicine and the radio transmitter. Your SEAL friend is well equipped." He coughed hollowly, one hand at his chest. "Too bad that damned plane crash nearly whacked me. Now I'm way off schedule."

"Off schedule for what?" Miki felt a weight settle over her chest. "I don't understand." But she was starting to pick up the threads and they made her sick. The man she had believed was an innocent victim was part of this whole dangerous mess.

Coughing harshly, Dutch leaned against the wall, gesturing with the revolver. "Your boyfriend should be in place at the island by now. It's time we went over to join him."

"My boyfriend? You mean Max?" Miki felt a stab of fury. Dutch had been playing possum, listening to every conversation while he followed orders from an unseen enemy. "Are you crazy? Max saved your life. After you went down, he swam back out to get you. If not for that, you'd be dead now. This is how you repay him?"

"The plane crash wasn't planned—at least the bad weather wasn't. First they'd follow you. Then I'd drop you, a civilian, down in an op zone, just to screw the hell out of everything. It was bound to bring the SEAL right into play, and it did."

"Who's *they?*"

"Government of the US of A, honey. Big eyes and bigger ears, and they want a piece of everything. You've been on their radar screen since that chip got put in your arm in the coffee shop back in Santa Fe."

"There's a *chip* in my arm?" Miki's voice rose, shrill with shock. "That's why it's hurt for all these weeks?"

"Afraid so, Blondie. You're in the middle of one hell of a big adventure." The pilot laughed hollowly. "Are you having fun yet?"

"Dutch, you can't—"

"Yeah, I can. I was just supposed to set you down in the ocean near the next island. Then the bad weather blew in, and I was lucky to get the damned plane down in one piece."

"You almost died. You could still die," Miki snapped.

He shrugged. "An acceptable risk. I'm tired of half-assed jobs carrying hack politicians and old entertainers around the Pacific. After this I'll have enough money to retire in style. Believe me, the only charters I'll be taking will be on my own vacations."

He leaned toward Miki, but Truman shot forward,

growling. "Get your damn dog out of my way. Otherwise, I'll shoot him."

Miki tugged vainly at Truman's collar. "He's not my dog. He won't do what I say."

"Make him do it." Dutch staggered a little, leveling his gun at Truman "You've got five seconds. Then I'll put two in his head."

Miki put one hand on the dog's rigid back. "Truman, stay here. Everything will be fine, honey."

The dog didn't move, his hackles rising as he growled at Dutch.

"Weird dog. He was watching me even before I pulled out the gun, and I was pretty damned quiet in the tunnel." The gun rose.

"*No.* Don't shoot him. I'll do whatever you want. Just leave the dog alone."

"No can do, Blondie. The dog's part of my deal and he's going to bring big bucks. Hell, anyone with eyes can see this is no ordinary Lab."

"What do you mean?" Miki edged forward and sank down on the ground as if exhausted. Behind her back, she was digging through the contents of her purse, searching for anything that could be used as a weapon.

Knitting needles against a revolver?

"The dog is high trained, probably biologically modified." Dutch's eyes narrowed. "Just like your friend Max."

Biologically modified?

Miki blinked. Suddenly all kinds of random details fell

into place, from Max's chemical sensitivities to his ability to withstand pain and his unusual sexual endurance.

She blushed a little at that last memory, remembering their off-the-chart sex, but she kept her face blank. "That's ridiculous. There's nothing special about either of them. I don't know who fed you this stuff, but they were lying."

Dutch's eyes hardened. "Makes no difference to me whether they're special or not. All I care about is getting paid and then getting lost." His face was sickly white as he brushed a hand across his forehead. "That's some damn storm outside. It's raining like a bitch out there. Hope I'll be able to take off." He laughed tightly. "That junk heap Vance made me rent was crap, but I've flown in all kinds of weather. This storm won't make any difference." He looked down at Truman, his gun level. "Time to go, kids."

Miki screamed and threw Max's medical kit at the pilot with all her might. Truman bounded over her, hit the bunker wall and threw his body at Dutch from the opposite side. The dog moved so fast that he appeared like a ghost image, something you saw in a blurred home movie. A bullet cracked, and she shot forward, kicking Dutch's legs with all her might while the pilot staggered, cursing between harsh, gasping breaths, trying to aim the revolver at Miki.

Truman slammed against Dutch's feet from the back, and the pilot lurched, barely managing to stay upright.

His gun fell, pointed at Miki's head. "I'll shoot him

if I have to, but I'll shoot you first. The dog's a hell of a lot more valuable than you are, believe me."

Miki's blood churned with fury, but she kept her face emotionless. "Go ahead and shoot then, you bastard. I hope Truman takes off your arm—and a few other body parts."

"Too bad I'm supposed to bring both of you with me." Dutch dug into his pocket.

"What are you—"

The pilot tossed something shiny onto the floor, and glass exploded.

The air filled with the acrid smell of camphor, menthol and rubbing alcohol, and Miki gagged as the scent became overpowering in the enclosed space.

Truman whimpered and sneezed loudly, the pungent scents overwhelming him.

Dutch nodded to himself. "Didn't know I saw that, did you? I was feeling like shit, but I wasn't totally out of my head, especially since the two of you kept putting all that damn water in my mouth." He smiled nastily. "Just goes to show, no good deed goes unpunished."

Truman huddled at Miki's feet, breathing loudly, his body rigid in an asthma attack. "Take him outside, Dutch. He can't stand that smell."

"I'll take him outside, don't worry. The three of us have an appointment with a man one island over. He tells me he wants his chip back."

Miki's hand crept to her burn scar. Max had been keenly interested in her story about the spilled coffee, and now she realized it hadn't been a coincidence. He must have known about the chip, but he hadn't said a word.

"Move it, Blondie. Open that door, walk out and tell the dog to follow you. No tricks, or he'll take a bullet along with you."

Miki had no choice but to do what he said. Cold wind brushed her face as she opened the door, hit by a sheet of driving rain. Down underground she hadn't had a real sense of how violent the weather had become. Now, looking up into dark, swirling clouds, she realized they were in the middle of a gale. "Where are we going?" The wind nearly drowned out her question.

Truman struggled to climb the sand beside her, wheezing loudly.

"To the nearest island. We'll take the boat Max was hiding."

If Miki hadn't known Max's real mission, she would have been furious at this revelation, but now she accepted that Max had hidden the boat as a precaution against an attack like this. "How did you know it was there?"

"Satellite photos. Believe me, I was well briefed." Dutch jammed a hat over his head, squinting into the rain. "The man I'm working for doesn't screw around, and he doesn't like your friend Max much, either. Something about the unit they served together in." He frowned as Miki leaned down, digging at the sand. "What the hell are you doing?"

"Getting my shrug. It's freezing out here, in case you didn't notice." She dug away the top of the shallow hole where she had buried her shrug. Funny, that seemed like weeks ago, Miki thought. How much she had changed in the space of a few hours.

Shaking off the sand that covered her favorite sweater, she freed the damp white angora. Dirty or not, it made her feel more prepared, more capable. Miki knew that the feeling was a complete illusion, but sometimes you took what you could get. At least she understood that most of her life had been spent grasping at illusions.

But not any longer.

"It's just a piece of crap yarn. Leave it and let's go."

"What do you know about yarn? I'm not leaving my shrug behind."

Dutch jammed the barrel of the revolver into the hollow behind her ear. "Get moving. Don't stop again."

"What about Truman?"

"I knew you wouldn't want to leave him behind. For the moment, your doggie friend has a pressing engagement down below." Dutch swung around, shoved the wheezing dog back through the open door into the bunker and slammed the door shut. "Stay, Spot, stay," he said, tightly. "Someone will be by to get you soon."

With the gun at her neck, Miki didn't have any choice but to hunch her shoulders and walk down the beach into the driving rain.

CHAPTER TWENTY-SIX

SHOWTIME.

Max yanked off his backpack, sprinting toward the heat anomaly. Crouching in the rain, he ran his hands over the ground and seventeen seconds later he found the point with the highest density of foreign chemicals tracked in by boots or machines. Then came a slow search, inch by inch, his fingers sifting through the dirt.

A tiny current of air brushed his fingertips, carried up from a hidden containment area beneath layers of rocky soil. Max pulled out one of Izzy Teague's newest gadgets, a silver box that would pick up a digital security signal anywhere within twenty yards, identify the broadcast pattern and automatically scan possible codes until it came up with the proper combination.

Max looked at his watch. It took two minutes and forty-six seconds before a yellow light began to flash, indicating code acquisition. Another LED told him the direction to the signal source. He crossed the clearing and found the signal coming from a strip of metal hidden on the fake palm tree Miki had identified. She'd been right on target, he thought grimly.

He locked in on the security frequency, triggered his unit to output the answering code, and waited.

Gravel skittered behind him and he heard the faint hum of a motor straining somewhere beneath the ground. Rocks groaned.

Then he was looking up at a six-by-six-foot square opening in the granite slope. A red light flashed on a small control panel just inside the open door.

Secondary alarm set.

Silently Max swiped the panel with Izzy's little box, watching numbers flicker across the LED screen. This time the search took nearly three minutes by Max's watch, and sweat mottled his forehead when the unit finally locked on to the correct code. Max triggered the relay sequence and the red light went out.

He traced the edge of the inside door until he felt a layer of oil and something clicked beneath his fingers. An inner door swung open. In front of him sat an eighty-pound circular piece of steel and aluminum alloy that had cost close to twenty million dollars in research and development expenses.

Time this little baby went back home to Mommy.

And there would be no time for subtlety. The betrayal had already begun, and he felt the seconds ticking past as he slipped the heavy guidance system into a specially insulated bag inside his backpack. When the pack was secured across his shoulders and anchored by waist straps, Max closed both compartment doors and reset the security codes.

The theft would be discovered within hours, assuming that Cruz's men made regular inspections of the unit. But with luck he'd have time to rappel down the cliff and be long gone before the alarm sounded.

With his precious cargo stowed, he stood motionless in the rain, hearing no sound but the faint cry of seabirds above the howl of the wind. When he circled back up the trail, he took a different route through the rocks to avoid meeting another security detail.

At the top of the ridge he clipped in his climbing rope, checked his carabiners and took a deep breath.

And swung out into cold, rushing wind, the rope straining beneath the new weight in his backpack while he quickly centered his body, bracing his feet against the cliff face. His hands were sure and steady, his breathing calm as he worked his way toward the water, playing out his line inch-by-inch.

Something whined past his ear. He squinted into the rain, expecting to see a small bird.

But there was nothing.

As he played out more rope, Max felt the burn of muscles at his thighs and shoulders. He was two hundred feet above the water now, his rope vibrating in the gale. Rain blurred his vision.

The whine hissed past his ear again, and something exploded inside his head.

Max fought grimly, trying to block the static. Only one thing could generate a beam of focused noise like that. Only one person was capable of casting an energy net that could attack with such painful accuracy.

Cruz.

MIKI WAS GOING TO THROW up any second.

Gripping the wall of the boat, she grimaced into a curtain of rain and sea spray. Small but stable, the boat jumped the waves despite Dutch's clumsy steering as they jolted across the bay toward the neighboring island.

Miki had hoped for a chance to grab his gun, but Dutch was too wary. Now she huddled with her back against the side of the boat, hideously seasick, shuddering every time they lurched into the air and slammed down seconds later.

With a groan, she twisted sharply, throwing up over the edge of the boat. When she finished, she saw Dutch looking back at her. He shook his head, grinning. They were about four hundred yards off shore now, with a long beach curving in front of them.

Where was Max? How was she going to get out of this mess? She knew that she couldn't rely on anyone but herself. If she was going to make a try for escape, it had to be now, while Dutch was watching the shoreline.

Waves frothed. Miki shut out the sounds of the rain and the motor. When Dutch turned away to scan the beach, she shot to her feet, tumbled over the rail and hit the icy water. She heard a dim shout and then she went under, slammed head over heels by churning currents, her sense of direction lost. She tried to swim away from the boat and with every stroke vivid images burned through her mind. Dreams of what should have been.

Her first photo chosen for the cover of a national magazine. A week in her oldest friend's mountain cabin in northern New Mexico, with no phones, no e-mails and clothes scattered over the floor. Max at her side, his naked body draped over hers, both of them too exhausted to move.

And maybe, just maybe…a baby.

One by one the images struck her as she fought to stay alive.

Something had shaken loose inside her, stirring up old and half-forgotten dreams.

She *refused* to die, damn it. She had survived her last crash and she was going to survive this. She had pictures to take, exotic beaches to visit and Max was going to fit into those plans somehow. At least, if she could get him to forgive her when this was all over.

She realized that she had been flailing at the water in panic, and now she focused, drifting while she searched for the dim light of the sky. A wave slapped her down in a painful somersault and she sucked in salt water, nearly blacking out.

No sky in sight.

Dimly she felt something brush her leg and tighten. Terror sent her clawing toward a faint smudge of gray above her shoulder.

She was fighting her way toward the surface when she heard the angry throb of a motor. The v-shaped wedge of a boat's prow loomed like a black arrow directly above her head.

She couldn't break the surface, but her breath was gone and her lungs burned, screaming for air. *Now-nownow.* She would die either way.

Something coiled around her foot, cold and slimy like seaweed, and Miki screamed, but sound was muffled by gray water.

Her terror spiked.

Then the thing yanked her hard, pulling her down into the darkness.

CHAPTER TWENTY-SEVEN

MAX CLOSED HIS MIND, shielding his thoughts against the energy probe that could only have come from Cruz.

Suddenly he heard his name, an angry shout cast high over his head. Beyond the sheeting rain, he saw a dark figure standing at the top of the cliff.

One slash with a knife, and the rope would be gone. Max would plummet two hundred feet and slam into the water, his neck crushed by the guidance system in his backpack.

But Cruz wanted something or he wouldn't have come to tackle this job personally. Max kept his descent smooth, braking his rope through interlocking carabiners. He wasn't going to make things easy for Cruz.

"Job well done, Preston." There was no mistaking that voice, stronger than it had ever been, full of confidence. "I figured they'd send you, given your particular skill set. But that device stuffed in your backpack is just a shell. I stripped away the guts of the unit before I stowed it. Why would I take a chance of you getting past my men?"

Max scowled into the wind. Whether he believed Cruz was irrelevant. The performance came first.

He expertly tightened the rope around his leg to fine-tune his descent while Cruz watched from the edge of the cliff. Max cursed silently as gravel shot down, slamming into his head.

"When are you going to wake up? Everyone in Foxfire is a guinea pig. Ryker will keep using you until there's nothing left. Then he'll toss you into the garbage, the same way he did me."

Max kept moving, closing his thoughts to the rogue Foxfire operative above him.

"We need to talk, Preston. I'll send a boat to get you. After that, if you're still so sure you want to leave, I'll let you go. No questions asked."

Like hell you will, Max thought grimly. He kept right on moving.

"Not interested? In that case, I happen to hold one more playing card, and it would be a major waste for her to die."

Miki. How had Cruz found her so soon?

Max thought of the set of pain pills missing from his medical kit. He'd only just begun to piece together the pilot's betrayal. Miki wouldn't have taken the pills, but Dutch could have. That meant he wasn't nearly as weak or disoriented as he'd appeared. If Max hadn't been so caught up in the grip of his lust for Miki, he might have made the connection sooner. Now she was Cruz's hostage, and he wouldn't let her live long.

Max forced his mind to be cold and calculating, the way Cruz had become. The drum of a motor made him turn as a boat headed toward the beach. He could make out Dutch's form, hunched over the wheel, but he couldn't see Miki.

If he'd harmed Miki, Max would rip him apart. But revenge would have to wait.

"She's a very resourceful woman. That's one reason I chose her to be the recipient of one of my older chips. And her travel plans were exotic enough to pull attention away from my movements."

If one of Cruz's chips was imbedded in Miki's arm, that would explain her continuing pain and the wound that didn't heal. It would also explain Max's odd sensory disorientation and the nosebleeds that struck when they were close. Max knew that Cruz's chips had been degrading during the months before his escape. The headaches and nosebleeds since coming to this island could be more signs of chip failure affecting both of them. In fact, Miki was damned lucky that she hadn't had a more serious reaction.

Not that Cruz would care about that. Everything was cold strategy to him. It had been his greatest skill in the Foxfire unit.

Max's eyes narrowed against the rain. He was fifty feet above the ocean now, his scuba gear and inflatable boat out of sight inside a small cave at the base of the cliff. He would be geared up and underwater in less than three minutes.

At least that's what Cruz would expect him to do, and expectation was everything.

Max looked down at his watch, calculating possibilities. It would be one hell of a tight switch.

He turned out of Cruz's line of sight, opened the face of his watch and tapped a short burst of code using a button hidden beneath the LED screen.

Showtime. Izzy would know exactly what the code word meant.

After that he shoved a small red pill into place inside his lower gum, careful not to puncture its hard gel coating. He sure as hell hoped he wasn't going to need it, but his orders were crystal clear. Get the weapon and get out.

He wasn't going anywhere with Cruz. Not alive.

He turned back, looking up the cliff, letting his tension show. "I don't see the woman, Enrique. Face it, your stooge Dutch was too weak to do anything after the pneumothorax from the crash. While we're at it, I don't buy that crap about the guidance system, either."

"No? Take a look over your right shoulder."

Max saw that the boat had stopped. Dutch was pulling someone onto the deck from the rear railing. The flash of bright red could only be Miki's Hawaiian shirt.

She must have tried to escape—and failed.

Something dug into Max's heart. He shouldn't have let her get involved. As soon as he had confirmation that she was an innocent civilian, he should have gotten her the hell off the island, despite Ryker's orders to ignore everything but the mission. Now it was too late.

He took a deep breath and shuttered his mind, putting away all trace of emotion. He had no other choice. The best protection for Miki now would be a swift, deadly counterattack.

He tightened his rope, peering through the rain. When he looked back at Cruz, he had shielded his mind completely. In the last months, Foxfire's science team had worked night and day to come up with a way to disable the man who had once been their strongest and most deadly member. Max hoped the mental shields he had been taught would hold Cruz off temporarily.

"Assuming I'm willing to talk, what's in it for me, Enrique?"

Cruz didn't move, a black slash against the churning gray clouds. "Name your price. Power, wealth, fame—any of them can be yours. I'll send a boat for you and we'll discuss it."

Max glared up through the rain. This was the opportunity he'd been seeking. He wouldn't get a second chance.

Careful, he thought. Cruz was vicious, but he wasn't stupid. "For starters, I want the woman. But after that I want a whole lot more. You're asking me to sell out my country, remember?"

"Your country already sold *you* out, Max. You're just another lab animal as far as Ryker is concerned. Once your chips start failing, he'll throw you into confinement, too. He'll test you night and day the same way he did to me."

Max didn't believe a word of it. Ryker wasn't a madman, only driven. He didn't make decisions without scrutiny, although Max couldn't remember the last time anyone from D.C. had come to inspect the lab—even the public parts of it.

"I don't care about Ryker or the suits back in D.C. If I do this, Enrique, I'm doing it for the money."

"And for the woman," Cruz said coldly.

"That, too. And if you're lying to me, I'll kick your ass all the way back to San Francisco."

Cruz didn't move. "I'm not lying."

As Max dropped the final feet to the cave entrance, his old teammate sent a wave of energy after him, rippling like smoke across the face of the cliff and burning down his spine. It was a basic distortion, part of Cruz's Foxfire training, but the effect was stronger than expected despite all of Max's new shields.

The cliff face seemed to catch fire and flame outward, ringing Max in heat.

An illusion, he knew. A sign of power meant to intimidate him. But it was one more proof that Cruz was changing, taking on strengths far beyond his original enhancements.

Max was about to walk into very deep shit.

CHAPTER TWENTY-EIGHT

MIKI WAS CAUGHT, her lungs burning, and in seconds she would pass out. Something gripped her leg, a slimy creature from the sea bottom she had been unlucky enough to disturb. Fighting her fear, she jackknifed vainly, searching for whatever was holding her ankle.

A black form loomed into view in front of her and she shot back in terror.

Huge, bulging eyes. Black and webby hands. Long, black body.

The snare left her leg, and two hands locked around her waist. As Miki sputtered and dug at the water, she realized she was looking at a man in full scuba gear. Suddenly she was surrounded by five more men. One of them pulled off his rebreather unit and slid it into her mouth, hovering nearby while she took shaky breaths.

It felt like a bad dream. Miki's eyes closed and the world faded to gray. So tired. So cold…

Something grabbed her, shaking her hard, and she came awake with a start, fighting the hands locked on her shoulders. When she opened her eyes, the masked face was back.

Creepy, she thought dizzily. Now he was holding a tiny waterproof light and some kind of plastic underwater writing slate. He tapped Miki's shoulder, then wrote on the slate with what looked like a big waxy crayon.

Friends.

Okay, this was abso-freaking nuts. Shuddering, Miki looked around her, ringed by big bodies and high-tech black wetsuits. She tried to work out the details, but she wasn't having much luck.

The man wrote on the slate again. Only one word this time. *Max?*

Miki realized he was holding the wax pen out and waiting for an answer. With shaking hands, she gripped the slate and wrote quickly.

Went to island. Looking for something important. Said hidden near palm tree on cliff.

The man whose breathing gear she was using nodded and then passed the slate around to the others. Miki wished she could see their faces clearly, but even through the murky water she sensed their intense focus and intelligence. One of the other men passed the leader his own breathing unit, and Miki gave a mental head slap. She made a move to pull out her mouthpiece and return it, but the man shook his head, motioning her to keep it. Then he held the slate in front of her again.

Gone how long?

Miki frowned and tried to remember.

Not sure. Less than an hour.

The man wrote quickly. *Need your help.*

Miki shivered with cold, treading the murky water. If she died now, who would miss her? Who would remember her for touching a life or changing the world in any way? That was what you were supposed to do, wasn't it? People said that everyone had a gift, and you were supposed to find that gift and use it fully before you died.

Right now it looked as if she had a ninety-ten chance of dying, and she'd done nothing of any importance in her life. This was her chance.

She nodded at him.

He wrote another line. *Will be very dangerous.*

He hadn't finished writing when she grabbed the board from his hand, crossed out the last line and scrawled in big letters.

YES.

One of the other men swam closer and squeezed her shoulder, giving a big thumbs-up. If the whole scene hadn't been so surreal, and if she hadn't had a mouthpiece locked between her trembling lips, she might have laughed.

But the danger ahead was anything but funny, and now the lead man was writing on the slate again, while one of the others pressed something heavy into her hands.

When she looked down, the slate said, *Kevlar vest. Put it on under your shirt.*

After Miki pulled her shirt back on over the black protective vest, he nodded and gave her arm another reassuring squeeze.

Max needs you. Can you do this?

She didn't hesitate, nodding hard.

Behind the dark masks, six sets of eyes probed her face, and she sensed how closely they were weighing her strengths and weaknesses. She wanted to scream that she was tough and they could count on her, that she'd anything to help Max, but they wouldn't hear and probably wouldn't believe it anyway. Then the man nodded at the others and she knew the decision to trust her had been made. He wrote one more line on the slate.

Can you keep a secret?

MAX SAW THE SPEEDBOAT surge around the bottom of the cliff, just the way Cruz had promised.

But they were going to play the last act by new rules. Ignoring the boat, Max slipped back into the water.

Ten minutes later, he dumped his breathing gear in a rocky crevice at the far side of the island. He hid his sealed rifle and removed a revolver from inside a waterproof case, then sprinted into the trees.

It wasn't hard to locate Cruz's camp. An hour before, there had been no signs of life here, but there was no more effort to hide. Now lights burned above the jungle and Max heard the rumble of machinery.

He made his way silently through the outskirts of the camp, where a dozen men unloaded crates with what appeared to be satellite communication equipment. There was no sign of Cruz, but his energy trail was strong, focused near the beach.

A twig snapped behind him. When Max turned, he

was staring into Wolfe Houston's face. Why in the hell was the new Foxfire team leader here in the jungle?

"Be careful." Wolfe frowned, bending closer. "He's unstable and probably paranoid. You saw Ryker's medical reports during the briefing. You know what you have to do."

Max kept his body relaxed as he laughed. "Nice job, Cruz. You almost had me believing you. But you made one mistake: Wolfe trusts me. When he gives an order he knows I carry it out without any further instructions. That's where you gave yourself away."

The man before him seemed to flicker, shifting colors like a photographic negative taking on tones and dimension in a chemical bath.

In a span of seconds Max was staring at the gaunt, powerful features of Enrique Cruz, not Wolfe Houston. Cruz looked sick, Max thought. He also looked deadly.

Max's gun was drawn, pointing at Cruz's head. "Where is she?"

"You'd put a woman above your mission? Ryker would have your ass and all the rest of you for that." Cruz pointed through the trees to the edge of the beach. "The boat will be here shortly and she'll be kept in confinement until I decide what to do with her. Dutch turned out to be very useful, managing to get hired in Hawaii at the last minute." Cruz's mouth twisted. "You broke one of Ryker's rules when you got emotionally attached."

"Maybe I've decided to set my sights higher than

Ryker's rules. But as I said, you'll have to make it worth my while."

"If you join me, there's nothing we can't do. I'll let you have the woman, for a start."

Max stood for a long time, staring into the rain. The timing was crucial now. Cruz wouldn't expect an easy capitulation. "You almost tempt me, Enrique. But the answer's still no. It's not enough."

At Cruz's signal, four of his men drove Max to the ground and cuffed him. Cruz hit Max hard. With his hands tied, Max felt the blow slam through his jaw and whip his head back. Blood spurted into his mouth and down his neck.

"I'll ask you again. Join me."

Max kept his face expressionless. "Not interested without more inducement. And just for the record, you were a rotten leader. You started liking the power and the ability to give orders, and you were afraid that someone would take that away from you. The day you put your own power above the safety of your men was the day you stopped being a leader worthy of my respect. You're nowhere close to being the man that Houston is."

Cruz hit him again, and this time Max managed to fall forward, away from the grip of the man in a faded camo uniform. Max grabbed at Cruz's arm, hormones and sweat burning into his awareness, painted through layers of adrenaline and more hormones. Max had each detail etched into his memory before Cruz shoved him away.

Now he had the information he needed, torn from those moments of physical contact. This was why Ryker had sent him, so he could read and record every detail of Cruz's physical and mental status. The weapon guidance system was valuable, but nothing in comparison with up-to-date information about Foxfire's rogue leader.

Max shielded his mind as Cruz squatted in front of him. "Something's different." Cruz touched Max's forehead and cursed. "You're blocking me, Preston. How?"

Max didn't answer, thinking of the rain and Miki's warm body. Thinking of their rough and primitive mating beneath a veil of water. He kept his mind deep in those moments, and through that energy he blocked Cruz.

"They've *done* something to you. Is it a new chip? Tell me, Preston."

Max leaned forward and spat coldly on the sand. *You are a dead man,* his mind whispered back, letting Cruz hear.

Not without my revenge complete. Cruz's eyes were like streaks of mud as he dug into the pocket of his vest and held out what appeared to be a black penlight. "I doubt you've seen this before. It was one of Ryker's favorite toys before I got away. He was testing a way to make our chips migrate slightly, using magnetics. I don't need to tell you how painful it is."

As he spoke, Cruz pressed on the barrel.

Pain stabbed through Max's neck like living slivers of glass. He felt the muscles at his shoulders clench.

Cruz triggered the unit again. Max had to bite back

a curse as the chip in his neck infiltrated deeper, tearing through tissue and nerves while the pain went on and on and rain hammered the beach. "Join me."

Max's cold answer didn't change, though Cruz repeated the order again and again, each time driving Max's chips deeper. Twenty minutes later, his face streaked with blood, he blacked out.

MIKI WAS CAUGHT SOMEWHERE between terror and a raw adrenaline high. In a gray blur she watched waves pound against the beach. What was she *doing* here facing bullets and pretending to be brave? She wasn't cut out for heroics.

Maybe not, but she wasn't backing down and she wouldn't screw up. Max and Truman both needed her. She took a deep breath and squared her shoulders.

"Do you have everything straight?"

The man who had written on the slate was at the wheel of Dutch's boat, wearing Dutch's clothes. The pilot was tied up and sedated, out of sight below the deck. In the heavy rain no one would notice the change.

Miki smoothed the torn shrug covering her shirt and nodded. "I remember."

"Good. It's going to get physical," the man who called himself Dakota said. "It's got to be convincing but I'll keep you out of range as much as—"

"To hell with staying out of range. Do whatever you need to do so you can get to Max," Miki said fiercely. "But once you're on the beach, they'll realize you're not Dutch."

The man steering the boat smiled faintly. "I've got a few tricks of my own, ma'am."

The old Miki would have hammered him with questions.

The new Miki zippered her mouth and focused on staying calm so she could give the best performance of her life. Dipping her hand into the boat's wake, she drenched her face and hair. The cold would help her focus.

Ahead of them on the beach a man pointed, running over the sand with a walkie-talkie pressed against his ear.

"You ready back there?" The question was low.

No. Actually, she was white-knuckle material, petrified that she'd screw up the way she had too many times before.

Miki took a deep breath. She didn't know who this Dakota was, but she was trusting him with her life. If he was a friend of Max, she knew it was the right thing to do. "No problem. I'll be fine. Let's bag this creep and go home."

"I'm with you, honey."

Their boat hissed as it touched sand and Miki slid lower, the perfect picture of a cowering woman. "Dutch" had his collar rolled up around his face as he leaned down, grappling with her.

A man in a camouflage uniform and an Australian bush hat walked toward them, an Uzi slanted over his shoulder. "Need some help?"

Dakota shook his head and grunted a graphic curse that made the man with the Uzi smile. "Hurry up. Cruz wants to see you pronto. He's in his tent up the beach."

Dakota released Miki and hunched over, hacking loudly. "Damned lungs."

Someone called out for Malovich, and the man with the Uzi ran back up the beach, his walkie-talkie screeching.

None of the other men paid much attention as "Dutch" yanked Miki out of the boat and shoved her across the sand. Her body blocked any view of his face.

"Let me go," she rasped. "You can't hold me. I'm an American and I demand—"

She was thrust sideways with an apparent backhand that sent her sprawling to the ground. Dakota leaned over her, holding her down with one foot. "There's no American embassy here so shut the fuck up."

She tossed sand in his face, prompting a string of curses.

Up the hill a cold voice brought all movement to a halt. "Bring them here."

Miki struggled to stand up and Dakota hunched over, coughing harshly.

"You can't hold me here." Suddenly something buzzed through her head, and pain shot up her neck. Her nose began to bleed again.

Two men stood near the tent above the beach, watching her as if she was a stray dog that had wandered into camp. Coughing loudly, Dakota pushed her forward.

Something felt wrong to Miki. Her palms were clammy with fear as the *wrongness* grew. She saw the man propped on the sand with a harpoon arrow protruding through his chest. In one quick glimpse she recognized the man who'd attacked her earlier on the beach. He hadn't died fast or easily.

Miki closed her eyes. She didn't know how he had ended up here. Another man was stretched out on the ground, leaning against a green tent. When she realized it was Max, her heart lurched. He was slumped sideways, his face swollen and smeared with blood. A man sat in a folding chair two feet away, watching him with eyes that missed nothing.

What she did next wasn't planned.

She ran forward, flailing at the two new men who tried to stop her. "What did you do to him?" She dug out a knitting needle she'd hidden under her shirt and jabbed it deep into one of the men's hands. "*Let go.*"

She twisted free and dropped to her knees beside Max, touching his face gently. He didn't move or give any sign that he knew she was there.

"Max," she whispered, her voice thick with emotion.

He forced open an eye, studying her blankly. "Don't know you."

The man in the chair stood up and pulled Miki to her feet, then slapped her hard. She bit back a moan, summoning all her anger to fight back, but her arms were pinned. Max's captor reminded her of the hungry wolves she had seen one winter pawing for food near a garbage dump outside Santa Fe. There was nothing that felt human in his eyes and his face held no expression as he shoved up the sleeve of her torn shrug and pressed the scar where she had been burned.

Twice he probed her arm until she was hit by waves of nausea.

"Dutch" shuffled along the sand, coughing as he came closer. He called a name and Miki realized it was Cruz.

Someone yelled. Gunfire cracked in the trees, and the next thing Miki knew, she was flat beneath Max's body, pressed into the sand while "Dutch" pointed a rifle at Cruz.

None of the three men spoke. They seemed to communicate without words, their eyes locked, and the unnatural tension between them made the little hairs prickle along Miki's neck. Who *were* these people?

Men were everywhere now, racing along the beach, charging out of the trees. More gunfire erupted. A man appeared in the back of the beached speedboat, shoved aside a tarp and sprinted toward the tent.

The man called Cruz didn't move. There in the rain he seemed to pull himself inside and shape the action around him. He raised his face to the wind, closing his eyes.

The rain grew harder, pounding against the tent and slashing at the trees.

Miki felt dizzy. Blood trickled from her nose as Max and a man who looked amazingly like Denzel Washington cornered Cruz.

Lightning arced through the sky, striking the tent until the air sizzled, acrid with ozone and burning nylon, and Miki flinched at the violent explosion, pitching forward. When she opened her eyes, Cruz was gone.

She saw Max on his feet, racing toward the trees,

with Smith right beside him. She could have sworn she saw a brown shape that looked like Truman hurtling out of the rain directly toward them.

Everything was chaos in the half-formed camp. No one paid any attention to her or to the Denzel lookalike. Miki was certain she'd seen him once in the hospital with her friend Kit's fiancé, Wolfe. He smiled slightly as he shoved aside the flap of the tent and pointed to the ground. "Stay down," he said. "We'll be fine. You've got the Kevlar and I've got the Glock."

Miki blinked at him. *Fine?*

She leaned over and was blindingly sick.

CHAPTER TWENTY-NINE

THROUGH A TUNNEL OF PAIN, Max ran after Cruz. Behind the hill a fuel dump exploded, marked by shouts and the hammering of feet while flames rose in an orange column. Without turning his head, he sensed Wolfe Houston and another Foxfire teammate, Trace O'Halloran, running parallel to him in the trees, fanning out to take their target in a pincer movement.

Trace, what have you got?

Max sensed Wolfe's growing impatience.

Energy trails everywhere, Wolfe. I'm getting multiple readings. Hell, they're all over the place. I can't pin them down. He's too damned good.

None of the men needed to speak aloud. From long practice their skills were honed to maintain a lethal silence. But now they faced an enemy who was one of their own kind, who thought the way they thought. Max wondered how much Cruz was picking up right now.

He knew Cruz's vitals. He'd read his pulse and hormone levels during their moments of contact during the interrogation, but Cruz had his own mental shields in place, and Max couldn't go deep enough to gauge the extent of Cruz's damage. All he could pick up was superficial structure changes. Ryker's scientists had equipped all of the field team with resonance chips to disrupt Cruz's old implants, and judging by Cruz's fury during their meeting, the chips had been successful.

But it would be dangerous to underestimate the man's resourcefulness. Like a cat, their rogue teammate always seemed to land on his feet.

Automatic weapon fire crackled behind them, but none of the men broke stride to look back. Their mission lay ahead in the jungle, with a man more valuable than any weapon guidance system.

A grove of black bamboo cracked and groaned in the wind, brushing Max's face with a shower of water. Suddenly Truman cut across the face of the slope. Max swerved sharply, jumped a fallen tree trunk to avoid the dog, and kept right on moving until the dog cut him off again.

What's wrong with Truman? Trace was at the top of the hill, looking back.

Something's got him spooked, Max thought back in answer. *Better slow down.*

You two stay back. I'm taking point from here on, Wolfe cut in.

Max started to argue, but you didn't question the team leader's direct order. He knew that Wolfe had a personal stake in bringing Cruz down after their prior encounter and the threat to the woman he loved. Max was starting to understand that last feeling very well.

He looked down as Truman bumped his leg. The dog's body was rigid, ears pricked alertly.

Air gusted as a bird shot over his shoulder, wings spread. Truman watched the hurtling flight, ears flat, his muscles tensed. One paw scratched a straight line on the ground.

Unspecified alert. Indeterminate danger.

Max slowed, checking the heavy vegetation along the slope. The heavy rain made vision difficult, and as Max trained his focus he picked up Cruz's energy signature, just the way Trace had said, projected along the trail. Max's skill wasn't half as strong as Trace's but he saw the ghostlike outlines of Cruz's projections as a shifting oily sheen in the air.

The gunfire came closer. A burst from an Uzi sent Max zigzagging to the left. When he turned around, Trace was hunched over, gripping his side.

Trace?

Took a round beneath the ribs. Hurts like hell, but I'll survive. You two go on and I'll catch up.

Max didn't hesitate. He would have made the same call if the situation were reversed.

We'll be back as soon as we can, Wolfe answered. *Stay low. He's close now.*

Max studied the slope, feeling awareness gather at the back of his neck. He was assaulted by the sudden smell of gasoline, carried on black, oily clouds from the explosion. For the other two men, the acrid smell would be unpleasant, but Max couldn't risk the contamination that would throw off his sensory work. Truman would have a similar problem unless the wind dispersed the smoke soon.

As he jerked a length of black cloth from his backpack and tied it around his face, something else bothered Max. He dropped to one knee, pressed his hand into the ground beside a wall of shifting bamboo plants, and picked up a dim impression of motion and what felt like the hum of machinery. He was trying to focus on the source when Truman went flat, ears back, body rigid.

A warning alert. Danger straight ahead.

Max stopped instantly. *Wolfe, can you see Truman?*

Yeah, and I wish I couldn't. Gotta be Cruz.

Max looked up and saw the bamboo wall part. Cruz stood in the middle of the trail, smiling coldly, holding out what appeared to be a computer disk.

Truman's teeth pulled back in a snarl, as if he was under silent attack. Max knew that Cruz had shown the ability to manipulate animals as part of his enhanced skills, and Truman would be a definite prize. But right now the Lab showed no signs of giving in easily.

Up the trail, Cruz's image seemed to waver and then reform. His lips moved, but no sound emerged, like a bad copy of a silent movie. Though Max searched the ground, he picked up no biomarkers or chemical layers.

Do you see him? he asked Wolfe.

Keep moving. It's an ID.

Image distortion, another one of Cruz's skills. Wolfe Houston would recognize the technique perfectly because he had always been the strongest of the team at the focused distortion skills.

What about the computer disk he was holding?

Max felt Wolfe's intensity as he stared up the trail. *Probably showing us what he thinks we want most. Don't trust anything you see, not even me. You know the code word. And if he takes you down...*

Understood.

Wolfe was warning that any image could be manipulated, friend turned to foe and foe to apparent friend. Without code verification, no one could be trusted. And if Cruz managed to take any of the men, the others were under order to kill him to avoid him being turned into a weapon in Cruz's hands.

Max picked up the hum of a wireless energy source somewhere near his feet. Sensors, he thought, reading the edge of a focused wireless network fanning out across the hill.

He pulled off his gloves and touched the tree trunk with his palm, reading patterns and searching for oil traces left by human skin.

Not here, but nearby. A dense line led up the hill.

He looked back at Trace, who was climbing awkwardly toward a flat rock, one hand pressed against his rib.

Trace, stop!

Max followed a faint trail of sweat and more of the amphetamine traces. Even in the rain, the layers were well defined. Immediately he projected the image to the others, who froze in mid-footstep.

But the warning came too late. The ground rumbled and soil heaved, giving way. Max plunged into a pit gaping open beneath him. By instinct, he managed to relax and shield his head, preparing for a fall.

He hit hard, dirt filling his mouth. His head throbbed as he crawled to his feet, staring up at the gashed earth and overturned bushes. A well-placed sensor had triggered a fall in what appeared to be one of Cruz's underground tunnels.

Max, are you all right?

Only a few scratches. Max ran a hand over the shifting earth. *Stay back, Wolfe. I'm picking up additional sensors, and the area looks unstable.*

Understood.

As the rain hammered on, Max moved to the center of the hole. Finding nothing significant, he squished on through dirt that was rapidly turning to mud.

And then he saw a weathered door. It was all but invisible, brown and mottled in the same colors as the ground.

Wolfe, there's a door down here. I'm checking it out. Max felt Wolfe's hesitation.

Negative. Not without backup. Trace is out of the picture and I can't get down there yet. Hold position.

We need a reading.

Wolfe's answer shot back, sharp and decisive. *Negative. This is Cruz's home turf and we're at a disadvantage. Are you picking up anyone in the area?*

No one, Max shot back.

Give me a second. I'll hitch my rope around a tree and you'll be out of there shortly.

Silently Max registered assent. Staying where he was, he pulled off his gloves and rested his palms against the newly furrowed ground.

Sweat. Layers of cortisol and adrenaline. The flash of amphetamines again, mixed with caffeine and tobacco.

Cruz kept his workers stoked and uncertain, always watching their backs. Max realized that it was a worst-case scenario of the way Ryker might handle the Foxfire team in a crisis. No one ever said that being nice got the job done.

Max didn't want to think about the similarities. None of them had done the things that Cruz had done. Most likely his chip degeneration had triggered a long dormant instability that had slipped past all the medical evaluations.

But a tiny voice whispered that the same chips could cause the process to repeat in any one of the team. Would Max wake up one day to find himself taking enemy fire from another friend turned foe, with all the skills of Foxfire technology turned against the team? What if it was Wolfe next time?

Impossible, Max thought.

Did you say something? Wolfe sounded a little distracted.

No.

Max couldn't analyze what made him go very still.

It might have been a hint of adrenaline in the air or maybe raw instinct.

He sniffed the air. Climate control. Not for personal comfort, but almost certainly designed for high-tech equipment that required stable temperature and humidity.

What the hell was Cruz making down here?

Max didn't move, wary of triggering another sensor.

Don't bother waiting for Wolfe. He's not coming.

Max stiffened as air brushed his back and a voice seemed to whine inside his ear.

We both know you'd give anything to take me down, Preston. So open the door and come on in. I'm here where you can get me. Unless you're afraid to see what I can show you because it will prove that I'm right. Ryker is nuts and the whole program is flawed.

The voice was hollow, disembodied, and Max couldn't register any physical signs of Cruz's presence, which meant this was more illusion.

Smoke and mirrors, the kind Cruz conjured best.

I don't need to see your world, Cruz. I already know it's as sick as you are.

Hell, you're so afraid that you're sweating, Preston. Ryker's got you so twisted around his finger you won't breathe without getting his approval first.

Max tried to contact Wolfe, but got no answer. Meanwhile, Cruz's ravings continued.

Where's your freedom gone, Preston? Where are the honesty and idealism you bought into? Ryker's made you all into his drones, shaped to his personal whim.

Face it—Foxfire isn't about the government or securing our borders, it's about Ryker and his personal quest for power. Why don't you ask him what he's doing in Lab 21? Ask him about South America and—

Max shielded his mind from the delusional ramblings. There wasn't a Lab 21 back at HQ. All of this was more of Cruz's paranoia.

You can dismiss me the way Wolfe did, but what happened to me will happen to you. One day you'll look in the mirror and you'll see my haunted eyes, my gaunt face. None of the medications will help. I'll be the only one you can turn to then.

Max tried to cut out the voice. It wavered like static from a distant radio, then came back stronger than before.

You want *to be Ryker's slave. I thought you were smarter than that, Preston. Guess I was wrong.*

Max's vision swam. He was hit by a sudden wave of dizziness, and when he looked around, the hole had vanished. Despite all Max's shielding, Cruz's image distortion patterns kicked in hard and all he could see was a high canopy of endless trees above him.

If you want to meet me, do it like a man, Cruz. Not like some dime-store magician.

I'm hardly dime-store quality. Remember, I cost the government ten million dollars to make.

I'm supposed to be impressed by all this hocus-pocus?

No, you're supposed to come and get me, unless I get you first. I intend to have those new chips you're carrying. Whether you're dead or alive when I get them is up to you.

The trees shook, and Max stared into desperation and sorrow. Whether it came from his mind or Cruz's, he couldn't tell.

"WHAT THE HELL HAPPENED?" Trace was propped against a tree, his face white. A dark stain was growing at his waist.

"Ground caved in," Wolfe said tightly. "One of Cruz's hidden sensors got tripped."

"Where's Preston?"

"He's good to go. I should have him out shortly." Wolfe wrapped his rope around a tree and knotted it securely. "How's that wound?"

"Hurts like hell. I've lost a little blood." Trace took a breath and grimaced. "I can still back you up. Say the word."

"The only word I'm saying to you is *rest.*"

"But—"

"That's an order, O'Halloran." Wolfe sprinted back toward the gaping hole, playing out rope until he came to the spot where he'd left Max.

Preston, where are you?

No answer.

Scowling, he tossed the rope over the edge and rappelled down. More dirt had fallen, mounded several feet high, and footsteps led across the soft earth toward the half-hidden door.

The door was open and Max was gone.

CHAPTER THIRTY

MAX FELT THE THREAD of contact break. Cruz was making this into a game, complete with taunting and trickery and threats. He'd always loved being tested and testing back.

The trees vanished over Max's head, and suddenly he was inside a tunnel beneath dim lights running along a low ceiling. The whine of generators seemed real, but Max knew that creating unshakable illusions was one of Cruz's oldest skills.

If Cruz wanted to play a game, Max would oblige him.

He rounded a turn cautiously and was hit by the pungent smell of animals from a narrow room lined by cages. Medical books and dissecting equipment were lit by high-wattage halogen lights, and Max saw refrigerators, microscopes and centrifuges similar to those in the Foxfire labs.

This was more than a simple storage area. Cruz was carrying on Ryker's research. The thought left Max very uneasy.

He watched a pair of lemurs swing from perch to perch in a high cage. Both appeared healthy and well fed, but agitated. Max picked up a black notebook on a shelf and flipped through the creased pages.

September 21—continued to check implantation problems.

September 25—sacrificed test animal.

October 1—muscle pattern control successful

All in all Max found records for twenty-six animals used in tests with various chip configurations, including full behavioral results.

Interesting, isn't it?

Cruz appeared in the doorway with an Uzi over one arm. Not an image this time, Max thought. The energy trail was too clear for that.

"Starting your own lab, Cruz? I thought you had enough of that at Los Alamos."

"I'm using what Ryker taught me, only driving in a new direction. I want his ability to shift chips once they're implanted. You saw that firsthand. How does it feel when they start moving inside you?"

Like hell, Max thought. He shrugged. "Why, so you can control us? If so, think again."

"I planned every step of this, and that bothers you. I knew Ryker would send someone once I unshielded the weapon area for his satellite. Face it—I'm ten steps ahead of you."

"What do you want from me, Cruz? Absolution or loyalty? Because I'm no priest and you're sure as hell no friend."

"What I want is for you to open your eyes. Do you think they'll let you have any say about your life? Do you think you can have any time with the woman after you leave this island? It's a dream. You'll walk away because they'll order you to."

Max tossed the notebook from one hand to the other, ready to move when he saw a break. "Maybe, maybe not. Now I get a question. Where did you hide the inertial weapon system?" he said coldly.

"Ryker whistles and you jump. Nice job they did on you. But there are too many things you don't know about the program, things that Ryker never plans to tell any of you. I'm going to enjoy watching your face when I show you his encrypted files. Then I'm going to drive your chips out your neck while you scream."

Max's lips curved. "You really know how to throw a party, Cruz."

"Tough talk. You won't be tough when four pieces of silicon slice through your spine."

Max was pretty sure Cruz was right, but he wasn't going to dwell on the possibilities. "You're not going anywhere. The whole team is on the ground right now, combing the jungle. You can't hide from all of us."

"I'm not interested in the rest of the team. Right now I'm only interested in you. Have you read your latest medical files closely?" Cruz held up a computer disk, his eyes locking with Max's. "I mean your real file, the private one Ryker doesn't want you to see. Remember what happened during the surgery after your training accident?"

"Broken bones. Kidney problems. Big deal."

"What about your partner?"

Max shied away from the memories and what he had been told about that long ordeal. "Drake died in transit to the hospital."

"Not true. Your partner was alive but in bad shape, dying on the operating table. Ryker didn't want to wait around, so they harvested his organs before they let him go—spleen, kidney and part of both tibias. You know where they went, don't you?"

Cold fingers crawled up Max's neck. "Not interested."

"You should be. They gave them to you, Preston. Ryker's medical experts decided you were more viable, and he had them pull the life support on Drake, but only after they'd taken any organs you might need. I saw your real files. You were side by side on two different operating tables that night. Ryker called the shots and let Drake die."

Max felt sick, and his uncertainty made him sicker. Why was he listening to a word from this traitor unless part of him had wondered all along? "I don't believe it. And if you want my chips, you'll have to take them out of my dead body."

"I expected you'd feel that way. Let's say you'll be my first living human test animal." Cruz raised the same little device he'd held in his tent, and pressed its switch. Instantly Max was swimming in pain, his nerves on fire, hammered by sharp movements beneath his skin, under his collarbone, along his spine. His chips were migrating just the way Cruz had described.

But Max hadn't come this far without backup scenarios. Wolfe and Trace would be coming after him shortly, and even the techno genius, Izzy Teague, had insisted on being part of the final op. His electronic tracking skills were second to none.

He grimaced, feeling a chip work upward past his collarbone and pierce the dermal layer, blood trickling over his shirt. The pain nearly blinded him, but he forced his mind to remain focused. "What about you, Cruz? You're having problems replacing your nutrients, and your body's burning too much energy at a constant temperature of 103. You're not sleeping, either."

Cruz's eyes narrowed. "You determined that from a few seconds of contact? That's very impressive. I'm going to enjoy those new chips of yours."

"What would you give me for a complete hormone assessment so you can replace everything you need? Your body will stop degenerating. That pain in your back will stop, too." Max smiled at the shock in Cruz's eyes. "What do you say?"

"What's your price?"

"You answer one question. I want to know what else you did to Miki Fortune. If you went to the trouble to insert one chip, I figure you didn't stop there."

"Busted." Cruz's laugh was a cold, reckless sound. "It's nothing she'll feel for a few months. Let's just say the woman you fell in love with—the woman you were screwing blind back in that bunker—has turned into my walking weapon. I control the detonator, the place, the time. When I choose, she'll go off. You'll understand if I don't disclose the details."

Max closed his hands to fists, battered by fury. Was this one more test by Cruz or was it real?

He couldn't risk Miki's life on a vague hope. "How did you manage it so fast?"

"Remember when Houston was in Santa Fe? Thanks to my contact there, I was experimenting with a few things I stole from Ryker's lab. Ryker was ready to test a new procedure on me, so I had to escape. I don't suppose he told you about that part of his plans, either."

Max looked at the caged animals and tried to dismiss this as another sign of Cruz's paranoia, but something rang true. There had been hints that Ryker and his lab team were working on wireless remote devices at Los Alamos, and the question was *when,* not *if* they would be available. "No biomedical chip with wireless activation could remain hidden from us. We would have picked up the energy sooner or later."

"You wouldn't have known where to look. It was only partially mechanical. For the rest, Ryker was experimenting with—" Cruz stopped suddenly. His eyes hardened. "I've told you enough. Now I'll ask you once more, and it's the last chance you'll get. Do you join me or do you prefer the unpleasant experience of your chips migrating out your spine and through the back of your neck?"

Max felt a clawing attack of pain, followed by crippling spasms at his back, a demonstration of what would come next if he said no.

Preston, where the hell are you?

About time. Max sent back an instant answer to Wolfe's mental probe. *I'm at the end of the tunnel marked E, in some kind of lab Cruz has down here. He's armed, and our discussion time is just about over. You might want to pick up the pace or I'll be the guy you find twitching on the floor in his own blood.*

On the way. Knock something over so I can figure out how far away you are.

Max leaned against the wall, his body hunched as he summoned up the picture of a man caught in overwhelming pain. "No more, Cruz." His voice was a low rasp. He stumbled, knocking a pile of beakers to the floor, where they smashed in a rain of glass. In a cage nearby the lemurs were howling and a dozen white mice darted in jerky circles while a lone parrot threw its body against the walls of its cage again and again, as if oblivious to its pain.

"Time's up, Preston. Make the choice. Let go of Ryker or let go of this slavery you call life."

Max knew if his chips moved much farther he would have serious tissue damage and death would come soon after that. But thanks to his physical contact with Cruz, he knew that Cruz had a pinched sciatic nerve and nerve damage in his right hand, resulting in slower response time.

Max pulled Miki's torn shrug out of his vest. He'd managed to snatch part of it amid the chaos at camp. It had negative affects on him, so he prayed it would affect Cruz the same way.

Max tossed the shrug at Cruz's head, dived under a lab table and scuttled for the adjoining room, ignoring the Uzi fire that drilled the floor after him. *Houston, did you hear that? Cruz is getting nasty in here. Hurrying up would be good.*

Almost there.

Max kicked over a huge metal cabinet and dove around the corner a split second before Cruz stitched a line of bullets across the tiles. Unholstering his Sig, he took cover next to a rolling cart full of test tubes.

When Cruz appeared he looked pale and shaken, the shrug dropped on the floor behind him. Max's assessment of the animal fiber had been right.

Point to remember for Ryker.

Preston, get the hell out of there. I'm twenty feet down the hall to your right. You head left and we'll run a pincer movement on him.

Copy. Max sent the silent answer as he ran to the next room and crouched out of sight, lining his Sig on the spot where Cruz would appear.

But the shadows didn't move. There was no noise in the hall.

You see him? Wolfe shot back.

Not from here.

Watch your back. There may be another door to the room.

Silence. Max heard the loud drumming of his heart.

Footsteps pounded in the opposite direction, echoing

hollowly in the underground corridor, and the two men sprinted toward the noise, weapons drawn.

They were surprised to see Truman emerge from a side corridor, followed by Izzy.

"What happened?" Max asked curtly.

"Dakota's up there with Miki. She kept telling me there was something strange about the shape of one of the bricks on the ground beneath the tent, and when she touched it, a tunnel opened up. The woman's got eyes all right." Izzy kept moving, checking the nearby rooms. "Where's Cruz?"

"Straight ahead of us, judging by the noise."

The Lab shot in front of Max, his muzzle raised as the footsteps echoed in the opposite direction.

"Truman, move out. We have to go."

The dog turned, his body rigid, blocking their way. He slammed his head against Max's leg, driving him back toward the corridor they had just left.

This time Max didn't say a word. Truman was too well trained to react by mistake. Something had to be wrong. As the dog continued to bump his leg, the men sprinted back toward the door at the site of the cave-in.

Wolfe?

The rope's still there. You two go up first. One of you will have to carry Truman. I'll stay here to clean up.

Like hell, Max thought. They were all getting out of this alive. He sniffed, picking up sulphur and the acrid smell of smoke as he turned a corner. The door was only a few feet away when a fireball burst along the corridor behind him.

He hit the door and the three men dove through inches ahead of the flames, Truman in front. As they scrambled for the rope, Max grabbed the dog and motioned Izzy up ahead of him. Cruz must have used a flamethrower, Max thought. But where was he now?

When Izzy was up, Wolfe gestured to Max, who pulled his way up one-handed with the dog cradled against his chest. Dirt rained down from a second fireball as Wolfe cleared the edge. They immediately ran for the beach, alerting the rest of the team to stay on watch for Cruz.

Max felt the spike of adrenaline amplifying the pain at his spine. An explosion rocked the ground behind him and the whole slope fell in, burying the tunnels and Cruz's hidden lab.

He stopped to look back, reading the scent on the air and the debris carried from the explosion. As the grass whipped around him, he saw a chopper rise above the trees. Cruz was inside next to a man in a camouflage uniform.

The clock's ticking, Preston. Who will it be next? Who can you trust?

Wolfe, Max called. *On your six.*

Got him. The Foxfire team leader was already shouldering a missile launcher and turning to follow the chopper as it thundered over their heads. Max felt a wave of dizziness hit him courtesy of Cruz, but he managed to keep moving.

Wolfe's rocket hissed free, struck the chopper and exploded. The back propeller was hit and the aircraft spiraled out of control, losing altitude fast. Wolfe took a second shot and this one hit dead center, debris hurtling over the beach. Fire mushroomed up as the fuel tanks exploded and the air filled with orange-yellow fury.

When the flames finally burned out, pieces of metal still hissed past Max like lethal hail. It was over, he thought, looking at the bits of twisted metal scattered over the ground. There was no way that Cruz or any other person could have escaped that kind of carnage.

The mission was complete.

As Max stood wearily, watching the oily black cloud rise into the air, he tried to feel some scrap of emotion, but there was nothing left. He couldn't summon a benediction for Cruz, or anything close to forgiveness.

He had his own questions about the story Cruz had told him, but they could wait. He had to get Miki into surgery a.s.a.p. to deal with Cruz's chip and whatever other implant he'd put inside her. After that Max had to figure out what kind of future they could have.

If any was possible. Cruz had probably been right about that much.

He realized that Truman was looking up at him, strong and steady. "Good dog. We owe you, buddy. How about a steak tonight?" Max closed his eyes as he was hit by a wave of dizziness. But he stood up slowly and squared his shoulders. His wounds could wait.

"Time to go home," he whispered to Truman.

CHAPTER THIRTY-ONE

"WHAT DO YOU MEAN, he's coming? You said that twenty minutes ago, so where *is* he?" Miki paced the beach, waving her arms, her face pale and anxious. "I want to see for myself how he is."

"He got a few scratches, that's all." Wolfe Houston offered her a bottle of water, but she pushed it away. "Izzy's almost done looking at him."

"This Izzy guy had better be good," she said flatly.

"Count on it."

"Yeah, right. All of you keep *saying* that Max is fine, but then you look away or clear your throats in that juvenile way that means you're hiding something but you think I'm too dumb to notice."

Wolfe cleared his throat and looked away.

"You see? Just like *that*."

The tall man named Dakota, who was still wearing Dutch's shirt, stood up and rubbed his neck. "You know, she could have a point, Chief. Maybe I should go check on Izzy and see what's taking so long."

"Great idea." Miki ran a hand through her hair and

then shot around so fast that she kicked up sand. "I'll come with you."

"Neither of you is going anywhere." Wolfe glared at the two of them. "Izzy knows what he's doing, and believe me, he doesn't like an audience when he works."

"Tough," Miki snapped. "He'll have to get used to it."

She stormed across the beach, her expression set, and Wolfe shook his head in irritation. He knew Miki well enough to realize there would be no holding her back without physical restraints.

"Do me a favor and keep her out of trouble," he said to Dakota. "Tell her anything you want, since we'll have to remove all her memories of today when we leave. Right now I've got to finish rounding up Cruz's people and then make a definitive recovery of his remains." There was something unreadable in Wolfe's eyes. He took a deep breath and then turned to glare at Dakota. "And stop calling me Chief."

"Sure thing." Dakota grinned and gave a little two-finger wave as he turned to follow Miki. "Chief," he muttered.

WOLFE RUBBED HIS NECK in irritation. He had to complete the recovery of Cruz's remains, capture all hostile forces and prepare a report in triplicate. Ryker would be furious that he'd lost a chance to take Cruz alive, but anything was better than allowing the rogue soldier to escape their net again. Now that they had the pilot in custody, they were gaining valuable information about Cruz's organization. Meanwhile, there was the question of Miki's additional implants to deal with, and Wolfe had commandeered a chopper for fast transport to the nearest secure medical facility.

He was glad it was nearly over. As he looked up into the sky, the sun began to peek through blotchy clouds. His gaze shifted to the smoldering remains of the fallen chopper, a sullen reminder of human greed and perversity.

There was a lesson buried in that wreckage littering the quiet strip of jungle, and Wolfe thought the message might be a warning about technology that advanced too far, too fast, beyond man's ability to keep pace.

No, that was wrong. The lesson was far simpler: choose your friends with care and then trust no one, even the friends you chose so carefully. Something about the thought left him angry. Most of his team's operations took place in tight situations that demanded loyalty and quick communication. When you were crouched in the mud or hunched over weapons trying to hide from an enemy strike force, your partner's loyalty meant your life. Period.

If you couldn't trust, you couldn't stay alive. To Wolfe it was as simple as that. Maybe that was why Cruz's betrayal continued to goad him so deeply.

He shook his head, putting the behavioral and medical questions out of his mind. He was relieved to have so many details to tackle now, because they left him too busy to wonder why Cruz had snapped, sliding down into madness.

What the hell was this Lab 21 he had mentioned to

Max? And his next question was always the same: if Cruz had snapped, couldn't any of them snap just as easily?

As he crossed the beach, Trace O'Halloran was sitting on an overturned ammo box, petting Truman. "You should be lying down, O'Halloran."

"Plenty of time for that after we're choppered out of here. Izzy tells me the round managed to miss anything significant." He frowned a little, scratching Truman's head. "By the way, what happened to Miki's hair? It looked like one side caught fire."

"It did." Wolfe hid a smile, remembering the story Dakota had told him. After two of Cruz's men charged the tent during the firefight, Dakota had dispatched one, but when he turned around, the other man was flat on the ground, howling in pain while Miki held him down with some kind of torch.

"How the heck did she make a torch?"

"Nail polish remover, a knitting needle, yarn and a set of matches. Or she might have said hair spray." Wolfe shrugged. "I'm not up on female grooming products. Thank God Kit isn't the high-maintenance type." At least Wolfe didn't think Kit was. They hadn't spent enough free time together in the last few months for him to know the extent of her likes and dislikes. He swore he was going to rectify that as soon as Ryker gave him some time off. Wolfe wanted at least a fragment of a private life, and he was determined to have it.

"Don't worry, my sister was never into all that stuff. Of course Miki is an entirely different story. You name the clothes or the gadget and she has it. None of us could ever figure out why the two of them were best friends." Trace stared out at the ocean. "She's something, isn't she? I thought she'd spit nails when she saw me. Now she's set fire to her hair. Hell, I never even knew it was blond. She must have been dying it all these years." His mouth hitched up in a grin. "Blondie strikes again."

"She saved our butts," Wolfe said quietly. "She got us close enough to dig in before Cruz knew what had happened."

"Yeah, and I'll thank her for that." Trace's grin widened. "But first I'm going to get a whole lot of mileage out of this hair story, believe me."

"JUST FOR THE RECORD, it's *not* about the sex." Miki glared at the tent at the edge of the beach, her thoughts churning. "It's about way more than the sex."

"I beg your pardon, ma'am?" Dakota looked at her curiously as they crossed the sand. He was tall and lanky, drop-dead gorgeous in a cowboy sort of way, Miki thought. And underneath those calm eyes was a brain that worked fast.

Any other time he might be exactly Miki's cup of tea.

But sometime during the last gut-wrenching, stomach-twisting and painful twenty-four hours, she had come to realize that there would be no other men. Her heart was already given.

Locked up, tied down, spoken for.

She closed her eyes, rubbed her face. When had it

happened? One minute she was enjoying her perfect job in paradise, and the next minute she was fighting for her life in choppy seas. Somewhere in the middle of the drama, the man of her dreams had commandeered her life and walked away with her heart.

Miki scowled down at the sand.

It wasn't *fair.* She didn't want to be in love. She didn't even want to be in *like.* She had pictures to take, dreams to chase and all kinds of rules to break. The whole idea of relationships and complications left her furious.

And frightened out of her mind.

She had seen a photograph in a book when she was twelve, and the photograph had made her realize what she wanted to do with her life. The picture wasn't pretty or soft. It had frightened her with its terrible beauty and stark drama of nature caught out of balance. Dark seas raged against stark granite cliffs in the Sea of Brittany beneath stormy gray skies. Looking at the photo, Miki had shivered, almost able to feel the cold bite of flying sea spray. She had known nothing about the artist who had taken the photo and she had lost the magazine soon afterward, but something about that image had haunted her, first with nightmares and later with a dream that she could capture an image with the same focus and raw drama.

She still wanted that dream, but she wanted Max, too.

She stopped walking so suddenly that Dakota almost bumped into her. "Something wrong?"

"You name it," she said grimly.

"Anything I can do to help?"

No one could help her, Miki thought. She was down for the count. If Max didn't feel the same way…

But as she stared at the clouds racing across the horizon, Miki realized you couldn't hold back change anymore than you could hold back the clouds. Life happened, and you didn't ignore a thunderbolt when it hit you in the center of your heart. You had to grab hold, hang on tight and see where it took you.

Even when you were dead certain you were going to screw up just like you'd screwed up all the other things in your life…

"WHAT DO YOU THINK you're doing?" Izzy scowled as the tent flap opened. "You can't come in here."

"I can't?" Miki shouldered her way through the door, determination on her face. She stopped suddenly, seeing that Max was alive. Seeing he was stretched out on a cot. Then seeing that he was naked.

"You'll have to leave." Izzy dropped a scalpel on a nearby cot and pulled a medical drape in place. "I'm just finishing here. The man's naked."

"So?" Miki looked over Izzy's shoulder, and her face went pale. "What's wrong with him? Why is there so much blood on his neck and his shoulder?" She wobbled a little, and Dakota and Izzy caught her, one arm each. "I'm—fine, really. I just want to know the truth. No more of these dumb excuses." She took a deep breath. "How is he really?"

Izzy smoothed a gauze bandage over Max's shoulder. "He'll be out a little longer because I gave him something for the pain. But he's going to live, if that's what you're worried about."

"I'm worried about a lot of things," Miki said quietly. "But living seems like a good place to start." She looked at Izzy for a long time, frowning. "I saw you at the hospital with Wolfe, right?"

"Definitely not." He dropped what looked like a small piece of metal into a glass container and then reached for a bottle of brown liquid. "And don't ask me again."

"What's that stuff?"

"Betadine."

"Because there are signs of infection?"

"No, but I'm taking no chances."

"What was that other thing you were holding?" Miki asked quietly. "The small piece of metal."

"Just an old bit of shrapnel. I'm almost done here. If you wait outside, I'll come get you. Then you can talk to Max."

Miki looked mutinous. "I want to stay. You won't shock me. I've spent plenty of time in hospitals," she said tightly. "My mother had cancer. She lived at home as long as she could, but…"

"I'm sorry to hear about your mother." Izzy glanced at Dakota. "Why don't you two go tell Wolfe that he can see the patient in about fifteen minutes when Max comes around."

Miki crossed her arms. "I'm not leaving until—" Suddenly her face went pale, and she grabbed for the wall of the tent.

Izzy caught her as she lost her balance.

"I—I'm fine," she whispered.

But there was a trail of blood from her nose, and her body was rigid. When he put this together with Max's conversation with Cruz, Izzy began to be worried. He was reaching for a piece of gauze for her nose when he felt her legs give way. Five seconds later she was out cold, and the nosebleed was coming full force.

"I'll take care of her," he told Dakota. "Go tell Houston to find out what happened to that chopper. We may not have a lot of time here."

"WHAT DO YOU MEAN, I can't see her? Like hell I'm staying away." His face hard with determination, Max crossed the beach toward Izzy and Wolfe. "Cruz didn't just put an old chip in place back in Santa Fe. He also inserted some new kind of implant. She could be in serious danger," he snapped.

"Take it easy." Wolfe blocked his path. "Izzy's handling this just fine."

"Handling *what?* We don't know what Cruz did. By the time we figure it out, it may be too late to help her."

"I've got a handheld x-ray," Izzy said calmly. "I've made a thorough scan of her arm. There was a chip in there and I removed it."

Max waited, his face strained. "What else?"

"One in her carotid vein, but I can't touch it. That kind of surgery is way beyond what we're set up for here."

A muscle moved at Max's jaw. "How long until that chopper gets here?"

"Any minute. There's a sub ready for us about twenty minutes away, and they'll take her right into surgery."

Max stared at Miki, her eyes closed as she appeared to sleep peacefully. "What's going to happen to her?"

Izzy rubbed his neck tiredly. "You want the bullshit line or the truth?"

Max started to answer, but sighed. "The truth. I think."

"The truth is, *if* we're fast and *if* she's strong and *if* we're lucky, she's going to be fine."

"That's three big ifs you're juggling there, Teague."

"Tell me about it."

Max ran a hand through his hair and frowned. "So what can I do to help? There must be something."

Wolfe put a hand on his shoulder. "What you need to do now is rest. She went nuts when she heard Izzy was working on you, and you can bet that you'll be the first person she wants to see afterwards."

Max prayed there was an afterward. Sitting on the beach with the sun on his back and the sea wind in his face, he prayed for other things, too. Impossible dreams, they whirled through his mind like old newspapers as he watched Miki sleep.

She was difficult, opinionated and quirky.

She was brave, quick-witted and unforgettable.

She had also told him she was getting married. But Max wasn't giving up so easy. He'd just have to talk her out of settling for anyone else but him.

And what was he going to do if she didn't feel the same way, not that he had any right to expect she did?

He blew out a breath and nodded at Wolfe. "So we wait. I'll give it ten minutes. Then I'm getting on the radio and chewing Ryker's—" His eyes narrowed as he continued to study Miki's face. "What happened to her hair? It looks as if she—"

"Burned it," Trace said, ambling up with a big coconut he'd just cut open. He dropped a piece of shaved coconut to Truman, who ate it neatly. "Happened when she used a blowtorch on one of Cruz's thugs. He went after her while Dakota had his hands full, and the crazy fool let him have it with a blowtorch. Burned off part of her hair in the process, but she got her man."

Max scowled. "Dakota should have been faster."

"Yeah, and pigs should fly," Trace muttered.

Max continued to frown. "Where did she find a blowtorch anyway? I don't get it."

Trace grinned. "Set fire to her hairspray and the knitting yarn. Or maybe it was nail polish remover and her shirt. Wolfe knows about that stuff, seeing as he's hot and heavy with my sister."

Wolfe's eyes slitted. "I never said—"

Just then the distant drone of motors had the four men turning to scan the sky. Truman waited expectantly, never moving far from Miki's side.

Max shot to his feet as the helicopters thundered closer. He ignored a stab of pain at his shoulder. "Let's get her ready to move."

Truman was right behind him, watching when he lifted Miki into his arms.

CHAPTER THIRTY-TWO

WHEN MIKI OPENED HER EYES, the first thing she saw was Max, draped over the edge of an armchair beneath a single lamp, sound asleep. She blinked, wondering where the chair and lamp had come from because there was no furniture in the bunker. And how had he gotten electricity for the lamp?

She felt a faint hum beneath her and glanced around the space.

Metal walls. Small metal bed. Low ceilings painted industrial gray. Where *was* she?

When she tried to sit up, pain stabbed at her back and upper arm, and she was surprised to see heavy white bandages in place, looking fresh. She closed her eyes, feeling a wave of dizziness as she tried to remember what had happened before she fell asleep.

It was something bad, she knew that. Something that had threatened Max. But despite her mental search, she could remember only a plane crash and a white sand beach. Other fragments came to her then.

Max pulling her from the wreckage.

Max introducing her to a big dog that looked more intelligent than most people.

Max pulling her beneath a spray of water while they fought to shove off each other's clothes in record time. His body had been amazing, his control unforgettable. Miki closed her eyes, her face filling with heat. She'd really done it this time.

She'd fallen hard, the way it felt when you fell forever. The once-in-a-lifetime kind of way that left you thinking of thirty-year mortgages and family insurance plans.

Scary.

She took a deep breath and ran a hand through her hair, frowning when she felt tiny strands snap off. The pieces were bumpy and dark, almost as if they'd been burned. What was that about?

None of it made sense, and she was tired, although she had just awakened.

Max would know what was wrong. She started to wake him up, but he looked worn out and the big bandage at his neck and shoulder reminded Miki of something bad, something to do with danger and how close they had both come to dying. There were other images that flashed and then vanished, but the more she tried to reach them, the more blurred they became.

Clearly, someone had treated her arm. She thought maybe they had given her medicine that left her woozy, unable to sort out the recent past. That much made sense.

She yawned, reaching for a glass of water beside the bed, but her muscles seemed slow and she ended up knocking the glass onto the floor.

Max shot upright, instantly alert. “Don’t move,” he said curtly. “You’re supposed to stay still. I’ll get whatever you need.”

There was something fiercely protective in his eyes, mixed with a tenderness Miki had never expected to see in a man’s face. She couldn’t speak, overcome by emotion.

“Are you in pain? Tell me, honey. I’ll go get Izzy for some medicine.”

“N-not pain.” Miki swallowed hard, suddenly panicked and uncertain and wanting too many things she had never dared to want before. “Are you hurt? I remember the crash and the island, then something dangerous happened. I was worried for you, and there were other people, but it gets all blurry after that.”

“Don’t worry, that’s normal.” A muscle twitched at Max’s jaw. He sat on the edge of her bed and took her hand into his, locking their fingers. “Whatever you need to remember will come back when the medicine wears off. Try to rest while I go find another glass for water.”

“Forget the water.” Her fingers tightened, holding him. “Stay here and talk to me instead. I was…afraid for you.”

“I’m just fine. See?”

She wanted to touch the hard line of his face and kiss the bruise at his chin. The force of her need to touch him left her breathless.

But she’d lied to him, tried to push him away with her story about a wedding being planned.

Funny, but I love everything about your face. Your mouth, when it curves in that way you have. The little scar above your right cheek.

The way your eyes narrow and darken when you kiss me.

Miki looked away, overwhelmed by the new emotions. She was frightened to feel so much, to want so much. She wasn't going to call the feeling *love*, though it sure as heck felt that way.

"Hey." Max cradled her cheeks and gently turned her back to face him. "It's me, remember? This is the guy you tried to deck one or twice. The helpless victim nearly asphyxiated by that shrug of yours."

"I can't remember what happened. Everything's still a blur." She closed her eyes, exhausted by the effort to make sense of things. "Have you seen my shrug? I really want to have it back. It's just a piece of clothing, but—"

"I told everyone to watch for it, and I gave them a description. It's bound to turn up, and as soon as it does, I'll bring it to you."

He'd done all that?

Something melted in a puddle inside her, and Miki felt herself smiling a loopy smile. "You did that? Wait—who is everybody?"

"The guys I work with. Wolfe Houston, too."

"I know Wolfe. He's going to marry Kit." She frowned, feeling her thoughts blur again. "They must have given me some animal-grade painkillers, because I'm really floating here. Up and down, up and down." She made a little rocking movement with her hand.

"That's because you're aboard a ship."

Miki felt him lift her hand and kiss her open palm.

The brush of his mouth made muscles tighten throughout her body. "Max, whatever we did on that island—" She swallowed hard. "I just want you to know that I don't hold you to anything. It was isolated, we were alone, and everything was upside down. People say things they don't mean in a case like that. They do things they don't usually do."

She felt his hand tighten. "You're saying that you don't remember what we did?" His voice was harsh.

"I mean that it's not important. I don't want you to think you need to explain or make excuses. We're both adults. Things happen, that's all."

After a long time he nodded. "Okay. If that's what you want."

Miki looked away. It wasn't what she wanted, but she was determined to play this lightly, to give him all the space he needed to walk away. "Funny, I keep thinking that you were hurt. But you *were* hurt. I remember now. And there were other people with us. They followed you, and one of them came after me. I think something happened to my hair."

Max gave a crooked smile. "You burned it, honey. I think everyone on board this ship has heard the story by now. You're the hero of the hour."

Miki felt a constriction in her chest. She loved it when he called her *honey.* It made her bones melt and turn sloppy. "Everybody? What kind of ship is this?"

"A Los Angeles–class U.S. submarine. We're headed home, ETA noon tomorrow."

Miki wondered why she didn't feel more relieved. She was alive and healthy, sans a little blond hair, but that was a good trade-off for still being the first part.

"What's wrong? You don't look relieved."

"No, it's fine. Great, actually." It was awful, Miki thought suddenly. She didn't want to go home until she had this thing—whatever it was—sorted out. Was it love, lust or medical insanity? More important, did *he* feel the same?

Just ask him, a voice whispered.

"Max, what I told you before—it was a lie. There's no other man, no wedding."

"Honey, wait. I want to tell you something."

She cut him off. "No, let me tell you first. I changed my mind. I don't want you to forget what happened. Things are still a little spotty, but I know what happened between us was important. It *felt* important, maybe the most important thing in my life. And I want you to feel that, too. So I'm not releasing you." She swallowed hard. "I never want to release you. And I'll make you feel guilty as sin if you try to walk away from me. Now."

Something came and went in his face. Then his eyes did that little narrowing motion, filling with dark emotion.

And he kissed her, at first gently and then hungrily. "I remember. And I don't want to be released. You're still sick, so you're going to have to take it easy. There will be all kinds of questions and a few government people you need to talk to. That shrug of yours is turning out to be interesting, and they may want you to make another one, just for testing. You'll have some experimental yarn, all you want and any kind of equipment. I know it's a chore but—"

"Free yarn? Hey, you can have my house and my car for free yarn. Especially that fiber you had in your pack. So this would have military importance?"

"More or less."

"Because of the way my shrug affected you?"

"More or less." He spoke carefully. "There are things I can't tell you, Miki. I'd rather leave it at that and not have to lie."

She looked at him a long time and then nodded slowly. "Okay."

"Okay? No more flurry of questions? No demands for complete disclosure?"

"I figure you'll tell me if you can."

"You've changed," Max said quietly. "Hell, I've changed, too. I never thought emotions could run so deep. Maybe I couldn't trust myself to care until now. If you give me some time, I think I can work this out, maybe find a way for us to have time to be together. That is, if you want those things."

Her only answer was to smile slowly, circle his neck and pull him down while she kissed him, her mouth hungry and hot, holding nothing back.

She couldn't think of a thing she wanted more.

Paradise felt like this, she thought dizzily. Rocking on a boat, locked in a kiss with a man who could give lessons in flamethrower sex.

She was going to enjoy every minute of it.